FIGHT DIRTY

CJ LYONS

THOMAS & MERCER

Text copyright © 2014 CJ Lyons

Published by Thomas & Mercer, Seattle

www.apub.com

Amazon, the Amazon logo, and Thomas & Mercer are trademarks of Amazon.com, Inc., or its affiliates.

ISBN-13: 9781477825785
ISBN-10: 1477825789

Cover design by Inkd

Library of Congress Control Number: 2014939863

Printed in the United States of America

PROLOGUE

Even as she fell, arms flailing against gravity, cereal, milk, and orange juice tumbling with her, she thought she was dreaming.

Ever since she'd arrived at the ReNew Adolescent Treatment Center, most of her dreams ended this way: a nightmarish hurtle through space, followed by jerking awake, eyes wide, gasping for breath, heart pounding so hard her pulse throbbed from fingers to toes.

A stunned hush filled the room as fifty-one other adolescents watched her fall to the floor, creating a colorful collage of her breakfast. One knee hit the blue linoleum. Hard. She bit her tongue against her cry of pain.

Rule Number One: No Names do not speak unless they are spoken to.

Her hand slapped onto a mushy pile of cornflakes and OJ, saving her from slamming face-first, but even the pain couldn't breach the numb exhaustion that made her brain clumsy and slow to admit reality.

This is all just a dream, a seductive voice whispered. Any second now, her alarm would go off, Mom would shriek at her to get her lazy ass out of bed, *Now!*, or best of all, Dad would be home, rumbling at Mom, telling her to take it easy on the kid.

How could it be a dream? The thought as sluggish as the rest of her body.

Rule Number Seven: No Names do not sleep without permission.

The other kids were a khaki blur surrounding her. Like her, they had no name, no identity, no reason to exist. Beyond them brightly colored posters mocked her with exhortations to "ReJoice!" and "ReFresh Your Spirit!"

Chairs scraped back and footsteps thudded, bloodred spots appearing in her peripheral vision as she thought about getting up, but the idea felt too far away to actually do anything about it. Part of her wanted to roll over, pull warm, soft covers up over her head, and ignore the dream.

Another part of her, the area of her brain in charge of survival, shouted at her that this wasn't a dream and she needed to move, to run, run, run!

Rule Number Four: No Names do not leave or enter a room without permission.

Laughter cut through the fog. She looked up. Surrounded by a sea of red. Too late to save herself. Because this was no dream.

This was hell.

CHAPTER 1

The prison guard pressed his palm against Morgan's ass as he waved his wand over her body. She smiled. It wasn't an "Oh baby, so very glad you pulled me aside for this special security screening" smile—although, sheep that he was, he obviously thought so. No, she smiled because she knew that if she wanted, she could kill him.

"You sure you're a lawyer, Ms. Wilson?" he asked, his palm sliding over her hip. The name on her ID was Amy Wilson, twenty-two, residing at 515 Gettysburg Street, Pittsburgh, PA 15206.

Her real name was Morgan Ames and her real age was fifteen. So she waited, assessing her avenues for escape. The guard's next words would decide if he lived or died.

They were in the administrative section of Rockview State Penitentiary's maximum-security wing. There weren't that many doors between her and freedom. The men guarding them didn't worry her, not as much as the electronically controlled locks. Men she could kill in seconds, but it would take longer to overcome those damn locks.

After she'd passed through the metal detector and had her bag examined, the guard had ushered her to a private screening room. It was small, no windows, walls made of standard construction materials. If she killed him, she'd have to keep it quiet—sound would carry easily through the walls. Beyond them was the reception area where, even though it wasn't quite eight in the morning, women and children waited to be allowed visitation time with their own favorite maximum-security inmate.

The guard, oblivious to his precarious fate, held her breast in his hand as he ran the wand over her outstretched arms. She felt his heat through the silk of her bra and blouse, scented his testosterone rising.

A part of her hoped she'd have to kill him. It was the dangerous side of her, the one she was struggling to control so she didn't end up in a place like this, surrounded by steel bars and razor wire. The part of her that had killed before—and enjoyed it.

"You're much too pretty to be a lawyer."

Her smile didn't waver. His words had just saved his life—although he'd never know it. "I'm just a paralegal. Have to get our client's signature, so we can meet a filing deadline."

"I knew it. Like I said, too pretty—and too nice." He released her and stepped in front of her. "I get off in a few hours—"

The hard part wasn't not killing him; it was not laughing in his face. But Morgan was good at what she did. It was why she could as easily pass for twenty as for twelve. It was all in the attitude and the costume. Match them to your audience's expectations, and no one doubted the rest.

"I'd love to," she said, raising her left hand to grab her leather attaché, letting the overhead light flick against the gold band on her ring finger. A band that was almost a match to the guard's own. "But my husband has plans. You might know him. He's state police, was in the barracks here for a while, Tom Wilson?"

The guard's leer morphed into a grudging nod of respect. Prison guards depended on state troopers for a lot of things, including saving their bacon in the case of a riot. No way in hell would one ever cross a trooper. "Sure, I know Tom. Tell him I say hi."

He yanked the door open and escorted her down the hall to the first of several locked sally ports leading to the secure interview rooms. Idiot never looked back. Despite his uniform and swagger, he was just another sheep, milling about, doing what he was told without thinking. Morgan's smile turned genuine.

The prison corridor was empty except for the two of them and the invisible eyes watching via the cameras positioned overhead. Industrial-grade vinyl flooring and featureless beige walls muted their footsteps. Fluorescent lights flickered above, trying in vain to give the appearance of cheerful sunlight, but the feeble attempt was overwhelmed by the all-consuming stink of sweat and desperation that wept from every surface.

He unlocked the steel door to an interview room. The room was the size of a walk-in closet, no windows except the one in the door, the only furniture a steel table bolted to the floor—a bar running across its top on one side—and two lightweight chairs. There was a bright-red panic button on the wall beside the door and another on the visitor's side of the table. Otherwise the walls were bare.

"He's on his way," the guard said, his tone now surly, as if she'd purposely wasted his time. "You know about Caine, right? He used to take girls like you, hold them captive underground in the dark, torturing them, raping them—you name it, he did it." His eyes tightened, holding back his own rapacious fantasies. "He's gonna love you; you're just his type."

With that he left, locking her inside to await the arrival of a serial killer.

✦

Morgan played her role for the overhead camera—video only, audio recordings weren't permitted, a violation of prisoners' rights. Funny world where men like Clinton Caine had rights. That's what happened when you let sheep run things.

She sat down and smoothed out her skirt, a lovely teal and charcoal houndstooth wool-silk blend, bought, not shoplifted, from the South Hills Galleria. Now that she was on her own, Morgan was beyond petty thievery.

She'd just unpacked her folders with the fake legal documents when the door opened. A man's shadow slid into the room even as he remained at the threshold, flanked by two guards, waiting for permission to enter. Permission was granted in the form of one of the guards giving him a shove, forcing him to stumble inside. He wore the orange jumpsuit of a maximum-security prisoner— as if she wouldn't have figured that out from the handcuffs that restrained his wrists behind his back and the shackles around his ankles.

He must have done something to piss them off. Last time she'd visited, a few months ago, they'd had the handcuffs in front so that he could at least walk upright with some semblance of dignity.

For the first time ever, he looked older than his actual fifty-two. His hair was unwashed, uncombed, silver streaks marring the chestnut-brown curls always certain to attract the ladies. His face was pocked with red sores, pustules with ugly yellow crusts. One guard unlocked one of his handcuffs, swiftly bringing his hands to the front where the cuffs were wrapped around the bar running the length of the table and snapped shut again with a click.

The prisoner sat down, his gaze never leaving Morgan. His eyes. They hadn't changed. Two holes burned into the darkest night sky. Glaring, blazing, yet absolutely indifferent.

Clinton Caine knew what it cost Morgan to come here, to allow herself to be locked inside a cement-block room, trapped behind the razor wire and steel fences surrounding the state penitentiary's maximum-security housing unit. He didn't care. Clint didn't worry about anything except Clint and his ridiculous fantasies of regaining his own freedom.

He remained silent until the guards left and the door closed behind them. Then he leaned forward as if reading the papers she slid across to him. "What'cha bring me, little girl? Better be something worth the cavity search this visit's gonna cost me."

Morgan hid her cringe. His tone was the same one he used when goading fish—his word for the women he kidnapped and killed. A tone that promised no amount of effort would ever be enough to earn a reprieve. His way of reminding her that she existed solely to please him.

He didn't realize that only two things kept him alive: the prison guards monitoring them outside the interview room and Morgan's promise to herself that she'd give up killing.

Good thing, because there was no one she'd rather see dead than this man. Clinton Caine. Her father.

His gaze flicked from the papers to her suit. "Better not be using my hard-earned money for all that fancy crap. This new lawyer is already costing me plenty."

How easily he forgot that while he'd enjoyed himself torturing fish, it was Morgan who had taught herself the skills needed to steal identities and get them money to live on. Didn't matter. To him, it was all his. The world belonged to Clinton Caine, along with everyone and everything in it.

"If you'd stop firing your lawyers—" she protested.

"That's got nothing to do with you," he snapped. "What I want to hear from you is some good news." He shook his head, mocking her. "You don't call, you don't write. If I didn't know better, I'd think you'd forgotten me, were gonna leave me here to rot."

He reached a hand to take the pen she was holding, caressing her palm intimately, reminding her of what they'd shared. All those women . . . all that blood.

Morgan looked past him, counting the blocks in the concrete wall. Her therapist had taught her to focus on what she wanted long term rather than giving in to her immediate impulses. Delayed gratification. As she counted, imaginary blood sprayed the white-washed blocks. A pretty arterial spray in the shape of a butterfly.

Wouldn't that be lovely?

"Why did you call me here?" she asked, blinking hard to erase her bloodstained fantasy.

"My smart new lawyer says the same as the other two, that those damn witnesses could sway a jury. Poison them against me." Clint bent closer to her, his breath wafting across the steel table between them, bringing with it the stench of rot and decay.

She pulled her pen from his grasp and tapped the stack of folders before her, redirecting his attention, hiding her disgust.

Masks. Morgan was a pro at slipping masks on and off at will. Clint didn't even notice the mask she wore now. Not that of a bored paralegal sent to do her boss's dirty work. No. Right now she was concentrating on not jabbing her pen into his jugular.

Veins were better targets than arteries. No muscle in their walls. Hit them, wrench your blade back and forth to shred them, and no amount of pressure would stop the gush of blood that followed.

"You listening to me, girl?" Clint demanded.

Morgan peered through her vision of gorgeous scarlet ribbons flowing from his neck, clashing with the orange prison jumpsuit.

"Sorry," she muttered. Only Clint could make her feel weak or the need to apologize for it. No one else. With the rest of the world she was fearless, relentless, capable of anything.

To Clint she was his little girl, eager to please and obey.

"I said start with those two Feds," he snarled, a spray of saliva accompanying his words. She kept her gaze focused on the table, didn't remind him that he'd gotten caught not by brilliant police work but by his own greed and refusal to curb his sadistic impulses.

"Jenna Galloway and Lucy Guardino." He savored the names of his targets, a smile growing like a cancer on his face. "Start with them, and this will all go away. We can go back to having fun. Just a dad and his baby girl going fishing."

Clint's victims, his fish, they weren't people, not to him—not to Morgan, either. But she was out of the fishing business. For good.

No way in hell was she going to end up trapped in a steel and concrete cage like Clint. Morgan twisted her fingers around her pen until her nails blanched white. No. Way. In. Hell.

It was the reason she'd given up killing. Too risky, even if her last few kills had been bad guys.

The rush of power that came with taking a life, that hadn't changed—in fact, it had gotten stronger, like an addiction, especially when added to the glow of satisfaction when she'd saved Jenna Galloway's life a few months ago. Clint didn't know that little detail. No way was Morgan going to tell him. About how she'd inserted herself into Jenna's life or that she was seeing Lucy Guardino's husband, Nick Callahan, for counseling as she embarked on her new path of self-restraint and nonviolence. Well, maybe violence if circumstances called for it, but definitely nonkilling.

"You can do it." Clint's head bobbed, eyes half-closed as he imagined Morgan carrying out his orders. "Get close. Use your blade. Have fun like I taught you."

His voice turned to singsong. Good thing his hands were cuffed to the metal bar at the tabletop, otherwise they'd be down at his crotch.

"I have to go," she said, shuffling the folders and pushing the button to summon the guard.

He didn't answer, his eyes now totally closed, head weaving in time with invisible screams. Then he jerked his chin once more and opened his eyes, his stare resting on her with the pull of the sun. No way to avoid it, no way to break free.

"Don't let me down, baby girl. You know someday I'll be out of here and we'll be together again. Together forever." The door behind him opened, and two guards entered. "You do as I say. Get the job done. Fast."

The guards unlocked his wrists from the table and pulled them behind his back, forcing him to bend forward, inches from her face. He had new wrinkles around his mouth, highlighting the pimples between the stubble of his salt-and-pepper beard. But the fiendish gleam in his eyes was enough to make her grip the edge of the table so hard her hands went numb.

Morgan held his stare without blinking or flinching. Clint was the only person on the planet who had ever inspired fear in her, and she refused to let him see it. It took all her strength to deny him that pleasure, acid filling her mouth, her throat too tight to swallow, eyes burning from not blinking.

He smiled again. Rolled his tongue across his upper teeth as if tasting an exquisite morsel.

"I'll see you soon," he promised as the guards led him away. "Real soon."

Once the door clanged shut behind him, Morgan slumped, head down onto the table, arms wrapped around her chest tight, forcing herself to stop shaking.

Should've just killed the bastard, she thought as her teeth clenched in a death grip.

CHAPTER 2

Jenna Galloway buttoned her black blazer and turned to look in the mirror. She frowned, fingers raised to brush the hair above her ear, debating whether to pull her hair back or leave it down. Left down looked too casual, made her seem young, inexperienced. Pulled back, she looked like a librarian, her red hair contrasting starkly with her pale skin.

Couldn't even blame it on poor lighting. Her loft occupied the entire top floor of her Regent Square building, the windows and skylights inviting the morning sun in from every angle to dance across the exposed brick and heart pine floors.

Andre Stone appeared behind her, wrapping his strong arms around her body and pulling her to his chest. Six two, solidly muscled, skin darker than midnight—except for the pale, twisted scars that marred his perfection. In Afghanistan he'd received burns on over 60 percent of his body along with other injuries. That was two years ago, but every day he pushed himself through a punishing set of stretches and exercises, fighting against the scar tissue determined to twist his flesh into useless knots.

He was in constant pain, Jenna knew. Yet somehow the pain had become part of him, a challenge that propelled him to rise above rather than allow defeat. Andre's pain and scars made him appear more of a hero than any uniform ever would.

When it came to dressing for their new careers as security consultants, Andre had it easy; he'd look appropriately intimidating in anything. Today he wore a simple long-sleeved black polo over his compression garment—the specialized shirt designed to keep his burn scars from becoming hypertrophied—and khaki cargo pants. He appeared every inch the battle-tested former marine that he was.

"Leave it down. And not the black," he said, sliding Jenna's blazer from her shoulders and tossing it onto the bed. "Makes you look pasty."

"More than a corpse at a viewing," she agreed. Red hair and pale skin always made dressing for success a challenge. Sexy she could do. Kick-ass federal agent she could do. But CEO of a fledgling security firm?

"I think the corpse would look less sallow." Andre unbuttoned Jenna's white oxford shirt. "The white doesn't help, either." He caressed the bare flesh of her belly with one hand, the other teasing her through her bra.

A surge of pleasure rocked her. "You trying to help me impress our new clients or get laid?"

He grinned. "Any reason I can't do both?"

"Yeah. That clock on the wall. Robert Greene and his wife will be here in twenty minutes."

"Plenty of time." He nuzzled her neck. She inhaled his unique mix of musk and testosterone, then turned to kiss him properly, allowing him to enfold her in his embrace.

Damn it. She was happy. Jenna didn't do happy—or even worse, contented. She didn't trust happy. And contented scared the crap out of her.

Before Andre, the most she'd allowed herself was the release of a one-night stand, maybe two. Not this. Three months of . . . bliss . . .

She hid her frown by trailing her lips down his throat, wondering when she was going to blunder into the next minefield. Her life was littered with them, secrets like IEDs scattered past, present, and future. When would one surface and destroy everything?

When would Andre figure out that she wasn't the person he thought she was? That she was a fraud, anything but the capable, confident, competent woman she pretended to be.

Who would get hurt the most? Her or Andre? She'd never had to worry about someone else before. Jenna had enough on her hands just taking care of herself.

She took a deep breath from her belly, squelching the panic before it got a foothold, just the way Nick had taught her. Released it slowly, took another.

Andre wasn't fooled. He'd never made it past high school, but he was smart—especially about people. Sometimes he scared her, how much he could read between words spoken out loud. He knew she had secrets, but he was also patient. Giving her time, space . . . respect.

It twisted her heart, his oh-so-loving patience. Some days she thought she hated him for it . . . but really, she hated herself. A familiar refuge, easy to return to, hard to walk away from, those lifelong feelings of self-doubt, self-loathing.

As if reading her heart, Andre gently disengaged from her, sliding his palms down her arms until their hands joined. "There's nothing to be worried about. You'll be fine."

"So says the man actually able to dress himself."

He chuckled and moved to her closet, returning with a peacock-green silk blouse. "Try this."

She put it on and turned back to the mirror. "Better. But shouldn't I wear a jacket?"

"You're not a US postal inspector anymore, Jenna. You don't take orders; you give them. Back then you wore a jacket because you needed the pockets to carry shit—now you're the boss; you've got people for that."

After Jenna resigned from the US Postal Inspection Service three months ago, she'd used her former federal agent status to push through a business license while Andre oversaw the conversion of the loft below her apartment to office space, and Galloway and Stone, Security Consultants, had been born. She'd only been with the USPIS for two and a half years, lucky that she'd lasted that long, but it'd been enough to garner her some positive press and enough notoriety to hopefully attract high-profile clients.

"You're going to start carrying my purse for me?" she asked, smoothing the blouse. It did look good.

"Sorry, clashes with my ensemble."

They hadn't anticipated opening their doors for another few weeks until a frantic call from the head of Pittsburgh's largest energy firm had provided them their first client. Their offices were still half-finished, but the reception area and the small client room at least had walls, even if no furniture except for some hastily rented tables and chairs.

"Greene's going to think we're amateurs," she said, fussing at her hair and finally adding a clip to pull back one side. She smiled, liking the asymmetry.

"No, he's not." He moved to stand beside her. "He's going to see a pair of competent security experts ready to handle any job he has. It's not about us impressing him; it's about him impressing us enough that we'll take his job before we're even officially open for business."

He had a point. She joined hands with his, stood up straight.

"We're ready." Jenna worked to convince herself as much as Andre.

"Of course, we are," he replied, no trace of doubt in his voice. Exactly what she loved most about him. No one had ever believed in her before—not even herself.

Well, no one except a teenage psycho-killer, Morgan Ames. For some reason Morgan had chosen Jenna as her role model, to the point where she stalked Jenna obsessively. Morgan had also saved Jenna's life once, risking her own, but Jenna tried not to dwell on the implications of that. She didn't like the idea of owing Morgan—liked even less the idea of Morgan's delusions that she was now responsible for Jenna's life and happiness.

Thankfully, Morgan had vanished. It had been weeks since Jenna had seen her. Maybe the little psychopath had finally gotten bored and drifted off to greener pastures . . . Jenna could hope.

"Now what's wrong?" Andre asked, one hand smoothing across Jenna's cheek and clenched jaw.

She hadn't told him everything about Morgan's past. Although Andre was no dummy, he knew there was something wrong with the girl. Jenna turned her face into Andre's palm, kissing the puckered burn scar there. Why upset him? Morgan was gone. Andre was here. Jenna was happy. Wasn't that enough to deal with without adding the chaos that was Morgan to the mix?

She pulled him down to her and kissed him deeply. "Nothing's wrong," she murmured. "Everything's perfect." She broke away, took another deep breath, and glanced at the clock. "Showtime."

They headed downstairs to their offices on the second floor. Pride warmed her, just as it did every time she glimpsed the frosted-glass door with their names on it in bold lettering. No one giving her orders, no protocols to adhere to, no bosses to answer to.

Andre allowed her the honor of opening the door. She walked inside, expecting the smells of drywall and paint, anticipating the sight of a few folding tables and chairs scattered around what would eventually become their reception area.

Instead she was greeted by a mahogany receptionist's desk sitting across from an intimate cluster of leather chairs gathered around a circular Brazilian heartwood coffee table—the same one she'd flagged in an interior design magazine. Beyond it, the consultation room, the only room with the drywall finished, had also been miraculously furnished exactly as she had imagined.

She turned to Andre. "Did you do this?"

He shook his head in confusion. Before he could answer, a petite, dark-haired woman emerged from the back office, her arms filled with file folders and steno pads. She wore a sophisticated designer suit and looked like any twenty-something executive assistant.

Except this woman—girl, really—was no one's assistant.

Jenna knew better than anyone that Morgan Ames was a natural born killer.

CHAPTER 3

Jenna," Morgan said brightly, although her attention was on Andre. He was the wild card here. Jenna, well, Jenna would do what was best for Jenna. She always did, which made her ridiculously easy to manipulate. And right now what was best for Jenna would be to follow Morgan's lead.

"I've got the small office ready for the Greenes." She handed Jenna the client files before turning to the coffeemaker in an alcove opposite the reception area. "Andre, I think you'll like this." She handed him a steaming cup of coffee. "It's your favorite blend. Kona and Sumatra Gayo."

He took the cup, holding it in front of him, ready to drink it or use it as a weapon. He never fully dropped his guard around Morgan—only showed how smart the man was. She smiled at him. It was so good that Jenna had him. After all, it wasn't as if Morgan could always be around to protect Jenna. Mostly from Jenna's own poor judgment and need for drama.

"Morgan—" Jenna started before she stopped and glanced inside the smaller office, now also furnished exactly according to Jenna's plans with intimately placed dark-red leather love seats and chairs. *Confessional chic*, Jenna's notes had read, *a place where clients can confide their darkest secrets*. Morgan thought it was a bit melodramatic, but no one had consulted her, and right now it was all about keeping Jenna happy.

Jenna stumbled, then finished, "Why—how—what the hell?"

This was the fun part, plunging off the cliff without a net. Morgan lived for this, relished the exhilaration that rushed her veins, adrenaline hitting harder than the purest cocaine.

She had no idea how much Jenna had told Andre, and it was Andre she'd have to win over. She knew how Jenna's mind worked—very much like her own, only dosed with unhealthy amounts of anxiety and self-doubt. Jenna would see the advantages to having her around. Not just to make use of her skills but also to keep an eye on her.

Not unlike the deal Morgan had made with their mutual therapist, Nick Callahan. *Wouldn't you rather know where I am and what I'm doing?* she'd asked at her first session with him. Easy choice for anyone who knew what she was capable of.

"Thanks again for letting me work here, earn money for college," she told Jenna, mimicking a schoolgirl's gush of enthusiasm. "I hope I've got everything set up just the way you wanted. I followed your plans exactly."

Plans that existed solely on Jenna's laptop and scribbled in a notebook kept upstairs in her loft. Jenna's eyes widened, and she glanced up at the ceiling, then raised an eyebrow. Anger sparked for a moment, replaced by fear.

That hurt. Not really, it took a lot more to actually dent Morgan's armor, but surely, after all the work she'd done, Jenna could show a touch of gratitude?

Andre set his coffee down without tasting it. "You did all this?"

He meant the question for Jenna, was looking to her to clue him in on how she wanted to handle Morgan. If Jenna was okay with her being here, he'd tolerate Morgan's presence. Just like her, Andre lived to make Jenna happy.

For totally different reasons, of course. Andre, poor guy, was in love. Hopeless case—you'd think a battle-scarred marine would guard his heart better. Morgan wanted something more than silly hormonal-driven emotions from Jenna.

Jenna was the key to Morgan's future.

If Morgan was to survive without killing in this world drowning in sheep and fish, she needed someone to anchor her, keep her from getting bored, and provide her with entertainment—even if it came in the form of a job.

Psychology 101. Far easier to quit an established habit working with a partner who was as devoted to your success as you were. Nick's counseling was helpful, but Morgan knew she needed more than his psychobabble to get what she wanted.

Jenna was perfect. She had so much at risk—more than Andre or their new business. If Morgan failed and was caught by someone like Nick's wife, FBI Agent Lucy Guardino, Morgan knew things about Jenna that would send Jenna to prison. Probably for the rest of her life.

Now that was motivation. Morgan liked the simple math. No emotions necessary, just an old-fashioned horse trade. She'd help Jenna—with both Andre and the business—plus protect Jenna's secrets, while Jenna would help her stop killing.

Made perfect sense. But would Jenna buy it?

She watched Jenna's expression go from frightened to merely wary. Knew she'd won.

Jenna turned to Andre, a fake smile stretching her face. "I figured we'd need the help with our first case, and Morgan was available. Guess I was right. Great job, Morgan."

Morgan smiled. No wonder her father had called it fishing. Was there anything more fun than conning people who knew they were being played yet still couldn't resist the bait?

"Thanks," Morgan said in her role of the eager assistant. "I've got all the supplementary background material on Robert Greene and his wife there." She gestured to the folders in Jenna's other hand. "Along with financials, recent company security issues, plus everything I could find on his daughter's death and the ReNew facility."

Andre raised an eyebrow at that. "Really? We couldn't get anyone to talk to us about ReNew after Mr. Greene called and asked if we'd take his case."

"What did you find?" Jenna asked eagerly, flipping through the pages. "Think there's enough for us to pursue the case? I was worried we'd have to tell him no."

Translation: Jenna hated to see their first big client get away. Greene's daughter had killed herself the same day her parents signed her out against the therapist's advice from the ReNew facility. He and his wife couldn't accept that they might be responsible for their daughter's death and wanted to bring criminal or civil action against ReNew.

Unfortunately there was no criminal case, and no lawyer would pursue a civil action without evidence—and without a way around the shields that protected ReNew since it was owned and operated by a church.

But, the more Morgan dug into the ReNew operation, the more it creeped her out. Not an easy thing to do.

"Still looks pretty skimpy." Jenna glanced at the clock. "He'll be here any minute. What do you think, Andre? Should we even bother with the meeting?"

Morgan suppressed an eye roll at Jenna's indecision and anxiety. Jenna was all about appearances; she loved playing the cocky, kick-ass investigator, but it was just a charade designed to mask her insecurities and poor judgment. Exactly what had almost gotten her killed last December. Good thing she had Andre and Morgan around to save her from herself.

Andre slid the file from Jenna's hand, turning to the photo of Greene's daughter, BreeAnna. Morgan didn't see anything exceptional about the girl. Brown—almost, not quite, blonde hair; brown eyes—almost, not quite, symmetrical; full lips that almost, not quite, masked a slight overbite. She was the kind of girl adults would smile kindly at, remarking about how someday she'd grow into her own—whatever the hell that meant.

"Kid was only fourteen," Andre said. "Don't you think someone should find out why she killed herself?"

Jenna didn't seem convinced. "Maybe I should call him, cancel."

The buzzer from the door downstairs rang.

"Okay, then. Guess we'll see what he has to say." Jenna brushed her hands together, ready to do business—Jenna was always better when she had something to quiet her perpetual-motion mind. A lot like Morgan that way, only Jenna didn't fear boredom as much as she feared her own memories. And secrets. So many secrets.

Morgan was slowly unraveling the tapestry of lies that concealed Jenna's secrets. It was for Jenna's own good. She would never use what she knew against Jenna; she only wanted to protect her. Jenna was her friend. Well, as close to a friend as Morgan had ever had. Morgan wasn't sure if their bond included anything like the kind of love Norms—her term for the sheep (those who milled around, living their bland, ordinary lives) and fish (the weak, victims, easy prey)—felt for each other, but her best bet to get what she wanted meant making Jenna happy. And wasn't that what friends did for each other?

Jenna didn't make it easy. But that was Jenna. She never made it easy for anybody.

She and Andre retreated to the smaller, more intimate office, while Morgan opened the door to Robert Greene and his wife, Caren. Interesting that it was the dad pushing this investigation—the mom barely showed up in any of the notes from the attorneys Greene had consulted before coming to Galloway and Stone.

Was the mother overwhelmed by grief? Controlled by the husband? Morgan wondered at the family dynamics. And where their daughter, BreeAnna, had fit in.

Caren Greene was thirty-four to Robert's forty-one—a stay-at-home mother until they lost their only child last month. Guess she was just a stay-at-home now.

Morgan took their coats, expensive cashmere, London tailored for him; Italian silk-wool blend with a Hermès scarf for her. He didn't wear a wedding ring; she did. Caren's gaze never left him, while he barely seemed to notice her, not until she slipped an arm around his waist and leaned her weight against him, threatening to collapse if he didn't reciprocate. His movements as he draped his arm across her shoulders seemed more reflex than a true offer of comfort.

Were either of them truly grieving their daughter? Morgan couldn't tell for sure. As if they both wore masks.

Finally something interesting. Were they like her? Fellow non-Norms, sociopaths and narcissists, people beyond the bell-shaped curve, fascinated Morgan. She loved to study them—their failures as well as their successes.

She led them into the consultation room. Jenna made introductions and seated the Greenes on the wine-red love seat while she sat opposite them in a black leather chair. Andre stood, leaning against the wall diagonal to their prospective clients. Morgan took a seat near the door, pretending to take notes, and wondered how Jenna would turn the secondhand gossip Morgan had uncovered about ReNew into a case worth pursuing.

Jenna hated to lose, and no way in hell would she risk disappointing someone like Robert Greene. His energy firm could provide Galloway and Stone with enough work to put them in the black before they even officially opened their doors.

But first Jenna would have to solve the mystery of their daughter's death—a death the rest of the world had decided was no mystery at all.

Morgan watched in interest as Jenna took the lead. "Thank you for coming, Mr. and Mrs. Greene. I'm afraid we have some bad news."

That caught them off guard. Caren Greene jerked upright, sliding to the edge of the sofa. "What do you mean bad news? Does that mean you're not taking the case?"

Her tone was a combination of disbelief and strident entitlement. Her husband placed a possessive hand on her knee as if intent on holding her in place.

"It means that any investigation into the ReNew treatment program would be prolonged and with little hope of gaining you the evidence you need to prove they caused your daughter's death," Jenna answered in a level tone.

"She killed herself the day we rescued her from that hellhole," Caren retorted. "Of course, it was their fault."

"Yes ma'am. But if you want to pursue legal action against them, you'll need proof of that." She glanced at Andre who took his cue.

"That will mean looking into your daughter's life as well as investigating ReNew. I'm afraid what we've found so far isn't very promising."

"Surely there have been other incidents," Robert Greene said. "Students who could act as witnesses—"

Jenna shook her head. "We found several complaints—not unusual given that they serve such a high-risk population of juveniles. However, they were all rescinded by the families involved. And because ReNew is church owned and operated, they aren't bound by the regulations restricting other schools, so there's no official government agency that could justify an inquiry."

"We know all that," Greene snapped. "We've been through that already with our lawyers."

"That's why we're here," his wife added. "We want you to investigate them. Find whatever proof you need to shut them down."

Jenna opened the folder Morgan had given her and leaned forward, sliding an eight-by-ten in front of the Greenes. It was a headshot of a distinguished-appearing middle-aged man with salt-and-pepper hair and a friendly smile.

"Reverend Amos Benjamin. Founder of ReNew." She tapped a manicured nail on Benjamin's forehead, the exact same spot a sniper would take a kill shot. "He's fifty-seven years old. Never married. No criminal record. His bio states he has a doctor of divinity, but our research wasn't able to confirm that."

"Because the man's a fraud," Caren said, sounding vindicated.

"Because the school closed and all their records were lost in a fire."

"Convenient." Greene pushed the photo away in disgust.

"He moved here from Ohio sixteen years ago and established the ReNew Foundation. Built his congregation over the next several years and then bought the land and began the community. He—or rather the church—now owns over two hundred acres, the church, a fellowship hall, the ReNew Treatment Center, and there are fourteen families living on the land in houses leased from the church with the plans to build eight more this year."

"It's a cult. He's building a cult—surely that's against the law?" Caren bounced in excitement.

"I'm afraid not. It's all legal. And we've no evidence of any classic cult behavior. His members are free to come and go. We couldn't find any disgruntled members with our brief background check." She meant Morgan's research, but Morgan simply sat quietly, studying the Greenes and how Jenna maneuvered them. She was setting them up for a big payoff, and even Robert Greene, Mr. CEO, didn't see it coming.

"In sum," Jenna said, "everything appears to be legit."

The Greenes bristled at that, but Jenna didn't give them time to jump ship. "Which means we're going to have to do a lot of digging to find their secrets. Anything buried that deep is going to take time and resources to unearth."

Caren gripped her husband's hand. "We have resources. Anything you need. But please, please, you have to find the truth. I need to know why my baby died."

CHAPTER 4

"Start by telling us about BreeAnna," Jenna said.

Caren nodded, glanced at her husband, took his hand—he didn't offer it, Jenna noted—and started. "BreeAnna's always been a sensitive child. High-strung, sometimes even willful. She was an early-bloomer, started puberty when she was eleven, and well, ever since, living with her hasn't been easy."

She made it sound as if her child had broken a lease agreement. The dad wasn't even paying attention; his head was turned to look out the window.

To Jenna's surprise, Andre spoke up from behind her. "Did you also have problems with BreeAnna, Mr. Greene?" he asked, his tone carefully neutral, but Jenna knew better. Andre's dad had died in prison when he was a toddler; his mom had taken off to parts unknown soon after until she'd also died, drug overdose, when he was ten. He had strong feelings on the sanctity of family.

Robert Greene took his time in answering, slowly turning back to face them. "Caren bore the brunt of it," he said, now intertwining his fingers with his wife's as if he spoke for both of them.

"But you both thought ReNew was the best place for BreeAnna?" Andre continued, his voice gentle now. He didn't mention that the mother had been the one to remove BreeAnna from the treatment facility against medical advice. Only hours before she hung herself from the upper balcony of their three-story mansion.

The couple focused on the floor in front of them, not meeting Andre's or Jenna's gaze—and not making eye contact with each other. Jenna restrained her own glare, irritated that Andre's questions may have scared them off. How were they supposed to investigate anything if they couldn't even get their own clients to talk?

"Can you give us specific examples of BreeAnna's behavior?" Jenna asked Caren, trying to get things back on track.

The mother stared at her husband's hand wrapped around her own. She made a choking noise, shoulders heaving.

Her husband glanced up, his gaze sliding off Jenna's, then placed his arm carefully around Caren's body, drawing her to him protectively. "What does this have to do with ReNew?"

"We need to understand everything we can about BreeAnna," Andre answered. "Her life, her dreams, her hopes." Caren flinched at his words, but the father remained impassive. "Why she grew so out of control that you sent her there."

Caren's head jerked back so hard and fast it hit the back of the sofa. "It was me. I made the decision. I'm the one who sent her there." Spasms ran up and down her neck as she choked back sobs. "It's all my fault. BreeAnna is dead because of me."

✦

Andre knew he'd pissed off Jenna with his questioning of the Greenes. He didn't really care. Why come to a brand-new firm like theirs to start with? Sure, Jenna had been in the headlines with her big-time cases when she worked for the Feds, but Andre was just a grunt. Yet even he could see there was something off with this case and the Greenes. Why were they so insistent on pursuing this investigation while refusing to give Andre and Jenna any facts to go on?

Greene didn't even turn the whole way around to face his wife. It was obvious he'd heard her confession before. As the father's expression turned to granite, Andre caught a flicker of guilt. Greene leaned forward, both hands gripped tight around his knees, leaving his wife without comfort.

Had the father no say in the decision to send his daughter to ReNew? Busy executive, how involved was he with his wife and family? Maybe Greene was having an affair; that would account for his distance. Andre made a note to look into the Greenes' marriage. With a child dead, nothing was off-limits.

"I did the best I could," Caren said to the ceiling, leaning back against the couch as if she couldn't support her own weight. "The school, ReNew, they had references—even from our minister. And I just couldn't take it anymore." Her chest heaved as she gulped down a breath. "I couldn't watch my family self-destruct like that. I had to do something."

Greene made a low noise, deep in his throat, and finally raised an arm to wrap around his wife's shoulders, pulling her to him once more. He glared at Andre as if her pain was his fault. Andre kept his face impassive as he stared back. Nice thing about his scars, they made for a helluva poker face.

Jenna broke the impasse, awkwardly handing Caren a tissue. Caren stifled her sobs, wiped her tears, but still didn't look up. "You don't understand," she said in a low tone, one suitable for confession—or a funeral. "I was trying to save her."

"It's okay," Jenna said, even though clearly it wasn't. "Tell us what happened."

Caren nodded. Andre had a feeling Caren Greene enjoyed the spotlight as much as she did the catharsis of baring her soul to strangers.

"I could take the smoking, her skipping school, the shoplift-ing, sneaking our liquor, even the marijuana," Caren started. "I mean, we were all kids once, right?"

Andre glanced up at that. Hardly overboard for a rebellious teenager. Of course, that was teenagers from his Homewood zip code—the kind of folks who wouldn't even qualify to work as ser-vants for a family like the Greenes. The ME's report had docu-mented a negative tox screen. BreeAnna had been clean at the time of her death.

Jenna made an encouraging noise. Caren continued, "She hated me. She really did. The things she said when we fought—and we fought constantly. Hateful, vile, things. She even hit me a few times. I tried to get her to counseling, to talk to the youth ministers at our church—she refused. Said I was the one who needed help, not her. That I was trying to control her life—"

Finally her husband joined in, although he still didn't turn to look at his wife. "She was a fourteen-year-old girl, Caren. Of course, she hated her mother for trying to set boundaries. You can't keep beating yourself up over it."

"Is that why you sent her to ReNew?" Jenna asked in a gentle tone. "Because she was becoming more violent?"

Caren shook her head, staring at the wrung-out tissue in her hands. "No. Not just that. I was bringing her clean sheets and tow-els when I found a bag full of lingerie on her bed. Expensive linge-rie she could never have afforded to buy. Things much, much too mature for her to ever wear. And then, in her bathroom, I found a pregnancy test."

That got Greene's attention. "A pregnancy test?"

Andre looked up. Why did Greene sound as if he was hearing this for the first time? If not from his daughter, then why hadn't his wife told him? Maybe Greene wasn't just a father who was absent physically; maybe he'd checked out of the marriage and his family altogether . . . or maybe it was the opposite. Maybe Caren hadn't disclosed anything to her husband because she was afraid of his reaction. Greene was solidly built, seemed like the type who might hit first and ask questions later, despite his veneer of a polished executive.

"No. It was negative, thank God, but that's when I knew I had to take drastic measures." Caren glanced up at her husband. "Not like you'd ever do it yourself. She had you wrapped around her little finger, could sweet-talk you into anything."

He grimaced. "My hours, I work hard, travel weeks at a time— is it too much to ask to come home and relax with my family instead of walking into a battlefield and being expected to referee?"

"She needed you to be her father, not her best friend," Caren snapped.

Greene slid his hand down her arm to intertwine his fingers with hers. He squeezed her hand. Offering support or reminding her they weren't alone, Andre wondered. It hadn't escaped his attention that Greene didn't ask who may have gotten his daughter pregnant.

Andre caught Morgan's eye. She raised an eyebrow, glanced at Greene, and he knew she was thinking the same thing. He cleared his throat, wishing Jenna was the one doing the asking. She had a way of making the most intrusive questions sound reasonable.

"We'll need to know who BreeAnna's boyfriend was," he said. "And if she had any contact with him after she came home from ReNew."

Greene's head jerked up, his expression thunderous. If it wasn't for Caren's grip on his arm, he would have come out of the couch. "Do you think we would allow our daughter anywhere near—"

Caren interrupted, her voice carrying over her husband's. "I have no idea who BreeAnna was seeing. She refused to tell me—it was one of the reasons why we were fighting so much, especially after I grounded her."

"How long after that fight did she leave for ReNew?" Jenna asked.

The tension in the room eased, as if answering a simple numeric question would give them the key to BreeAnna's death.

"Two nights later," Caren said. "I tried to talk to her, about the sex—she was only fourteen for God's sake—about whoever the boy was."

Or man, Andre added silently. Fourteen-year-old girls didn't find a way to the mall and shoplift expensive lingerie to impress fourteen-year-old boys.

"But she became more and more out of control. Explosive is the only word I can use to describe what she was like. Then, that last night, I caught her trying to sneak out, run away, and I thought, this is it. If I don't do something here and now, I'm going to lose her forever." She paused, eyes closed, face up to the ceiling. "So I made the call. I sent her away to that place." She opened her eyes, stared directly at Jenna. "I will never, ever forgive myself."

After a moment of silence, Greene said, "Is there anything else you need to know about our private life?"

Life. Singular. As if his daughter and wife lived for him, through him, three lives intertwined as one.

There was a lot more they needed to know. Impatient with Jenna's dancing around the issue, Andre asked, "Why did you withdraw BreeAnna from ReNew early?"

Caren's shoulders slumped as violent sobs rocked her body. Once again, her husband glared up at Andre as if he was to blame for her pain instead of the weight of their grief. Jenna shook her head at him, scowling as if he'd made a rookie mistake. He frowned back at her. He might not have her training, but he knew enough to see that the Greenes were holding out on them.

Caren's sobs grew in volume, crowding the small room as if her grief had a life of its own. It was clear they wouldn't get more now. Might be best to question Greene alone, Andre decided. The more emotional Caren became, the more rigid and stoic the husband grew. They fed off each other.

Where had BreeAnna fit into the family's delicate ecosystem?

"I think that's enough for now," Jenna said. "But we'll need to talk to BreeAnna's friends, teachers—see if any of them had any inkling she was about to kill herself."

"Electronics," Morgan reminded her. Andre looked over at Morgan—she'd been so still and quiet, he'd forgotten she was there. He wondered what her take on the Greenes was. But Morgan's poker face was even better than his own. He hoped Jenna knew what she was doing, bringing a kid like Morgan into the mix.

"Oh yes," Jenna said as if it was her idea, "any electronics she might have had access to and her passwords if you know them."

"Why do you need all that?" Caren asked, one hand fisted at her throat as she glanced up.

"We'll need to show BreeAnna wasn't suicidal before she entered ReNew. Even better would be any indication she shared with her friends that something happened there that drove her over the edge."

"She was only home a day, isn't it obvious?" Greene said.

"If all you want is reassurance, that's one thing. But if you really want to see ReNew closed down, save other families from the pain and suffering that you're going through, then we'll need hard evidence."

Andre had a thought. "How about a psychological profile?"

Jenna nodded. "Good idea. We can ask Nick—Dr. Callahan is a psychologist who consults with us on difficult cases like this one."

Caren twisted in her seat to glance at her husband. "I'd like that," she told Greene, her voice now laced with steel. "I can't stand the thought of anyone thinking this was my fault."

The woman's emotions jackknifed so quickly, Andre wondered how anyone kept up. Being in the same room with her was exhausting.

Greene didn't seem too happy about the idea but finally nodded. Caren turned back to Jenna. "Do it. Whatever it takes to shut down that awful place before any more children die."

CHAPTER 5

"If shutting down ReNew is your goal, we can do that." Jenna paused. Baiting the hook, Morgan knew. If their initial interview with the Greenes was any indication, nothing about this investigation would be easy. "But I need you to understand it will mean using unconventional means. Usual methods of gathering evidence, financial records and witness statements, aren't going to work. Not with their money shielded by the church and the witnesses all being underage troubled teens."

"I don't care what you have to do," Caren practically shrieked. Her husband squeezed her knee again. This time she shoved his arm aside. "We have the money. Whatever it takes. Just do it. Find the bastards who did this to my baby girl, and make them pay. I don't care if you can prove it in court or not. Just shut them down."

"Now, Caren—" Robert Greene ignored Jenna to stare at his wife. "You need to calm down. Think this through."

Caren launched herself to her feet. "I'm tired of everyone telling me how I should feel. My baby is dead!" She whirled to look down at her husband. "They killed her, goddamn it. Your own daughter. Now do something about it!"

Greene blinked, his expression totally blank for an instant. Morgan wondered if anyone else noticed. But then his face crumbled with grief, and he sucked in a breath as if struggling to pull himself together. He looked down at the dark cherry floor, past his wife out the window, finally back at Jenna. "What kind of unorthodox techniques are you talking about? Nothing illegal?"

Caren sank back onto the couch. Instead of appearing satisfied that she was getting her way, she seemed unhappy she was no longer the center of attention. "Who cares what they have to do?"

Watching Jenna manipulate the parents was like watching a conductor and his orchestra. Morgan noted how she toed the fine line between pushing the parents to get the info they needed and pissing them off so much that they'd walk. Seemed like with the Greenes that line was as thin and fragile as a spider's strand of silk.

Jenna waited a beat, letting the emotions settle to a mere simmer. "We could send someone in. Posing as a student."

Morgan straightened at that. Not liking the implications. Jenna was trying to manipulate more than just her grieving clients.

"You mean undercover?" Caren said, clearly liking the idea. "Like they do on TV?"

"Something like that. We'd create an identity, a false background of emotional disturbances, drug use, minor criminal offenses—basically a typical picture of a troubled teen."

"Like BreeAnna," Greene said.

"Yes. Like BreeAnna." Jenna's voice brightened, and she studiously ignored Morgan's glare. "It would be expensive—you know ReNew expects full tuition up front. Plus we'll have the costs of building the cover identity. And while we have an operative for the undercover investigation, we'd need to hire an actor or actors to play the role of her parents. Mr. Stone and myself are too well known."

No one asked Morgan what she thought. Just like no one had asked her if she wanted to go undercover at a residential treatment center, locked in with a bunch of messed-up kids and the adults who controlled them.

No way in hell was Morgan going anywhere near that prison masquerading as a school. She stood and opened the office door.

"All right," Jenna said, hurriedly. "We'll need a retainer up front plus expenses billed by the hour." She handed their contract and liability waiver to Greene. "I'll give you a minute to look that over, then we'll answer any questions you have and begin collecting our intelligence. We'll be back in a minute."

By the time she and Andre had the door shut behind them, Morgan was halfway across the reception area.

"Morgan, wait," Jenna said, pitching her voice so it wouldn't carry through the door to the office where the Greenes sat. "Hear me out."

Most people felt fury as something hot, something that made their blood rush so they couldn't think clearly. Not Morgan. Just like fear, anger left her chilled—and her mind moving with lightning precision. Gauging reactions, calculating choices, sifting possibilities, searching for the path with the greatest reward and least pain.

Getting locked up was exactly what she was working so hard to avoid. It was why she'd sworn she wouldn't kill again. And Jenna, the person closest to a friend, wanted her to waltz into the one place where Morgan would go insane?

Morgan didn't even slow at Jenna's voice. But she did stop at Andre's hand on her shoulder. He didn't grab her or pull at her. Merely laid his palm down, stopping her just as she reached the outer door.

"It's a bad idea, sending you in," he said in a low voice that wouldn't carry back to the Greenes. "You don't have any training. You're too young and inexperienced to be put in that position."

Morgan slowly turned. This is why she loved Andre so much. He knew she wasn't a normal teenager—although he had no clue about who she really was—yet, he never treated her as anything but normal. Until she proved him wrong, he would accept her as she was.

His friendship was another benefit of living life as a Norm, fitting into this warped society where emotions ruled instead of cold, hard logic.

He looked down at her, now with both hands resting on her shoulders, and said, "I'm sorry, Morgan. We'll find another way."

"Stop treating her like a kid, Andre. She can do this. Hell, you want to do it, don't you, Morgan? That's why you wanted this job, right?" Jenna said it like a challenge—no, a dare. Her voice held a touch of triumph as if Jenna expected Morgan to fail her. Prove to her that any faith she had in Morgan was misplaced. Or simply payback for Morgan resurfacing in Jenna's life, spying on her, intruding in her business. "C'mon, let's get back inside."

Before Morgan could say anything, Andre rushed to her defense. "Jenna, don't bully her." He turned to Morgan, so tall that she had to crane her neck to meet his eyes, but she didn't mind. "We'll think of something else."

"Like what?" Jenna argued. "Morgan, you did the background research on ReNew. Did you find anything more than what I did? Any way to shut them down, any evidence of wrongdoing?"

Morgan didn't blink. She merely stared at Jenna, not breaking her gaze.

"C'mon," Jenna continued in a friendly tone. "You said you wanted to be here, a part of our team. You're perfect for this. Who else could pull it off?"

Morgan was not about to allow Jenna to manipulate her like Jenna had their clients. Jenna would just have to learn to accept the fact that Morgan wasn't going anywhere. She *was* a part of Galloway and Stone. Whether Jenna liked it or not. But that didn't mean Morgan would be taking orders from her.

"Sorry," she said in a businesslike tone. Much more business-like than Jenna's. "I've got an appointment. We can discuss this later."

And she was out the door before Jenna could make a move.

CHAPTER 6

"Why did you do that?" Andre asked as the door slammed shut behind Morgan.

"Do what?"

"Treat Morgan that way. The girl once saved your life. She almost died for you, Jenna. You act like she's a piece of garbage stuck to the bottom of your shoe and all you want is to scrape it off. Can't you see how much she looks up to you?"

Jenna's laughter was both surprising and unpleasant. Not her usual full-bodied laugh that warmed his insides with anticipation. This laugh was tainted by contempt. And accompanied by a look of pity.

"You have no idea who or what that so-called girl really is, Andre," she said in a strained voice. "Trust me. You don't have to worry about Morgan going inside a school filled with a bunch of emotionally disturbed and violent juvenile delinquents. It's them you should worry about."

"I'm not an idiot." A spray of spittle escaped his lips—the mouth the burn surgeons had reconstructed didn't work quite as well as the one he'd been born with, especially not when he was too upset to focus on using the right muscles. "You don't think I believe that whole emancipated-minor, got-her-GED-early bullshit, do you? But I do remember how she acted when you were the one in trouble. She'd kill for you, Jenna. And she'd take a bullet for you."

He paused, took a moment to draw in his breath, tried to temper his emotions. "I'm just saying, don't toss that kind of loyalty aside like it's nothing. I have no idea what happened between you two before I met you, but it's clear that girl is trying her best to do right by you. Least you could do is have enough respect not to treat her like she's some trained monkey you can order about as you please."

It was the longest speech he could remember making, his anger propelling the words out so fast he wasn't sure Jenna even had a chance to absorb them. Sure, he hadn't trusted Morgan when he first met her—he had a feeling he might never.

SCKs they used to call them in Afghanistan. Stone-Cold Killers. Dangers to themselves and every marine and civilian around them. No fear but also no boundaries.

Morgan reminded him a lot of them. So, no, he didn't believe her or trust her. But that wasn't what had him so upset. It was seeing Jenna act this way, totally out of character from the woman he'd grown to admire and respect.

"What happened, Jenna?" he asked, reaching across the space between them to lay his hand on her hip. "You can tell me. What did Morgan do?" Besides almost getting herself killed while rescuing Jenna from the Zapata cartel in December.

Jenna turned her face away, biting her lip. He thought she was about to say something, to finally tell him everything, but instead she shook her head. "Ask your friend. Nick Callahan."

Nick specialized in trauma and PTSD. He'd helped Andre cope with his own demons after returning from the war and now was seeing Jenna. Jenna never talked about her sessions with Nick, but Andre knew her demons went deeper than what had happened with the Zapatas.

"I'd rather hear it from you," Andre said softly. He knew how valuable it was to own your story, to find the strength to share it with those you loved. Telling Jenna everything he'd done in Afghanistan had been the turning point in his own recovery. He wanted her to know she could trust him in return.

She spun away, squaring her shoulders. "Later. We need to get back to our clients."

"You still want to take this case?" he asked. "You know we might never be able to give them what they want. Is it for the money?" Jenna had expensive tastes, and her final paycheck from the US Postal Service had quickly been eaten up by the cost of renovating the offices. Lord only knew how she'd paid for the new furniture Morgan had acquired.

She stopped, a small inverted V forming between her eyebrows. Glanced up at him without raising her chin, making her look like a little girl ready for a scolding. "Is that what you think? That I'm doing this for the money? That that's why I want to send Morgan undercover, do anything we can to bring down ReNew?"

Andre hesitated, then went for honesty just as he always did. "A contract with Greene's company would be a huge win—"

"A fourteen-year-old girl killed herself," she interrupted. "Don't you think someone should find out why?"

Andre smiled. She raised her face to meet his gaze. He grazed a finger along her jaw, tracing its strong, willful lines. This was his Jenna, the woman he'd fallen in love with. Headstrong, volatile, moody, yes, but once she found something worth fighting for she never backed down.

"Okay, then," he said, opening the door for her. "Let's get back to our clients."

✦

Morgan sat in her car, an Audi Quattro she'd picked up at the airport's long-term parking along with her latest house to crash in—God bless anniversary cruises—and listened to Jenna and Andre's discussion. Morgan had button cameras with mics scattered throughout Jenna's loft and the office space, all tied to an app on her phone. Oh, how Morgan loved technology.

As she eavesdropped on Jenna and Andre arguing about whether or not Morgan should go undercover as a juvenile delinquent, she was torn between the challenge of proving herself to Andre and anger at Jenna's lack of concern over her welfare.

They were both wrong—and both right. That was the problem with Norms. They always tried to figure every angle, including the emotional ones. If they just looked out for Number One like she did, they wouldn't have to worry about quirky, random influences like emotions and everyone would be the happier for it.

And this whole suicide thing? She totally didn't get that. The girl, BreeAnna, was out of the detention facility, reform school, treatment center, whatever you wanted to call it, it was still a prison. She was free. So why the hell did she hang herself?

Life was too damn precious. At least Morgan's was. Suicide. The only situation she could even remotely imagine would drive her to such an extreme final option would be if she faced what her father now faced: being locked away under someone else's control.

A few of the fish her father had caught had gone that route, killed themselves. Taken the easy way out, he'd called it. It made him furious, would send him off on a rampage. Not because he cared about the women or their lives—they were under a death sentence as soon as he took them. Rather because it was an act of defiance, taking away his power, spoiling his fun.

Morgan understood that. Power was everything. She even kind of admired the fish who'd had the nerve to defy her father.

But killing yourself when you were walking around, free to do anything you wanted? That was just wasteful.

She glanced at the clock. Nick would be breaking for lunch in twenty minutes. Perfect timing. She called his private cell, knowing it would go to voice mail while he was in with a patient, but it was part of their negotiation: no dropping in without notice.

"Hey, I'm bringing lunch," she told the machine. "I want to talk about suicide." She smiled. That should get his attention. "See you soon."

As she ended the call another came through. Jenna. She debated letting it go to voice mail, then decided it was better to go ahead and get the inevitable over with. Jenna would fume and fuss, she would ignore her, and in the end they would do things Morgan's way. What choice did Jenna have?

"I don't know what you're thinking, barging in on my life like this," Jenna started. "But I warn you, Morgan—"

"I've taken out all the cameras from your loft," Morgan lied. "All I want is to help you and Andre start your business."

"Yeah, right. Like walking out on us just when we need you is really going to help."

Again with the sending Morgan away to rot inside a prison for kids. Jenna wasn't getting rid of her that easily. No way. "I can help you more from out here. Just give me a little time, and I'll dig up all the dirt you need on the Greenes or ReNew or whatever."

"Maybe we don't need your help. Maybe we're better off without you in our lives at all." Jenna paused for dramatic effect. Morgan rolled her eyes. "Maybe I should tell Andre the truth about who and what you really are."

"I'm surprised you haven't already." Morgan's tone was one of boredom. "Doesn't matter to me. I never asked you to lie to him— you know that's the one thing Andre hates. Lies. He's an honest man, Jenna. If you want to keep him, you should be honest with him as well."

Jenna sputtered. Morgan grinned and stopped for a light even though it was yellow. "I don't need any relationship advice from you. Just leave us alone."

"Which is it, Jenna? I thought you wanted me to go under-cover, solve this big case for you, so you can get the rest of Greene's business." The light turned, and she sped through the intersection and turned into Nick's office building's parking lot. "Don't for-get, Jenna. I know some things about you that would be best left forgotten."

"Like what?"

You'd think a former federal agent would have a better mem-ory. Especially about little things like homicide. "How about video of you taking out those two gangbangers last December? You could plead self-defense, of course. After all, the Zapatas pretty much declared open war on any cops. But I have to tell you, Jenna, that video of you creeping up to their car and shooting them without warning . . . it makes you look pretty damn guilty."

Silence. Morgan strolled across the street to the café Nick liked. She'd just reached the door when Jenna finally answered. "What do you want?"

"Nothing. Just to work with you and Andre. I can be a huge help, Jenna. You'll see."

CHAPTER 7

Morgan was glad Nick was working out of his private office today instead of the VA clinic. More privacy, less interruptions. As usual his reception area was empty—he didn't actually have a receptionist, just a sign that asked patients to be seated, a buzzer, and a tasteful clock that counted down the time until he'd be free.

On the walls were photos of Pittsburgh: the Point at sunrise, a nighttime cityscape taken from across the river on Mount Washington, a haunting image of a lone rower parting ghostly mist on the Allegheny. Each carried a subliminal message of hope—no kittens or smiley faces, just the idea that life could go on, no matter the obstacle, just as the city had.

Morgan ignored the photos and the comfortable seating and crossed to the door, opening it without knocking, to enter Nick's inner sanctum. He was alone, jotting notes into a patient file. He didn't look up, instead raised a finger in the universal gesture for silence and patience.

A few months ago that would have annoyed the hell out of her. A few months ago, it might have led to bloodshed. She smirked as she unpacked their lunch on the coffee table in front of the sofa and chairs on the other side of the office from his desk. Look at her, acting all sheep-ish, blending in.

Finally Nick closed the file, carefully placed it in a locked drawer—not locked against her, no lock would keep Morgan out if she wanted access—and smiled at her. Not many people smiled at Morgan and meant it. She appreciated that Nick never lied, not even with his smiles.

"Smells good," he said, taking off his reading glasses and joining her on the couch. "Loretta's?"

"Pulled pork, corn bread, green beans with those little cherry tomatoes you like, and banana cream pudding for dessert."

"With the Nilla wafers?" His Virginia accent came out as he asked about his favorite dessert.

"Of course." She waited until he'd made his way through most of his food—see, she *could* learn patience—before asking, "What do you know about juvenile residential treatment centers?"

"Privately held or state run?"

"This one is private. Connected with a church. ReNew."

He wiped barbecue sauce from his chin and thought. "Never heard of them. My work is with adults, but I've counseled a few parents who were considering placement for their kids."

"So you think they're a good idea?" she challenged him, surprised by the emotion coloring her voice. His gaze snapped up to meet hers, obviously surprised as well.

"It depends," he said cautiously. "On the child. What they're struggling with. On the center and its staff. It's like any treatment, you need the right fit. What's all this about?"

She stood, abandoning the rest of her meal. "I don't think it's right. Locking kids up when they haven't broken the law, just because their parents think they aren't perfect enough."

"Morgan, I'm sure the parents have good reasons, want what's best—"

"You tell me, Nick. What would your own daughter have to do in order for you to lock her up like that?"

He pressed his hands against his knees as if getting ready to stand. She was surprised he didn't. One of the few rules she'd agreed to was that his daughter was off-limits. But she wasn't talking about Megan specifically; she truly wanted to know where a normal father would draw the line. Not like she had any experience with normal fathers.

Nick sat for a moment in silence, considering. Another thing she liked about him; he wouldn't give her the easy answer just to shut her up.

"I don't know," he finally said. "I guess I'd have to have tried everything else first and still be afraid that they might hurt themselves or someone else."

Hurt themselves or someone else . . . Bree's parents hadn't seemed too concerned about that. Although Caren Greene had said Bree hit her, she didn't seem afraid.

Of course, now that Bree was dead, maybe there was nothing to be afraid of. Maybe the parents had acted in what they thought was Bree's best interest . . . maybe all they wanted now was forgiveness, some way to assuage their grief.

Morgan stomped one foot in frustration. She just didn't understand them. Sending their daughter away, locking her up behind bars to "get help," acting now like nothing that had happened was their fault . . . none of it.

One thing she was certain of was that places like ReNew shouldn't exist to begin with. Yeah, there were kids out there who were messed up. Violent. A danger to themselves and others—like Morgan. But they needed help from their parents . . . access to professionals like Nick.

Maybe some of them deserved to be behind bars—like Morgan. But that should be up to the justice system to decide, not parents.

She tried to imagine a girl like Bree, someone without the defenses Morgan had built up, ripped from the only life she'd known, and locked away . . . for Bree, it must have been a fate worse than death.

Death . . . why had Bree chosen death *after* she'd been released from ReNew?

She turned back to Nick, who watched her with a studied gaze. "Why do kids kill themselves?"

CHAPTER 8

Nick hid his smile at Morgan's question. Morgan never identified herself as a child or teen. She'd never been a "kid," and she knew it. Knew herself and what she wanted and needed with more insight than any adult. He admired her for that clarity, but it made working with her a challenge.

Of course, if he'd wanted safe, he could have taken the job his old college roommate had once offered: milking rattlesnakes for their venom.

He glanced up. Morgan never wore her mask of civility when they were alone together—she respected him too much for that. But sometimes the way she looked at him, eyes devoid of emotion, dead to humanity . . . made it difficult to remember she was a person in need like his other patients. Nick worked mainly with newly returned soldiers struggling with PTSD, and they were often just as deadly as Morgan, some of them even more out of control than she was. "Why do you think anyone might be driven to end their life?"

She scowled at his retreat into a more normal psychologist-patient power paradigm. They both knew this was anything but a normal counseling session and that he wasn't the one with the power here.

Then she shrugged. "Okay, I'll play along. I've watched their videos, seen their online suicide notes and journals. Read what other kids say about them. Seems like it's always about bullies or broken hearts or not fitting in."

"But you don't buy that."

"Of course not. No one can hurt you like family. Why isn't anyone looking at the family, the parents, the people in charge?"

Nick noted her use of present tense. "Is that how you felt when you were with your father?"

Morgan didn't experience or express emotion the same as the 98 percent of the population who weren't psychopaths like she was. But that didn't mean she didn't have feelings.

The sadistic bastard who was her father had forced her to partner with him in his brutal killings at such a very young age. Anyone would have been warped by that. Nick feared it might be too late to repair the damage her father had done to Morgan's psyche, but he had to respect her for trying.

She took a moment to choose her words. Not because she was worried about shocking him—he knew what her father had done, what she had done, in intimate detail—he was way past shocking. No, Morgan prided herself on being as honest as possible during these sessions. Her no-bullshit rule, she called it. Said she didn't want to waste their time with silly mind games.

It was a sign of respect for Nick, which he appreciated, but even more so a sign of her realization that learning how to control her impulses, how to live in a world populated by her so-called Norms, was the only way she was going to avoid her father's fate. To Morgan, prison, being under someone else's control, trapped, caged, was a fate worse than death.

It gave him hope that someone as damaged as she was realized the importance of change. Not that there was any cure for sociopathy, but he could help her not to kill; he could teach her how to think about other people. They'd always be objects to be used for her own means, but if she could learn to keep her goals aligned with the rest of society, she could live a long, productive, maybe even happy life. Without killing.

"You saw your father again, didn't you?" he asked when the silence lengthened.

Even now, with all the progress Morgan had made, the man still had a powerful hold over her. Made sense. He'd created Morgan, shaped her psyche, molded her until she would obey him without thought or hesitation.

She didn't answer, but the way she clasped both hands around one knee, as if resisting the impulse to pull her legs up to her chest and curl up into a fetal ball, told him everything he needed to know.

"When I was with my father," she finally answered his earlier question, "it was like I was two people. One inside my body just living—eating, breathing, sleeping, doing. And one outside looking down, judging my performance. Was I acting excited enough to satisfy him? Did I look like I was enjoying myself as he tortured one of his victims? Did I rush in to help and join in on the fun fast enough?"

"That's not uncommon in traumatic situations."

"I know that," she snapped.

He smiled and tilted his head in acknowledgment. For a girl who hadn't attended a traditional school past fourth grade, Morgan knew everything there was to know about any subject that interested her—and abnormal psychology was a definite interest.

"My point is, you know that now. You couldn't have known that when you were younger. Why do you think you started to use that disassociation technique?"

"Survival," she answered without thinking. "If I'd shown any weakness, any hint I might rebel or resist, he would have killed me."

"Would you have ever killed yourself?" Any other patient and he would have had to carefully couch the question, dance around it until they were comfortable answering honestly. Not with Morgan.

"No. Of course not. It's my life. No one else's. I'm not about to surrender, to give up." Rare emotion colored her tone. Not anger like a normal fifteen-year-old. More like impatience that he even needed to ask.

"That's why you don't understand these other kids, the ones who killed themselves." He paused, then took the gamble and pushed her a little further. After all, that was the point of these sessions, inching her away from being a killer, even if it was only by a hairsplitting micrometer at a time. "You value life. Despite the number of people you've seen your father kill, despite the people you have killed yourself, you still see life as something precious and valuable."

"*My* life." She blinked hard. "If I can value my life, growing up with the father I had, why couldn't they? They were so young— how did their families twist and warp them to the point where they couldn't see the value of their own lives?"

She stood abruptly, catching Nick off guard, but he was able to suppress his flinch. Morgan rarely showed any emotion, much less allowed it to control her. But now her face was flushed, hands fisted at her hips, ready for violence.

"You know what?" she continued, rocking her weight back. Perfect position to throw a punch—or stab someone, Morgan's particular specialty when it came to lethal weapons.

Nick took a deep breath, flushing any fear from his system. Her fury was focused on the empty air before her. Space where he was certain she saw her father's image.

"I don't think there is any such thing as suicide," she said in a voice that didn't allow for any disagreement. "Not for kids."

Nick raised an eyebrow, not wanting to break into her thoughts but also letting her know he was paying attention.

She continued, eyes narrowed with fury. "I think they're all homicides. I think the grown-ups in their lives are the real killers."

CHAPTER 9

After leaving Nick, Morgan sat in her car and used her phone to do some preliminary investigating. Not on the Greenes or ReNew or the legal options reviewed in the files she'd given Jenna. This time she wanted to get to know the girl, Bree.

BreeAnna. Silly, pretentious name, but coming from a Caren with a *C*, she guessed it made sense. Oh, look there, Caren with a *C* started life as plain old Karen with a *K*. Karen Ann—no *e*—Puykovski.

Morgan wasn't surprised. The Greenes seemed to care more about how they appeared to the world than about the fact that it was obvious neither really knew their own daughter. Guess it was up to Morgan to discover the real Bree.

She started with social media—the twenty-first century's answer to teen angst and self-expression. Bree's Facebook likes included a wide variety of topics, including the David Tennant *Doctor Who*, but not chinny-chin goofball Matt Smith or the new guy, Morgan was pleased to note. Girl had taste. She'd also liked over two hundred fan pages for TV shows and characters and movies and brand names . . . hmm, but had only eleven friends.

Not Miss Popularity. Or maybe Facebook wasn't cool enough for Bree and her friends. Morgan tried the private school that Bree attended, easily hacking into their student forums from her phone without even needing to fire up her laptop. Idiots. They had tons of expensive security measures built in but had never bothered to change the default administrative password.

Good thing she wasn't a predator trolling for victims. Morgan snuggled back into the Audi's leather seat and searched for mentions of Bree in the student conversation threads. It was pretty clear they weren't monitored, despite a bright-red warning at the top of each discussion. Even more obvious that the few fellow students who knew Bree existed didn't like her.

No overt bullying but snide comments about Bree's appearance, speculation as to her sexual orientation, an entire thread with photos and videos of Bree at a party a few weeks before she was sent to ReNew. Bree was shown making out with both girls and boys, obviously oblivious as she was passed around like a party favor. The posts were followed by pages of congrats to the junior whose older brother had slipped Bree the Molly and booze and arranged for the photos.

No one voiced any objection or defended Bree. Morgan drilled down on the photos and videos. They'd been shared 3,012 times. Just from the school's private forum. A quick search online found tens of thousands more shares.

The kids who posted them weren't dumb: none of them showed any faces other than Bree's and nothing overtly pornographic.

Made her wonder what other photos were out there, being shared privately.

She hacked into the school administrator's records and found that the week after the party Bree had talked to the guidance counselor and asked to withdraw from school. The adults, including Caren—a note said Robert was out of town, what a shock—the principal, and the guidance counselor, met to discuss Bree's future and together decided it wasn't worth jeopardizing her academic career by withdrawing her over a childish prank.

The principal also noted that the party had taken place off campus, was not associated with any school events, and that there was no evidence that Bree had not taken the drugs and alcohol voluntarily. Covering his butt while keeping the Greenes' tuition despite the cost to Bree.

No wonder the kid started acting out. All she'd wanted was to escape, start over.

If anyone could understand that, it was Morgan.

Morgan also knew how hard it was to do alone. She'd tried for months after her father was arrested, even attempted attending school, blending in as a Norm. She'd met girls like the ones at Bree's school and guys like the ones at the party. It had taken all her willpower not to kill.

She'd finally decided if she was going to give up killing, stay out of jail, then she needed accomplices—just like her father had needed her. So she'd begun following Jenna and Lucy, figured if they were smart enough to catch her father, then maybe she could learn from them, maybe even someday do what they did. After all, there was a high percentage of sociopaths in law enforcement.

Thanks to her father's upbringing, as warped and twisted as it was, Morgan had the strength to start over, the tools to make it happen, even if those tools—Nick, Lucy, Jenna, and Andre—hadn't exactly volunteered to help her. Plus, she knew what she wanted, had a goal to hang on to, keep her focused and on track.

Bree had had none of that. Was that why she'd seen suicide as her only escape?

Morgan knew she'd never kill herself, not even to avoid prison. Used to be that knowledge would force her to take bigger chances, tempting fate in outrageous ways—not unlike her father. When she was young, she'd bought into his fantasy that they were both special, above and beyond mere mortals.

After seeing Clint fall so hard and so fast, she realized how wrong he was. If she wanted to survive in this world filled with fish and sheep, she had to learn new ways.

She'd already learned a lot while out fishing for prey for her father: blend in; if someone notices you, make sure they don't notice *you* but only the mask you're wearing; think twice, act once, and make it fast; deny everything; make them smile and say yes and they'll like you; find a sucker to blame, then make your escape.

If Morgan had been the junior at Bree's school who had arranged for that *Best Prank Ever!*, she would have seen Bree as the perfect victim. She might have used, abused, and discarded Bree all in the name of a good time.

Bree would have been powerless against her.

Morgan didn't do regret. But having been on both sides of the equation: the predator and now trying to blend in with the sheep, she understood better the cost to the victim. Funny, when she was little, watching her father work, bathed in blood, she never really thought about what his victims felt.

Until Bree. Nick would be proud of her. Morgan's father? He'd disown her as weak, damaged beyond redemption.

She glanced at Bree's pathetic Facebook page with her smile full of hope gleaming from the profile photo, then dialed Jenna's number. "Where are you?" she asked, even though she could easily check the GPS tracker she'd planted on Jenna's phone. Part of playing a Norm.

"Headed over to the Greenes' home. Why? I thought you didn't want to have any part of this case."

"Maybe I've changed my mind."

"Even if it means going undercover at ReNew?" Jenna's voice sounded eager. Morgan blinked slowly, imagining the other woman's triumphant smile. Jenna loved to win.

"I'm on my way." Morgan hung up and put the car in "Drive." She didn't like the idea of going to ReNew, not at all. In fact, she hated it. She hoped she could find some solid leads at the house, anything that would provide an alternative angle to the case.

But damned if she was going to let Bree down. Not again. Not after every other person in her life had abandoned her.

CHAPTER 10

Morgan arrived at the Greenes' Sewickley Heights home; Jenna and Andre pulled into the drive right behind her. The house sat alone at the end of a cul-de-sac, surrounded by an eight-foot-tall fence made of twisted iron bars with delicate curlicues to mask wicked points at the top. It wasn't on a golf-course-sized lot like many of the newer mansions nearby, but made up for its lack of land with haughty, disapproving grandeur. The house was a simple three-story brick colonial. Aligned between the twelve-foot-tall windows were wide white columns, soldiers guarding a maiden's virtue.

The drive was circular, which meant that Jenna parked her black Tahoe directly behind Morgan's Audi.

"Nice car," Andre said, eyeing the Audi.

Morgan cursed beneath her breath. Should have known a guy like Andre, always looking to do the right thing, wouldn't let anything slide. "Thanks," she replied in a perky voice. "I'm borrowing it from friends while they're taking a cruise."

"Thought you were only fifteen? Could have sworn Jenna said something about you being an emancipated minor."

So that was the story Jenna had gone with. Surely she could have picked up on Morgan's cues this morning and told Andre she was older. As always, it was up to Morgan to clean up the mess. "You're so sweet. I'm way older than that."

Jenna was halfway up the steps to the front door and turned to look back at them impatiently. "Come on. We've got work to do."

Morgan dashed up the steps to join Jenna. "You told him I was fifteen?" she whispered.

"No." Jenna frowned. "Oh, maybe when he first met you back in December. Seriously, Morgan, don't expect me to keep your lies straight."

Andre caught up with them. Jenna straightened as if preparing for battle. "Morgan, you take the girl's room and talk to any staff. Andre, you've got the mom, and I'll take the dad."

Divide and conquer. After what Morgan had seen of the Greenes in the office earlier, it seemed like a good plan. They reached the front door. To Morgan's surprise, Robert Greene opened it himself. She had the feeling he did it on purpose, trying to show them he was a self-made man, down-to-earth, blah, blah, blah . . . Anything but a man who'd had no earthly idea what was going on with his family while he was off fracking his way to billions.

The front entrance was the size of a ballroom. An empty ballroom. Except for the grand staircase leading up to the second floor and a large chandelier suspended from the ceiling three stories above them. Balconies made of dark wood broke up the space at the second and third floors, but there was no sign of the rooms beyond them.

With the tall windows flanking the door and the arched skylight above it, the space should have felt light and airy. But it didn't. Instead the house felt heavy, as if gravity had folded in on itself, making Morgan's shoulders sag with imaginary weight.

Each footstep was a chore, resulting in an echo that could make a heart ache with emptiness. Morgan didn't believe in ghosts—how could she, with the number of tortured souls her father's murder spree had created?—but something haunted this house.

"I know you came to see BreeAnna's room," Greene said. "But before you do, I had an idea that might help. Caren's waiting for us in the den."

He led them through an archway that opened into another immense room filled with stiff toile-covered furniture that had high backs and not enough padding to look at all comfortable. Then into a dining room that could seat two dozen at the mahogany table that appeared as if it had never been used, through a butler's pantry filled with china, past a caterer's nook, through a large kitchen equipped better than most restaurants, and finally into a room at the rear of the house that had rows of plush leather couches lined up facing a projection screen.

Caren lounged in the front row, sipping a martini. One wall was taken up with a well-stocked bar, and the opposite wall held DVDs and actual movies on reels like a cinema. Morgan could just imagine the three Greenes sitting in the dark, side by side yet utterly alone during their "family time."

American dream, her ass.

"Caren," Greene said, gesturing to the bar, giving them permission to make their own drinks since clearly they weren't guests he was obliged to serve. "I was just about to tell them my idea."

He slid in beside her, jostling her to sit up straight. She finished her drink in a slow sip, but he didn't take the empty glass from her or offer to get her a refill. Morgan had the impression Caren had already had one refill too many.

"So," he said, leaning forward eagerly. It was the first hint of nerves Morgan had detected in him. "I realized that no one at ReNew has ever seen me. There'd be no reason for them to have any idea what I look like. I thought I could help out. Play the father when you go undercover."

He sat back, beaming, waiting for their cheer of approval. There was no place for them to sit, unless they wanted to sit behind the Greenes or on the floor in front of them. Andre settled in, leaning against the wall opposite the bar while Jenna paced the small space between the Greenes and the screen.

Morgan decided to push Greene, see if she could figure out why he was nervous. And why he wanted to insert himself into their investigation.

"Why is it that no one at ReNew knows you, Mr. Greene?" she asked, sliding in beside him on the couch. Caren jerked her head up at that, staring at her. Hey, if he was supposed to be playing her father, she needed to know him better, right?

Greene relaxed into the leather cushions, basking in the attention of the two women on either side of him, and sipped at his whiskey, taking his time. "I was out of town when BreeAnna was enrolled at ReNew. Work."

Something in his tone made it sound as if he'd had nothing to do with the decision to ship his only child off to a facility guarded by razor wire and steel bars.

Caren picked up on it as well, straightening, one hand possessively on her husband's thigh. "We had, of course, discussed it," she said. "Options to deal with BreeAnna. But Robert wasn't there when things came to a crisis." She sighed, enjoying her role as martyr. "I had to make the call myself."

"You took BreeAnna to ReNew?" Jenna joined in. "Could you walk us through the admission process?"

Caren squirmed. Robert answered for her—he did that a lot, Morgan had noticed. "ReNew has an emergency transport team that will pick up the child. Caren called them."

"She was so out of control. She'd never have gone on her own. I was worried that she'd hurt me—or herself." The last came as an afterthought.

"How did that work?" Jenna asked.

"I called them, agreed to the extra fees—"

"Forty-five hundred," her husband grumbled. "For a twenty-minute ride."

Caren ignored him. "They told me where to meet them. I told BreeAnna we were going to a movie, but before we got there I pulled into the parking lot where the ReNew van was waiting. They had her out of the car and into the van before I had a chance to turn the car off and unbuckle my seat belt."

"She had no idea what was happening?" Andre voiced Morgan's own thought. She'd helped her father grab fish that way, knew the panic and terror that kind of blitz attack produced. For the first time, Morgan understood a piece of what Bree had gone through.

Caren shook her head. "They said it was better that way. So she couldn't try to run away or do something. Said by law, they aren't allowed to chase any juvenile who runs—for their own protection—and we couldn't risk that, could we?"

"Yet she was calm enough to get in the car and want to go to a movie with you?" Morgan asked, ignoring Jenna's glare commanding her to leave things alone.

"Thanks to Caren's quick thinking," Robert put in. "She gave BreeAnna a Valium, calmed her down before things could escalate."

"Walk us through what the men did." Jenna moved the discussion back to tactics. "Did they restrain her? Search her?"

"First, they put a hood over her head—to disorient her, I guess," Caren answered. For the first time a hint of regret entered her voice. "They yanked her out of the car, and she was screaming, trying to hit and kick."

She swallowed and turned her head away to stare at the bar. "She called out—for you, Robert." Her voice broke. "She kept yelling 'Daddy, Daddy.' They handcuffed her hands behind her back and did something with her ankles—I couldn't see, it happened so fast—but then she was facedown on the pavement. Two men, one at her shoulders and one at her knees, picked her up and laid her in the van. They closed the doors, and after that I couldn't hear her scream."

Caren paused to try to take a drink, frowning when she found the glass empty, her hand trembling as she set the glass down. Andre moved forward to rescue the martini glass before it toppled over and set it on the bar, ignoring Caren's silent plea for more.

Finally she continued, "I followed the men to ReNew, met the administrator, Mr. Chapman. By then it was after ten at night, so I didn't meet anyone else. Oh, except the student leader, Deidre. She was so sweet and helpful. And Mr. Chapman was very kind, assured me BreeAnna was in good hands—even showed me her on a video monitor before I left. She was sound asleep, looked so peaceful." She sniffed. "And I, I left her there. I thought they could help her."

Her voice rose, then faded. Everyone was silent for a moment. Caren's fingers curled into the muscles of Robert's thigh, but he didn't move to touch or comfort her.

Morgan forced a mask of serenity, relaxing her hands before she could slash Caren with the blade nestled in the sleeve of her jacket. How could a mother betray her own daughter that way?

And the father, he'd just let it happen. Kept his distance, as if he was above it all.

She had the sudden thought that the Greenes weren't all that different from her own father.

Maybe for BreeAnna, escaping ReNew, returning home to these two, wasn't much of an escape. Could that explain why she'd killed herself?

"And you weren't there to pick her up, either? Never visited her, sent her any photos?" Andre asked Greene.

"No." Greene didn't even seem flustered by the questions. "I was on the road, but I wanted both my girls home. After talking it over with Caren, we decided it was better for BreeAnna to live at home while she got the help she needed. So Caren went to get her, and when I got off my plane, there they were, both my girls, safe and sound."

Right. A real Hallmark moment. Then why was his daughter dead less than ten hours later?

"Like I said," Greene continued. "No one at ReNew has ever seen me. The only thing they know about me is my credit rating. So instead of wasting time and money hiring an actor, I say we do this. Tomorrow. I'm tired of waiting for answers."

He glared at each of them in turn, the CEO demanding his board's approval.

"At least let us look around BreeAnna's room, first," Jenna broke the silence. "Make sure we're not overlooking any other avenue of investigation."

Andre stepped forward, offering Caren his hand. "Mrs. Greene, is there someplace we could talk? Your impressions about what you saw at ReNew and how they operate would be most helpful."

Caren simpered and stood, smoothing her dress. Morgan felt Robert stiffen, watched his lips tighten as Andre led Caren out. He didn't like the idea of Caren talking without him there to monitor her, but Andre had given him no chance to make an excuse.

The Greenes were hiding something—but then why push forward with the investigation at all? The police were satisfied; BreeAnna's death was a closed case to everyone except her parents.

What were they so desperate to find? It definitely wasn't the truth.

CHAPTER 11

Morgan wondered what rich-girl rebel decor would look like. She found Bree's rooms on the top floor of the mansion. Bree had an entire wing to herself on one side of the open space above the foyer, while the other wing consisted of two tastefully appointed guest suites.

On Bree's side of the floor, the first room at the top of the stairs was a music room with wide windows, hardwood floors, and a baby grand piano taking up most of the space. One wall held a large whiteboard covered with musical notations, pages of sheet music with scribbled notes attached by magnets.

Interesting. Why didn't her parents mention that Bree was a musician? Must have been half-decent to have her very own grand piano to practice on. There was also an expensive computerized keyboard and recording equipment, microphones, and headsets.

Other than the music, the walls were bare. No photos, no inspirational posters, not even any shelves with CDs or more sheet music. No place to sit, either, other than at the piano or keyboard.

Was this a place to learn music? Or to be force-fed it?

She left the music room and found a small kitchenette next door opening into another room that appeared to be where Bree did her schoolwork. An antique desk sprawled across one wall, floor-to-ceiling bookshelves on either side filled with volumes that appeared to have never been opened. Classics and actual paper encyclopedias and reference books. As if someone had mail-ordered a kit labeled "Student destined for Harvard."

There was a leather sofa along the opposite wall and on the coffee table actual water marks, indicating this was where Bree actually worked. Nothing to indicate what she was like—at least not until Morgan got down on her hands and knees and peered beneath the sofa.

Neat stacks of paperback novels, pushed beyond the reach of the maid's vacuum. Talking animals and knights riding dragons and fairy queens, judging from the titles and cover art. All with spines broken many times and pages rubbed raw. None with any explicit content, they all appeared aimed at a younger audience than Bree's fourteen.

Her mother had described a girl gone wild, complete with drug use, shoplifting, and a pregnancy scare.

Which was the real Bree?

Morgan put the books back where she'd found them and went into the remaining room: Bree's bedroom. Another room mail-ordered complete with everything except personality. This time the product description would have read "Girl's princess fantasy done in shades of lavender and rose with cream-colored accents."

The bed was a four-poster, complete with frilly canopy. The walls were adorned with hand-painted cels of Disney princesses. The only hint of the room's occupant came from the small mountain of stuffed animals occupying the bed.

That and the evidence bags stacked against the far wall, their bright-orange labels clashing with the princess-pink wainscoting.

There, Morgan found Bree's phone, iPad, and laptop. She grabbed them and their chargers. Jenna could work on them later—she was pretty good at computer forensics, even if she did fall short of Morgan's cyberstalking capabilities.

There was a final bag, this one brown paper instead of clear plastic. Brown paper—that meant the police had been trying to preserve biological evidence. She knelt before it, fairly certain she knew what she'd find inside.

She flipped her knife open and sliced the orange evidence seal. The top of the bag had been folded over itself, each fold firmly creased as if whatever anonymous evidence tech who'd closed it hoped it remained sealed.

Paper crackling beneath her fingers, Morgan unfolded the top and opened it wide. Puzzled, she stared into the shadows lining the interior before withdrawing the contents and laying them carefully on the bed.

Who the hell killed themselves wearing Hello Kitty pajamas?

✦

They met at the cars twenty minutes later. Jenna took possession of Morgan's electronic plunder, handing it off to Andre, who secured it in the rear of the Tahoe.

"Anything from the mother?" she asked Andre.

"Tears and blubber. Fell apart as soon as I got her alone. Only thing I can tell you is that she and Greene have separate bedrooms." He shrugged. "No idea if that means anything or not."

"I called Nick. He can come tomorrow, around noon, take a crack at her. Hopefully before her happy hour starts." Jenna eyed Morgan in a way that Morgan really didn't like. Appraisal and judgment. "Greene didn't give me anything, except more of his woe-is-me, I-have-to-work-so-hard story. According to his version of reality, he's an all-American guy with an all-American family who has been victimized by some evil cult."

"Might be true," Morgan said, playing devil's advocate. "A lot of these privately run adolescent treatment centers basically forget about any actual curriculum and instead use coercive tactics to brainwash the kids."

Jenna didn't look impressed. "I read that *New York Times* report, too. Innuendos about other programs won't do us any good. We need concrete evidence."

"What about BreeAnna's room?" Andre asked. "Any help there?"

"Apparently she was a pretty serious musician—or her parents wanted her to be." She told them about the music room. "Other than that, everything was normal. If anything, a bit juvenile for her age. No signs of any age-inappropriate clothing or that sexy lingerie Caren was freaked out by."

"Confiscated and long gone," Jenna said.

Morgan exchanged a glance with Andre. "Or the mom lied about why she exiled Bree. Maybe there was something else going on, some reason she wanted Bree out of the house."

"Evidence," Jenna chided. "Not speculation. Evidence." She glanced around them, the house almost totally dark except for a single light over the front door, the porch shadow looming over them in the dim light of the setting sun. "Let's get back to the office." She handed her car keys to Andre. "I'll ride with Morgan, meet you there."

Jenna said nothing as Morgan steered them past the gates surrounding the Greenes' mansion and down the lane. Instead she seemed to be waiting for Morgan. To do what? Apologize for walking out earlier?

Finally Jenna made a *humphring* noise deep in her throat as if she'd swallowed a nasty piece of gristle but was too polite to spit it out. "I don't like our clients."

Morgan resisted the urge to roll her eyes. For someone trained in objectively collecting and evaluating evidence, Jenna was one of the most judgmental people Morgan had ever met.

"But," Jenna continued, "you did good back there. Playing them off each other, trying to get them to expose what was really going on. Too bad it's clear we won't find the truth behind BreeAnna's death inside her home. Which means there's only one place left to go."

As if Morgan hadn't already figured that out. "So you're inviting me onto the team?"

"We both know the word *team* isn't in your vocabulary. You'll do what's best for you, Morgan. Which means I can't trust you. Never have and never will."

Morgan was silent. Couldn't really argue with that. But Jenna needed her if she was going to save this case and grab Greene's business for the firm.

"But," Jenna continued, "I am willing to offer you a trial run."

"How generous of you, seeing as I'll be the one locked up behind bars."

"And there will be some ground rules. First, Andre has to sign on. After I tell him the truth about who you are."

"Already told you I have no problem with that. You're the one keeping secrets from him, not me."

Jenna cut in, her words overlapping Morgan's as if what Morgan had to say didn't matter. "Second, you and I start on a clean slate. No more spying, no more threats about exposing anything you may think you have on me."

"Not think, know," Morgan muttered. Did Jenna have any idea how much she sounded just like the Greenes? Superior and entitled?

"And finally, anything happens, anything goes wrong"— Jenna's tone dropped—"and I go to the authorities, turn you in."

"For what? There's no warrants out, not on me." Only thing Morgan's father had ever done for her—kept silent about her part in things. Mostly because he was covering his own ass, but she'd take what she could get.

"I'm sure I can think of something." Jenna twisted in her seat to face Morgan. "Do we have a deal?"

Since Morgan was getting exactly what she wanted—invited on board the Galloway and Stone team—the answer was yes. But she knew Jenna needed to feel like she'd somehow outmaneuvered her.

"Are you going to make me go undercover at ReNew?" Morgan asked in a petulant tone. She'd already decided she'd go—her curiosity about Bree's death was too strong to ignore and Jenna was right, ReNew was the place where she'd find the answers.

"That's part of the package. All or none. Are you in or not?"

Morgan drew out a dramatic sigh. "I'm in."

CHAPTER 12

Morgan spent the night worming her way into Bree's online life. The most exciting thing she found was that by mentioning Steven Moffat on Tumblr, Bree had stumbled into the middle of a Whovian GIF war. Since Bree shared everything with her own page, it seemed she enjoyed the attention from both sides, accidental as it was.

Eight hours later and that and the slutty-party pix were the sum of Bree's social life—her entire life—as best that Morgan could document. She hadn't been able to find more explicit photos from the party where Bree had been drugged. Made her wonder who had come along to clean up that mess. Certainly not Bree's mother. Had Greene found time in his busy schedule to salvage his daughter's reputation? Then why hadn't he pressed charges or at least allowed her to transfer to a different school, one where she wouldn't have to face her tormentors daily.

The sun was just coming up when she closed down her laptop. Morgan didn't have the same sleep cycle as the rest of the world; she tended to catch short naps when she felt like it rather than sleep during any prescribed hours. She didn't understand why the rest of the world clung to their archaic day-night rotation. After all, sleeping only when you needed it meant less time spent being vulnerable. When the rest of the world was asleep was when she and her father had wreaked the most havoc.

Sheep and fish snoring away, practically begging for it, her father would sneer.

Feeling restless and still uncertain about her upcoming under-cover mission, Morgan took the Audi out for a drive. She sped out of the city, no rush hour congestion yet to slow her down, and opened up the Quattro on the county highway leading to ReNew.

About forty minutes out of the city she crested a rolling hill topped by brown fields, waiting for spring to thaw frozen earth, and spotted the ugly squat outline of the ReNew compound in the distance. Had to be it—what other structure would boast towers at each corner, spotlights glinting in the sun, the rigid vertical sup-ports of a high fence lined up like soldiers at attention?

She coasted down the hill, and the glimpse of ReNew blinked out of sight.

The Audi roared up another hill, and the prison came into view once more. She refused to think of it as a school or residential treatment center or any other bullshit. It was a prison pure and simple, and her job was to get what she came for and escape.

She found a good vantage point, pulled over, and grabbed her camera with the long lens. A gravel drive led through a set of gates into the compound; brown grass spread out on both sides. In the distance, Morgan could make out two basketball hoops and what looked like a soccer field. Beyond it, only trees.

The building itself was single story, looked like an elementary school with its windows covered with bright banners and posters, a stark contrast to the grey cinder-block walls. No bars—at least not on this side, the only part of the building easily seen from the highway or by the public. Surrounding it was church property, the congregational buildings half a mile down the highway, separated from the juvenile facility by a large forested parcel. If she craned her head in that direction, she could make out the church's steeple glinting in the sunlight, a beacon above the thick trees.

Idyllic setting, the pamphlets promised. More like isolated, except for the cars and trucks speeding past on the highway beyond the fence.

Superior attention to your child's physical and spiritual well-being away from modern distractions and temptations. After successfully completing our twelve-step, faith-based redemptive program, your child will return home ReFreshed and ReNewed!

Morgan couldn't wait to see what they meant by that.

Although the ReNew compound exuded a sense of security, up close Morgan saw it was mostly illusion. Designed to reassure the parents who exiled their children here, no doubt.

The twelve-foot fence surrounding the building and grounds was simple chain link, no razor wire. The towers were for spotlights, no signs of any guards patrolling outside at all, and the gate, while formidable in appearance, was controlled via a simple keypad. All for show—who needed to worry about the gate when you could climb up one of the light towers and down the fence on the other side?

These people were amateurs when it came to external security. Which meant they must be good at psychological manipulation—made sense, how better to control a juvenile population?

Morgan's father was a master at stripping his captives of their identity, turning them into mindless puppets who'd never dream of freedom. By the time he was done, the concept of escape was meaningless. He'd often even leave their chains or prison doors unlocked.

All they had to do was try . . . but they never did. He always laughed at that, how easily sheep and fish learned their place on the food chain. With him at the top, of course.

Morgan hated those mind games—because she knew he was playing her as well. Telling her she was different, special like him, but at the same time whittling her psyche to fit the role he wanted her to play.

If she could survive her father, outwit him, then these idiots didn't stand a chance.

CHAPTER 13

Morgan got to the Galloway and Stone office at eight twenty, ten minutes before the Greenes were due to arrive. She'd dressed in what she thought a rich, pampered, suburban teen would wear: torn Juicy Couture jeans, a Jessica Simpson designer top, a retro-style denim jacket.

Morgan hated it, parading around, dressed like a fish. Which was why she'd chosen shoes she could run in. Just in case.

Jenna took in her outfit and nodded in approval.

"You sure about this?" Andre asked in a rumble of concern. Morgan couldn't help but smile—she loved it when he worried about her. The fact that he still did, even after she'd shown up so unexpectedly yesterday, meant she had a chance of maintaining her mask, her sheep's clothing.

"I'm sure," she told him. "Those kids need help."

That earned her a quick hug—surprising since Andre knew she didn't like being touched. "You'll be fine," he assured her. "We'll be monitoring everything. Anything happens, we'll get you out straightaway."

"They'll probably take all my stuff." Morgan gestured to her outfit. "How are we going to get any bugs in there?" She had a few ideas—and wasn't leaving anything to chance—but she wanted to give Jenna the lead. It made everything easier when Jenna thought she was in charge.

In answer, Jenna gestured to the receptionist's desk. Lined up on it were a pair of glasses with thick frames complete with a rhinestone-encrusted designer logo on the sidepiece, along with a ballpoint pen, and a stack of three pennies.

"Jenna thought this might call for some specialty items," Andre said. "What do you think?"

"Nice job." Morgan tried the glasses on for size. They actually did have a bit of a prescription—enough to fool anyone glancing at them, but not enough that she couldn't get used to it. Might cost her a few headaches, but that was the least of her worries. She examined the sidepieces. "Audio and video?"

"Yes, but unfortunately no transmission. Just a USB upload." Jenna demonstrated by pulling the end off one of the stems.

"So I can record, but you guys can't hear me?" Not exactly the kind of backup Morgan had in mind.

"That's why you'll have the other two," Andre said. "Both are audio only but they transmit. Voice activated, so you should have several days of battery life. We thought you could leave one in administration and the other in the therapist's office."

He pointed to their floor plan of the ReNew facility. The single-story building had begun life as a school for the ReNew congregation's children, but then had been reinvented as the treatment center. More profit, less government oversight, Morgan guessed. "If you need us, all you need to do is make your way to either room."

"Both of which are locked on the other side of the security doors leading into the detention wing," Morgan pointed out.

"Yeah. Any thoughts on that?"

"Standard procedure is to do a cavity search and strip you of all your clothes," Jenna reminded her before Morgan could suggest any classic prisoner smuggling techniques.

"How about something I could hold in my mouth? Like a fake cap over my molars?"

They exchanged glances. Andre said, "It'd take a visit to a dentist—we don't have time before you go in this morning."

"Worst comes to worst, start a fire," Jenna told Morgan. "The church might be able to skirt the school and HHS codes, but no way is the fire inspector letting them off the hook."

"Start a fire in a facility with fifty kids trapped behind locked doors and windows? Let's hope it doesn't come to that," Andre said.

"And that they don't only turn the fire alarm system on when there's an inspection scheduled," Morgan added.

Andre frowned. "Maybe we should delay another day. We need more intel about how things run inside ReNew. And we haven't finished our research into Greene's company or interviews with former ReNew students—"

"All of the ones I've contacted have nothing but praise for the 'good Reverend Doctor Benjamin' and his practices," Jenna interjected. "Even the three families who filed complaints withdrew them at the request of the children involved. Now they all swear that ReNew saved their kids' lives, steered them straight."

"Sounds more like a cult than a treatment program," Morgan said. Her own research had revealed more of the same—as if everyone had read from the same script.

"All the more reason to wait and do more recon," Andre argued.

Jenna turned to Morgan, hands on her hips. "Your call, Morgan. You up for this or not?"

Typical Jenna making this more about challenging Morgan and less about logistics. But Morgan's curiosity was piqued—not just about what lay behind the lily-white facade of ReNew and

Reverend Benjamin, but about why BreeAnna had killed herself. She'd never felt this invested in someone else before, this need to understand. It was a new experience, and she wanted answers. Only one place to get them.

"I'm good to go." Before she could say anything more the Greenes arrived, ready for their final debriefing and preparation.

Morgan slipped into her new glasses and practiced palming the fake stack of pennies as Jenna played hostess and served coffee. This morning Caren seemed calmer and Robert was the one who fidgeted nervously while they went over the plan.

He caught her staring at him and laughed. "Never did anything like this before. Going undercover. Have to admit, it's a bit exciting."

Morgan gave him a banal smile and turned to shuffle her notes, then rose as if she'd forgotten something in the other room. Andre followed her. No surprise, he'd picked up on the weird vibes from Greene as well.

"This isn't just about his daughter," she told Andre once they were in the reception area and out of earshot.

"I know. He hasn't mentioned BreeAnna once since they arrived." He frowned. "There was nothing on BreeAnna's electronics. Jenna and I couldn't find anything linking Greene or his company to ReNew, other than BreeAnna, could you?"

"No. But you're right, he acts like he's getting ready for a corporate takeover rather than exposing the people responsible for his daughter's death."

"Do you want to cancel?" His voice deepened with concern—a tone she'd only ever heard him use with Jenna before. Clearly Jenna still hadn't told Andre the truth about Morgan's past.

Whatever Greene was up to, it would be best to let this play out, get everything into the open. She could handle him. And the only place left to find answers for Bree was inside ReNew.

"No. But while I'm inside, don't stop digging. There's something fishy about Greene—both of them."

The office door opened, and Jenna leaned out. "Problems?"

Andre answered before Morgan could say anything. "No. I forgot something upstairs. Could you help me, Jenna?" He turned to Morgan. "We'll be back in a minute."

"Andre, I'm fine. You don't need to—"

He shook his head. "Just give us a minute, okay?"

Jenna glared at Morgan as if this was her fault and followed Andre out the door while Morgan returned to keep the Greenes busy while they waited.

Caren hadn't said five words since they arrived. She sat slumped on the couch, eyes glazed. More Valium and booze? Morgan wondered.

"Is it always like this, before an op?" Greene asked, his words rushed. "And you have such interesting gadgets to work with. Makes me feel like James Bond."

"Yes," Morgan answered, mirroring his tone and posture. "Kind of thrilling, isn't it?"

He stood and grabbed the folder with the backstory she had prepped for him. "Guess I'd better go over my role once more." He moved to stand in front of the window, murmuring to himself as if addressing an invisible audience.

Caren didn't follow him with her gaze. Just sat, staring at . . . Morgan pivoted to see what the mother was staring at. The coffee table strewn with files and paperwork and BreeAnna's school photo.

Morgan moved to sit beside Caren. She didn't react, didn't even blink. Her coffee sat untouched on the table beside the folder with the photo paper clipped to the front.

"You miss her, don't you?" Morgan said in a soft tone.

Caren nodded, finally blinked.

"I'll bet that house gets lonely with your husband gone—even when it was you and BreeAnna."

"She despised that house," Caren whispered. "Said it was a prison. Most of the time that's what we fought about—she wanted us to move, anywhere, just get out of that house, that school . . ."

"Because of what happened at the party? That was, what, three weeks before she left for ReNew?"

"You know about that?"

"It's my job. Was that when she started acting out?"

"I guess. Robert's gone all the time, for months. He thrives on it, the wheeling and dealing. Says that's the best thing about owning the company, he can get his hands dirty doing what he loves and let his staff take care of the boring stuff."

Why was it every conversation with these people led away from their daughter and back to Robert Greene? With BreeAnna paying the price when she wanted something more than being locked up like a trophy in his trophy house with his trophy wife.

Was that all this was? Maybe none of this—not Caren's histrionic mood swings and Robert's demands that they destroy ReNew—had anything to do with why BreeAnna killed herself and everything to do with protecting Greene's ego?

CHAPTER 14

Andre led Jenna upstairs to her loft. Usually he relished taking a moment to enjoy the way the morning light scattered across the polished floors and wide open spaces, but today he was distracted. It wasn't often that Andre felt nervous before an op—almost never, in fact—but after three tours in Afghanistan, he'd learned to trust his gut.

"We need to cancel," he told her once the door was closed behind them. "There's something not right about this."

"What?" she demanded, moving past him to lean against the arm of one of the twin leather sofas that sat perpendicular to the entrance. "Everything's fine. We're getting paid, we're starting our business with a major client, and we're getting rid of Morgan for a few days. The trifecta of perfection, seems to me."

Andre studied the space she'd put between them—a sure sign that she wasn't about to compromise. But this wasn't a debate about which restaurant to order takeout from. They were talking about potentially risking Morgan's life—or at the very least, making her life miserable for the foreseeable future.

"There you go again. Talking about getting rid of Morgan, like she's not even a person. Jenna, seriously, I don't think you see how you change when you're around her—and not for the better. You become someone I don't even know, someone I'm not sure I want to know."

"Like you don't change when you're around her? You turn into Mr. Big Brother. Always protecting her. You think you know her so well," Jenna scoffed. "Let me show you who your little friend really is." She whirled around to the front of the sofa where her personal laptop sat on the coffee table, punched a few keys, and pivoted the laptop to face him. "Little fiend is more like it."

Andre crossed from the door to the sofa, taking the seat beside her. He watched as a grainy security camera video played. There was no sound—there didn't need to be.

A girl, maybe ten or twelve years old, dressed in a winter coat and hat, came into view, her back to the camera as she crossed an empty lobby. The camera was obviously situated in a small-town police station—no, sheriff's station, he realized as he spotted the insignia on the deputy who opened the office door and smiled at the girl, crouching down to her level, then inviting her through to the office behind him.

There was nothing after that. Andre glanced at Jenna who nodded tight-lipped at the screen. A few seconds later a dark fluid that showed black against the light-colored floor seeped from beneath the closed door that the deputy and girl had gone through. Blood. A lot of it. Too much of it.

A minute later the door opened again and the girl reappeared, this time in the company of a teenage boy. She leapt over the blood and smiled up at the camera as if performing for an audience.

It was Morgan. Behind her, framed in the open doorway was the deputy's body.

Andre slumped back, stunned. "Morgan killed a police officer? Why? How?"

"Did you see her smile? She enjoyed killing him, Andre. That's the point, that's what you can never forget. As to the why and how, her father is Clinton Caine."

"The serial killer you and Lucy Guardino caught. He made her do this? She's just a kid—"

"Clint always worked with a partner. First his wife, then when she got sick and died, his son. Started taking the boy fishing—that's what he called it when he stalked and kidnapped his victims—when he was just six. But the kid never had the heart for helping his dad, so Clint hit the road and found another partner."

"Morgan? How old was she when he took her?"

"Ten. Young enough to control and train. He taught her everything she knows—how to hunt, how to lie, how to manipulate, how to kill."

Andre had heard about Caine and his decades of torturing and killing women. To be a kid, growing up with that as your entire world . . . it explained a lot about Morgan.

But it sure as hell didn't explain Jenna's actions.

"How could you not tell me? You let me invite her into my home, introduce her to my Grams," he said. "You knew what she was—"

"You knew as well, Andre. Don't tell me you didn't feel it when you first met her."

He had. An animal instinct to avoid a predator. Andre had ignored it—he was used to being the defender of the pack, the big, bad, ugly monster that predators ran from.

But not Morgan. She hadn't run. No. She'd sidled close, snuck under his guard. "Why isn't she locked up?"

"For what?" Jenna scoffed. "That tape isn't enough to charge her, especially as there's no physical evidence."

"Has she killed since? Is that why she's here, to hurt you?" Fear threaded his words.

Jenna looked away with a strange grimace twisting her face. "She followed Lucy home to Pittsburgh. Has some crazy idea of giving up killing and becoming a normal girl. Figured Lucy with her perfect husband and perfect family was the one to show her how."

"I can't imagine Lucy putting up with that." The FBI agent would never allow someone like Morgan near her family.

"No. So Morgan began stalking me instead. Back in December when the Zapata cartel declared war on Pittsburgh, she came along for the ride."

"Zapata was going to kill you. She risked herself to save your life." He'd felt grateful to Morgan for rescuing Jenna. But maybe her actions had been more self-serving than self-sacrificing. What did saving a life even mean to someone like Morgan?

"She enjoyed killing Zapata's men. Enjoyed the idea of playing the hero for once." Jenna's tone was bitter, the words spilling from her in a rush. "Enjoyed getting away with it even more."

Andre thought about that. "She values her freedom."

Jenna nodded. "About the only thing she values."

"Maybe she's serious about giving up killing. If it ensures her freedom, keeps her out of jail—"

"That's what Nick says." She sounded like she didn't believe the psychologist. Nick was one of the smartest men Andre had ever met, but he had to admit, sometimes he was too much of an idealist, always wanting to see the best in people.

Then he realized the implications. "Wait. Does Nick know about Morgan because you and Lucy told him? Or—"

"He's seeing her. Even he won't call it 'treatment.' Says the only thing she'd learn from conventional therapy is how to better blend in and take advantage of people. But he and Lucy decided it was the best way to keep tabs on her since we have nothing we can lock her up for."

Andre thought back to when he was a kid, running with the gang until he was arrested. He remembered sitting with the lawyers and the marine recruiter. With as many members behind bars as on the streets, going to prison was seen by the Rippers as graduating to "Killer U." At least with the marines, he'd also be serving his country, protecting civilians, learning to channel his pride and anger into something more than banging for colors. "I'm not sure prison is the answer for someone like her."

"I know. She'd come out even more vicious than her father ever was. Another Caine set loose on an unsuspecting population." She shuddered, but it wasn't real. Almost as if Jenna had rehearsed this entire conversation. She was like that, always anticipating the worst, trying to prepare and guard against it.

Which meant that Jenna, despite what she said, for whatever reason, wanted Morgan to stay. Andre thought about that. He was sure it was about more than protecting the population against a budding psycho-killer trying to redeem herself. Wished he understood the bond between Jenna and Morgan, but like so much about Jenna, he resigned himself to taking his time and being patient.

"I guess we're stuck with her. Like guardians, teaching her how not to kill." He wrapped his arm around her shoulder and pulled her to his side. "I know it seems hopeless to you, but I was twelve when I got jumped into the gang. Despite all that, I turned out okay, didn't I?"

"That's different. You're different."

"Not so sure about that. The only difference I see is that I had people watching out for me. People like Grams, then my squad, and Nick helping me when I came back, and now you." He kissed the top of her head. "Seems like we're the best chance Morgan has."

"If she slips up? We're talking people's lives here."

Andre was glad she couldn't see his face. Because although he meant what he said about helping Morgan, no way in hell was he about to let her hurt anyone ever again. Especially not Jenna.

Morgan might have learned how to kill from her father, but Andre was a battle-hardened marine, twice her size. If it came to it, he'd put her down as quickly as he would a rabid dog.

CHAPTER 15

When Jenna returned without Andre and wearing a conservative grey sweaterdress that made her look ten years older than she was, Morgan knew something was up.

Jenna shot her a glare, then to the Greenes she said, "Slight change of plans. We need more intel before we can commit to placing an operative inside ReNew. I'll be accompanying you instead of Morgan."

Robert Greene spun to face her. "No. That's not what we discussed."

Jenna didn't back down. "Nevertheless, it's what has to happen. You and I will go inside ReNew as prospective parents, learn their security routines, get a better feel for what Morgan will be facing. Then we can safely send her inside—if we need to."

Greene's face tightened. "You're wasting time. We all know sending the girl in is the best way to finish this."

Morgan watched, interested. Finish what, she wondered. Sending her in wasn't going to end the Greenes' fight against ReNew—in fact, any evidence she collected would only be the start of their battle . . . if that's what they were really looking for, ammunition against ReNew.

"Andre wants to see you," Jenna told Morgan, dismissing her from the conversation.

Didn't matter. She was just as happy not to be going to ReNew—at least not until she understood Greene's motives better. As curious as she was about what happened to Bree while inside the treatment center, she wasn't foolish enough to allow anyone to use her as a pawn.

She walked up the steps, wondering if Jenna had found something out about the Greenes. Maybe she'd discovered new info on ReNew that had made her change her mind about sending her in this morning?

The door to the loft was open. Andre waited on the sofa, but he didn't turn to look at her as she entered, despite the fact that she knocked. The March sunlight came in through windows and the overhead skylight, reflecting from a thin sheen of sweat that covered his scalp.

Morgan stayed close to the door, keeping her exit clear, not sure why she suddenly felt uncomfortable being in the same room as Andre, but she wasn't one to ignore her instincts. "You wanted to see me?"

"Jenna told me the truth," he finally said, still not looking at her. Instead he stared at a blank laptop screen. "About you. About your dad. What you two did together."

The air in the room sparked with emotion—all of it from Andre. If anything, during fight-or-flight situations like this, Morgan felt less than nothing. She was too busy calculating the odds, assessing each possible response, and deciding what would get her what she wanted.

He turned. Slowly, as if he were an old man too heavy for his years instead of a twenty-six-year-old former marine in excellent shape. "I just have one question."

Silence grew as his gaze held hers. Morgan didn't flinch, didn't blink, although every ounce of her energy folded in on itself like a fist closing, ready to strike.

Not physically—she wouldn't stand a chance against Andre, not when his guard was up. But the right words could bring even the strongest man to his knees, and she knew exactly where Andre's weak spots lay. He had people he would protect, people he would die for.

His grandmother. Jenna. Nick. Even Morgan herself, once upon a time.

"What?" she prompted him, weary of the wait. "What do you want to know?"

His jaw tightened, making the scars crossing his face bulge. "Do you regret it? The things your father made you do, the women you killed together. Do you regret any of it?"

She opened her mouth, ready to tell him what he wanted to hear, but he held a hand up, stopping her. "Please, Morgan. The truth. You owe me that much."

Anger flashed through her at the thought that he assumed she owed him anything, but she doused it with a calming breath like Nick had taught her.

Owe? She didn't owe anyone anything. No debts, no regrets—it was part of her new way of life, the one she and Nick were working on building. A set of tools to survive, a wolf loose among so many unsuspecting sheep. Deciding when she owed a debt, navigating those human interactions others took for granted, was a challenge she took seriously.

She hated the thought that anyone felt they deserved a piece of her. Her freedom was too valuable to squander.

But she did respect Andre—a lot. She even liked him, enjoyed having him in her life.

If there was any chance that he would continue to be a part of her life, she'd have to risk telling him the truth. Andre's bullshit meter was too well honed for anything else.

"No," she answered. "I don't regret any of it."

His eyes blazed, hands clenched into fists, but he didn't raise them. Instead he slumped forward, hands dangling uselessly between his knees. "So it's true." His words emerged with a sigh. As if he hadn't truly believed until now. "And people call me a monster."

Morgan gave in to her impulse, moved across the space separating them, and gave him a quick kiss on the top of his head, now in easy reach with her still standing and him below her on the sofa. He flinched—he should, because he was vulnerable sitting like that, so close to her. She could have just as easily slit his throat.

"Trust me, Andre," she whispered. "You're no monster."

He shied away from her touch but didn't look up. She perched on the arm of the sofa. "How can I have any regrets when I wouldn't be here today without that time with my father? How can I regret my life, Andre?"

Usually she never explained, but she was curious what his response would be. Would a man who'd seen battle, who'd killed with his own hands understand?

"And those women?" he asked.

"If they had lived, I would be dead now." It was the simple truth.

The one thing her father had promised her was that she would never live to see a day behind bars. A fate worse than death for a wild one like her, he'd said.

As if she didn't see the truth behind his words: if they were caught, she was one more potential witness. If she and her father had been caught together, her father would have killed her himself—to silence her.

Andre's hands clenched and unclenched, and she knew he was remembering the men he'd killed.

"When was the last time you killed anyone?" he asked.

"I'm not like my father," she answered, annoyed that he saw her as some kind of out-of-control psycho-killer on a rampage, dropping bodies left and right. "His hunger drove him. He was reckless, impulsive."

"And you aren't?" He turned to meet her gaze, his own accusing her.

"No. I am." She smiled. "But unlike my father I have something I'm passionate about, something strong enough to give me control."

He stared at her in disbelief. "And what's that?"

"The last time I killed anyone was the night I saved Jenna." She stood and gathered her breath. It would be the first time she spoke the words out loud to another human, not even Nick. "I won't kill again because I don't want to ever end up in a cage like my father. I want to live a long and happy life, Andre. Outside of prison. I want my freedom."

"That's it? That's what keeps you from killing?" He pushed to his feet, standing too close, inside her kill zone. And he knew that. She liked that he showed no fear, understood he was challenging her on purpose. "You enjoyed the killing, the chaos, the power over others, didn't you? It was fun for you and your father."

A spray of spittle accompanied his words, but Morgan didn't back up. She decided to give him the truth.

"It was," she admitted. "I was a kid in a candy store, and nothing I wanted was off-limits. My life with him—it didn't feel real; it was like some crazy, mad dream. I'm older now. I understand the consequences. I know what I want, and I'm going to get it."

It was just that simple. And that hard. She met his gaze, watching the range of emotions twisting his face. Disgust, fury, skepticism. Despite his scars—or maybe because of them—Morgan could read Andre better than she could others. Most people never saw beyond his mask of scars, but they didn't distract her.

Finally resignation filled his eyes. Nick had that same look every time she came into the office. As if Morgan was a burden to be carried.

She didn't care. If Nick and Andre helped her get what she wanted, she didn't care why they did what they did. She didn't ask for their help; she didn't owe them anything. These men of... honor was the best word she could find . . . they assumed responsibility without being asked or told.

That was their weakness. She might respect Nick and Andre more than most Norms, but damned if she wasn't going to use any advantage given her.

"I want to tell you to leave, to never come back," Andre said. "But where would you go? Who would watch over you, stop you if you lost control? Who would die or be hurt if I did that?"

Morgan had no answers, so she gave him none. Instead she waited for what she knew was coming. Was curious to compare it to the ultimatum Nick had given her when he first began working with her.

"But I warn you, Morgan," Andre continued as Morgan hid her smirk. He sounded exactly like Nick had. "You hurt one person—good, bad, I don't care—you take one step out of line, and I will end you."

Andre's threat hit harder than Nick's. Because, unlike Nick who would never entertain the thought of violence, Andre wouldn't simply call the cops or try to send her to prison. He'd kill her. "You know I can, and you know I will."

Keep your friends close and your enemies closer. Good to know where she stood. She nodded her assent, her respect for Andre a notch higher.

Still. If their positions had been reversed, if she'd been him, facing a monster like her, she wouldn't have hesitated to finish things once and for all. Killing her now, whether or not she kept up her end of the bargain, was the only solution to the threat he faced—but men like Andre and Nick, they were blind to that. Had to follow their rules. Their code of honor.

Andre should have killed her. Prevented any worry and saved future bloodshed and pain.

And they both knew it.

CHAPTER 16

As angry as Jenna was, it wasn't difficult to play the sullen, frumpy wife as Greene drove them out to ReNew. She hated changing plans so abruptly, hated even more the reason why: Andre's so-called gut feeling.

She didn't even have the satisfaction of blaming it on Morgan. Andre had wanted to cancel the undercover op before she told him the truth about Morgan. He would come around to her way of thinking, she was certain, but she couldn't let their clients see his discomfort, so she'd arranged this field trip to buy some time. And hopefully regain Greene's confidence. Who knew, maybe she could ferret out some overlooked piece of intel that unraveled the entire ReNew setup?

The thought cheered her a bit. The Greene Energy headquarters were between her office and ReNew, so she and Greene had driven there in separate vehicles and she'd left her Tahoe behind since his Lexus SUV fit their cover story better. It wasn't often that she had the opportunity to sit doing nothing in the passenger seat, staring at the mindless scenery. She hated it. Hills and cows and trees filled the horizon in every direction. Barely any homes—more barns than houses, in fact. How did people live like this? So out of touch with civilization?

"I'm not paying extra for this little field trip, if that's your game," Greene said, his first words since they'd left the office.

Jenna flipped down the sun visor and adjusted the scarf she'd tied around her head, hiding her red hair as much as possible. She wiped off most of her makeup as well, smudging what was left to make her appear a bit haggard. Even her own mother wouldn't recognize her, she thought with satisfaction. Anyway, she intended to let Greene take the spotlight. Her role was the mousy partner, watching from the shadows.

"We don't intend on charging you extra." It wasn't about the money, she knew. It was about her usurping his control. From the start, Greene had wanted to drive this investigation at his pace and in his direction. Now he was upset his plans had hit a bump in the road.

Maybe it was for the best. After all, he'd come to her for her expertise. If she was going to win his trust enough to gain the Greene Energy corporate contract, she needed him to respect her and accept her authority. Ruffling feathers and delivering the goods would both be required.

"What do you intend?" he asked, his tone skeptical.

"I intend on evaluating the situation and providing you with the best plan of action to achieve your goals. You want to bring ReNew down, this is the first step."

He frowned, staring out through the windshield. "I still want the girl to go in. I need to know what my daughter went through. What those bastards did to her."

"We can definitely discuss that option." Maybe it wasn't taking down ReNew that he wanted so much as a reason to blame them—instead of his and Caren's inept parenting—for BreeAnna's death. If so, sending Morgan in and recording her experiences might achieve that.

Or it could result in hours of boring footage that wouldn't answer any of the Greenes' needs. Maybe Andre was right; she should meet the people involved and evaluate ReNew for herself before risking sending Morgan inside.

They reached a single-story building surrounded by a tall fence. Greene slowed, then pulled into the gravel drive, stopping before a gate and giving his fake name into the intercom. "James Renshaw and wife to see Reverend Benjamin. We have an appointment for ten o'clock."

There was a pause before a man's voice answered. "Please wait."

Greene sat, not fidgeting. Now that they were here, he seemed more relaxed. *A good thing,* Jenna thought. Less likely to say something stupid and blow their cover. A car, a late-model Cadillac ATS, approached them from the school. The gate slid open, and it pulled up alongside.

The driver, a man in his midtwenties wearing a navy-blue suit with a crisp white shirt and conservative tie, rolled down his window and gestured for Greene to do the same. "I'm Sean Chapman, the director of the ReNew Treatment Center. Nice to meet you, Mr. and Mrs. Renshaw. If you follow me, I'll take you to the good Reverend Doctor."

"No. We were told to meet him here. So we could see the facility for ourselves. We were promised a tour," Greene protested. Jenna touched his arm in a calming, wifely manner, her gaze directed downward.

Chapman didn't rattle, despite Greene's bluster. "Of course. We'll answer all your questions and concerns. But the good Reverend Doctor was detained at the church, and he would very much like to meet you in person. When he heard about your daughter's circumstances, he felt your case warranted his personal attention."

He made it sound as if Reverend Benjamin was granting them a papal boon. *Guess they liked "Renshaw's" credit report,* Jenna thought with satisfaction. If ReNew was more about profit and less about saving souls, she'd created a fake persona they'd find irresistible.

"It's okay, honey," she said, adding a hint of cower to her tone. "Please, maybe he can help."

"Not like anything else we've tried has," Greene said, playing along. He nodded to Chapman, who drove past, then reversed the Lexus to follow.

They returned to the highway and drove west into a forested area. "If we don't get a look inside," Greene muttered, "this entire trip will be a waste of my time."

His time, not Jenna's, she noted. "Don't you want to meet the man you hold responsible for your daughter's death?"

That earned her a grunt. The trees gave way to allow room for a large sign with a brightly colored sunrise logo, inviting all to turn right to "ReNew" their souls. Chapman took the turn, and they followed.

This two-lane drive was well maintained as it curved through the forest. Then, at the top of a hill, the trees ended and a spacious meadow was revealed. At the center was a large white building. Its shape, with a sloped metal roof, resembled the barns they'd passed on the highway more than a church, but at the center of the roof was a wide steeple with a tall cross on top of it, reaching to the sky.

Despite the fact that it was the middle of a weekday, there were several cars in the parking lot, but Chapman didn't bother with it. He led them up the circular drive and parked directly in front of the main entrance. Greene parked as well and exited the SUV. It was Chapman who came and opened Jenna's door for her and helped her down from her seat.

"Welcome to ReNew," he said, waving his arm as if unveiling a work of art. "We know it's not as grand as other religions' cathedrals, but we enjoy the quiet simplicity of it."

He ran up the steps and across the porch to swing one of the wide doors open for them. "Besides," he continued with a grin as they crossed over the threshold, "it's paid for. Not many churches around here can say that."

Inside they were greeted by the sweet, if off-key, tones of a children's choir rehearsing. The cynic in Jenna wondered if the performance had been staged for their benefit.

"This is our worship hall," Chapman told them as they entered a wide open space surrounded on all sides with large windows. No stained glass or fancy iconography. Just whitewashed walls and plain windows except for one large arched window at the far end that featured the ReNew sunrise logo. Below it was a simple wooden cross suspended above a raised stage.

No pews, instead there were plain wooden chairs—very much like Jenna's own kitchen chairs—arranged in a semicircle around the stage. Some of them had been pulled to the corner where the children sang to accommodate several beaming mothers.

"Our services can be rather informal," Chapman explained. "After the good Reverend Doctor concludes his instruction and all testimony has been heard, we often break up in smaller groups to discuss the Bible passages. It makes worship become a true community event instead of an empty ritual."

A thin blonde woman appeared from a door behind the stage and hurried to greet them. She wore a gossamer-thin dress that reached her ankles, and Jenna wondered that she wasn't freezing—it was only fifty degrees outside, and the church felt drafty and chilly.

"This is Deidre, our student leader." Chapman made introductions as Deidre arrived, her cheeks flushed and appearing a bit out of breath. She ducked her head and made a tiny movement that was almost but not quite a curtsy.

"I'm so pleased to meet you, Mr. Renshaw, Mrs. Renshaw," she said. "Your daughter isn't with you?" She sounded disappointed, but Greene took it as a challenge.

"No," he snapped. "There's no way in hell I'd trust my only child to total strangers."

Jenna placed her hand on his arm, a subtle warning. "It's my fault," she explained. "I was so desperate. She was so out of control yesterday that when I called, I didn't think we could wait."

"Is she okay?" Deidre asked, concern filling her voice. "So many of these children, when they feel out of control—"

"She's fine," Greene said.

"We can't trust her in school," Jenna put in. "But my mother is watching her today." She sighed dramatically. "Morgan is too much for any of us to handle. We hope your program—"

"Let's not keep the good Reverend Doctor waiting," Chapman said, steering them down the aisle to the door Deidre had come through. "He can answer all of your concerns, I'm sure."

They skirted the stage and came to a simple whitewashed door. Chapman knocked and opened it. "The Renshaws," he announced them. He positioned his body so that he and Greene entered first. Jenna wondered if it was intentional, placing the men before the women. Either way, it suited her plans. She hoped to keep the focus on Greene, so she could observe without notice.

She entered the room—an office, furnished with a large wooden desk, nothing fancy or expensive, several mismatched chairs, and bookshelves overflowing with religious texts. The closest thing to a vanity wall were the framed photos of the Reverend surrounded by smiling parishioners of all ages, digging in a community garden, painting a mural with children, earnestly discussing a Bible passage with a group of teens.

The photos were nothing compared to the man who rose from his chair behind the desk to greet them. He wasn't tall or broad-shouldered, yet he dominated the space, commanding attention as he beamed at them, the light from the window behind him making his salt-and-pepper hair gleam. He reached out a hand to Greene, shook it, and nodded to the chairs. Greene took the one in front while Chapman held the chair behind it for Jenna.

She sank in it, unable to tear her gaze away from Reverend Benjamin. She found herself leaning forward, not wanting to miss a word or gesture he made. It was a familiar feeling, one that she'd missed and yearned for for years—ever since her grandfather, the Judge, died.

He'd been the center of her universe as a child—she lived to please him, to earn the slightest glance or smile. Reverend Benjamin looked nothing like Jenna's grandfather, but she couldn't fight the wave of emotion that overwhelmed her. Being in his presence made her want to do more than please him—just like with her grandfather, she felt herself wishing he'd look at her, favor her with a request, give her the chance to serve him, to earn his praise.

Charismatic, that was the word people used to describe her grandfather. *Men wanted to be him; women wanted to be with him,* she'd once heard her mother say.

The Reverend remained standing, relaxed, arms open in greeting. Without speaking a word, he dwarfed Greene, conquering the younger man's innate alpha male nature and establishing himself as the dominate force. She glanced at Greene, expecting him to be bristling with challenge. Instead he leaned forward in his chair, chin tilted down, waiting for the Reverend's lead.

Jenna sucked in her breath, long-buried memories snaring her like weeds whose roots survived a blaze. She tried to swallow, but her mouth was dry. She pushed back in her chair, crossing her arms and legs. The feelings she had for her grandfather, the things she'd done to earn his love, she'd fought long and hard to keep those buried, a secret from everyone—especially herself.

The Reverend sensed her vulnerability. And her shame, she was sure. Because he turned his attention away from Greene to focus on Jenna. Then he smiled.

"Mrs. Renshaw," he said, his voice a sinuous chord that echoed throughout her body. "I'm so glad you came to us. I read the information you gave Director Chapman, and I truly believe we can help your child. Trust her with me, and she'll leave here with her spirit ReNewed."

Then he smiled, and it was as if the room filled with warm sunshine. Jenna's posture relaxed, almost against her will. "I promise you, I will save your little girl."

CHAPTER 17

At first Morgan had been furious to return from her discussion with Andre to find that Jenna had absconded with Greene, leaving her to escort Caren home. *Better that than being stuck in the office with Andre*, she thought as she gathered Caren's coat and purse—the woman seemed incapable of even these simple tasks. Morgan decided it was a good thing Caren hadn't driven herself to the office as she led her to Morgan's borrowed Audi.

"I'm glad he's going out there himself," Caren murmured as Morgan maneuvered them through the city traffic. "He'll see that I made the right decision. It wasn't my fault."

Morgan rolled her eyes at Caren's recurring theme and changed the subject to something she actually cared about. "I saw Bree's piano. She must have been very talented."

Caren shrugged. "Her teachers thought so. Of course, they also insisted that she wasn't fulfilling her promise." She turned to face Morgan. "That's what private instructors being paid two hundred dollars an hour say when they want to keep their job but also want you to know a child is too lazy to ever improve."

Lazy? Morgan thought of all the carefully composed scores and notations that filled the wall of Bree's music room. "Maybe she wasn't lazy. Maybe there are limits to talent. Not everyone can be a genius."

"Tell that to my husband. He bootstrapped his way up from the West Virginia coal mines, digging coal by hand at times. First in his family to go to college and own his own home. He doesn't believe in limits."

Sounded like Greene. No wonder the man acted as if he was the sun and the rest of the world revolved around him.

They left the city and traffic thinned. A short time later, Morgan pulled up in front of the Greenes' mansion. The house looked even less welcoming now than it had last night, despite the clear skies surrounding it.

She walked Caren up the steps. "Won't you come inside?" Caren asked as she opened the front door.

Morgan took a step back as if the oppressive atmosphere she'd felt last night was trying to force her away. "I really should be getting back," she lied.

Caren's balance wavered, and Morgan wondered, not for the first time, if she was already drunk. Or popping pills. Maybe both. Not even ten in the morning and the woman could barely walk. She clung to the heavy brass doorknob and turned to face Morgan.

"Please, I don't want to be alone." She squinted at Morgan, struggling to focus. "Come inside. I'll tell you a secret."

Probably where she hid her liquor and pills. But Morgan played along. "What kind of secret?"

Caren smiled and pulled Morgan over the threshold, closing the door and leaning against it as if preventing Morgan's escape. "A secret about BreeAnna." Her voice echoed through the high ceilinged foyer, and she put a finger to her lips. "Follow me."

She staggered up the stairs, Morgan following, one hand braced against Caren's back to keep her from falling. "What about BreeAnna?"

Caren said nothing until they were inside her suite of rooms. She dropped her coat and purse to the floor, kicking them to one side, then collapsed onto a love seat. The entire room was filled with skinny French furniture, pieces that tried to appear like antiques but Morgan could tell they weren't. Froufrou wallpaper and drapes, crystal vases with fake flowers, and other knickknacks designed to evoke a feeling of a cultured world traveler.

She almost snorted in derision at the contrast between the studied decor and the woman slumped on the love seat, eyes closed. Morgan was about to leave, thinking Caren had fallen asleep, when the older woman spoke.

"It was his idea to bring her home," she said in a singsong, her words slurred. "He blamed me for sending her. Said I needed to control her. As if." She opened her eyes and made a grab for Morgan, missing by inches. "I could never control her. No one could. He made her come home, made me bring her home."

Morgan stopped. Listened and thought about the meaning behind Caren's words. "Robert didn't want Bree at ReNew."

Caren shook her head vigorously. "No. No. No. He did not. He. Wanted. Her. Home. ASAP." She punched the air with her index finger. "But here's the secret. Not even Robert knows."

She drifted into silence, eyes closing once more. Morgan knelt beside her, gripping her hand. "What didn't you tell Robert, Caren? What's the secret?"

She squeezed her eyes tighter, as if denying Morgan's presence. Morgan changed her tone and caressed Caren's forehead.

"It's okay," she crooned. "You can tell me. You'll feel so much better. Tell me, Caren."

"It's all my fault. All my fault," Caren said, eyes still closed tight.

Morgan kept soothing the older woman's forehead, stroking her hair. Waiting. She was afraid Caren would drift asleep before saying anything more, but finally her eyes fluttered open.

"It's all my fault. I made her come home. Because that's what Robert wanted. And Robert always gets what he wants. Always." A strangled sob choked her to silence. She swallowed hard and continued, "BreeAnna's dead because I made her come home. She didn't want to come. She wanted to stay. There. At that awful place."

"Did Bree say that?" Who would want to stay locked up rather than return to freedom? Morgan couldn't even imagine it. Maybe ReNew was a cult, had brainwashed her.

"No. Bree didn't say a word. Not to me. Not when I came for her, not on the ride home, not before she, she—" She choked up, her inhalation gurgling with tears.

"Why do you think she wanted to stay at ReNew?" Morgan asked after Caren had recovered enough to blow her nose and speak clearly.

"Horrid place. While I was waiting for them to get her, I overheard a girl in the hallway, arguing with Mr. Chapman, the director. The girl was screaming. In a rage. Said Bree had to stay, that he shouldn't take her away. Said Bree hated me, hated her life here."

She stared into Morgan's eyes with a sudden ferocity and gripped her hands tight. "My baby girl would rather stay locked up in that hellhole than live with me. I drove her away, and when I made her come home—"

She released Morgan and collapsed back against the cushions, curling up into a fetal ball, sobbing. "All my fault. I made her come home and now she's dead. She's dead. Because of me."

CHAPTER 18

Jenna found herself torn between conflicting feelings—physical and emotional. The Reverend's words made her stomach tighten in both anticipation and fear. Memories overwhelmed her, and she lost sense of time, could only dimly hear Greene's voice as he continued the conversation without her.

She wished Nick were here so she could seek his counsel, but that would mean exposing her secrets, and there was no way she'd ever tell him the truth.

She thought of Andre. He could never, ever know the truth, either. But thinking of him brought no fear of being exposed for who, for what she really was. Instead her mind filled with the memory of how she would burrow into Andre's embrace after they made love. He'd wrap his arms around her, offering warmth and comfort. And never once asking for anything in return.

Focusing on Andre, feeling his hands glide down her body, hearing his voice murmur, low and soothing, that gave her the strength she needed to shove the memories—the good along with the bad—behind the barricades she'd spent decades constructing.

She blinked and glanced over at Greene, trying to clue back into the conversation. "The girl is willful, stubborn," he was saying. "She refuses to obey any rules, accept any consequences."

"Out of control," the Reverend finished for him.

"Yes, exactly. Totally out of control." Greene didn't seem at all uncomfortable with the Reverend's magnetic dominance. Instead Greene was relaxed in his chair, his chin bobbing in agreement with the Reverend's pronouncements.

The girl, Deidre, and the administrator, Chapman, had moved to stand side by side behind the Reverend, their bodies almost touching. Both stood tall, soldiers at parade rest. The Reverend had resumed his chair, his fingers templed before him as he considered their fictional problem child.

"In my experience," he said, sounding more like a grandfather than a man of God, "children like your daughter are almost impossible to handle in the home setting. I commend both of you for being able to keep her from harming herself or someone else, but I sense we've come to a crisis."

Greene nodded and leaned forward eagerly. "It's only been a little drinking and acting out, but—"

"But you see that it's the tip of the iceberg." The Reverend smiled at Greene as if he were a particularly astute student. "I totally agree. I've been doing this for several decades, caring for these wayward young souls, and I can assure you, Mr. Renshaw, that anything you know or think you know about your daughter's behavior is only a tiny fraction of what is actually going on."

Chapman took his cue and handed the Reverend a folder. The Reverend opened the cover and allowed it to fall against the desk, the small noise sounding like a judge's gavel. "Take this latest incident. Drinking, out at night at an older boy's house, bringing a younger girlfriend along—" He looked up suddenly, his gaze now stern. "You do realize if the authorities got involved, your daughter could be labeled a sexual predator and charged as an adult?"

"No, please," Jenna said with a gasp, playing her role. "She's only fifteen. She didn't know what she was doing—it's those boys, it's their fault."

"But who placed the younger girl in that dangerous environment with those older, predatory males?" The Reverend shook his head. "I think we can help Morgan. I really do—but it won't be easy. Or quick. She'll need to learn to take responsibility for her actions, to accept the consequences and learn control."

Greene was nodding eagerly. "Yes, exactly. That's why we're here." He turned to Jenna. "I think we've finally come to the right place." Without waiting for Jenna's answer, he faced the Reverend. "When can you take her? When can we bring her?"

Jenna stood up, startling them all and bringing their focus on her. "Wait. I want to see where she'd be staying, learn more—"

To her surprise it wasn't the Reverend who answered her but rather the student leader, Deidre, who came forward and took Jenna's hand in her own. "Of course, Mrs. Renshaw. Let me show you." She glanced back at Chapman and the Reverend who both nodded their approval. Before she knew it, Deidre led Jenna from the room, leaving the men behind. Jenna looked over her shoulder, hoping Greene wouldn't blow their cover, but she had no choice but to follow—especially as Deidre still clung to her arm.

Instead of leading her out of the building, Deidre took her into an adjacent room. There were several chairs gathered around a wall-mounted wide-screen TV. "Sit here."

Jenna obeyed—the girl, she wasn't sure how old Deidre was, late teens to early twenties, was oddly persuasive. A lot like the Reverend that way. Jenna wondered if they were related. The body language back in the office had implied that the administrator, Sean Chapman, might be involved with Deidre. He'd looked at her in a way that was almost possessive.

Deidre reached for a remote and took the seat beside Jenna. "You understand how disruptive it would be to interrupt the students' day with strangers touring, so we created this video to show families a typical day at ReNew."

The video, complete with a mellow acoustic guitar playing in the background, began with a panoramic view of the ReNew grounds. "Both Director Chapman and myself live on the campus. We also maintain a small but effective security staff." The ReNew logo filled the screen, then was replaced by still shots of smiling teenagers staring attentively at a teacher, followed by more of the same—teens gathered together listening or discussing or eating or playing basketball. The girls outnumbered the boys by about three to one. They were almost all white and good-looking, to the point where Jenna wondered if they were students or hired models.

As the video ended, Deidre continued, "While our focus is, of course, on behavior modification, following traditional twelve-step tenets, we strive to ensure that each student graduates from the program not only with their spirit ReNewed but also better equipped for the responsibilities of adulthood."

Jenna glanced up at the sweeping statement. "How can you possibly know that?"

Deidre didn't take offense at Jenna's skepticism. "I'm sure you've already done your homework and read the testimonials of our prior students from our website. Let me share with you my personal testimony." She took both of Jenna's hands in hers and leaned toward her until they were almost head to head. "ReNew saved my life."

"How so?"

"We only had my mom, my brother and I, and we lost her when I was ten. He was seventeen, and he did a good job of taking care of us, well, as good as he could. But, by the time I was twelve, we were living out of our car, broke, hadn't eaten in a few days. As you can imagine, a big brother isn't the same as a parent, and the more chaotic our life became, the more I rebelled, acted out. A wild child, my brother used to call me. I began stealing. I used to lie to adults and panhandle for spare change. I even imagined I'd be better off on my own and tried to run away."

"What happened?" Jenna asked, transfixed by the younger woman's story despite herself. No, not a story. Deidre was telling the truth, of that she was certain.

Deidre inhaled deeply, bit her lip, then released it once more. "We were on our way to the city, so my brother could find work. Stopped for the night at a rest stop. No food, no money, not sure if we had enough gas left to make it to a service station or how we'd pay for it once we got there. And, of course, stupid, stubborn selfish twelve-year-old that I was, I picked a fight. I can't even remember what it was about. But that night after my brother fell asleep, I decided I'd had enough. We'd been on the road long enough that I knew there were ways women could make money, using their bodies, and I decided that I wasn't a little girl and I could take care of myself. So I propositioned the next male driving alone who parked near us."

Jenna stared at Deidre. Deidre nodded. "I know. I was an idiot—but that's just how out of control I was. I didn't care about consequences. I didn't want to think, I just wanted to leave my life behind. Thankfully that first driver in that first car was the good Reverend Doctor. He brought my brother and me here, gave my brother a job, and my brother enrolled me in ReNew."

"You wanted to attend?"

"Heck no. I hated him for it—thought he was abandoning me. I fought, kicked, screamed my way through the first few months. Until one day, I stopped shouting long enough to listen. To understand how messed up I was. To calm down. To let my guard down and admit that I couldn't make it without help."

She released Jenna's hands. "I've been here ever since. Trying to repay the Reverend by helping others who were like me. But honestly, without ReNew, I would have died years ago. The good Reverend Doctor didn't just save my soul, he saved my life."

CHAPTER 19

I can't believe you were thinking of sending Morgan in there without talking with me first," Nick said to Andre as they drove to the Greenes' house for their meeting with Caren to begin the psychological autopsy. Nick drove—Andre preferred to ride shotgun, keeping his eyes and hands free to focus on the environment around them.

To Nick's surprise, Andre jerked upright as if on alert. But the road was clear. Nick glanced over and realized Andre wasn't staring at their surroundings, but rather at Nick.

"Who are you worried about?" Andre's tone was flat. "Morgan? Or the kids locked in with her?"

Oh. Jenna must have finally told Andre the truth about Morgan. "I couldn't tell you, Andre. Patient confidentiality."

He didn't tell Andre that it was Jenna's confidentiality he was protecting. Morgan didn't care who he told about their sessions, had made it clear that he was free to talk to Lucy or Jenna or anyone because as she put it, "I won't be confessing anything anyone can use against me."

She was wrong, revealing vulnerabilities that she herself was blind to. Despite Morgan's permission, Nick had kept their sessions private, just as he would for any client. But Jenna had specifically asked him to not tell Andre what she'd told Nick about her first encounter with Morgan, and Nick had honored that, difficult as it was.

"Bullshit. You knew what she was, and you let me invite her into my home, introduce her to my Grams. You let that, that—" he sputtered into silence.

"That kid who's trying to get her life together?" Nick supplied.

"Hell no, don't go playing Mr. Everyone Has Some Good In Them with me. She's a stone-cold killer. And now I have to figure out what to do with her before she hurts someone else."

"Sending her into a volatile situation like ReNew is hardly the answer." Nick allowed his own anger to edge his voice. Andre wasn't a patient anymore—he was a friend—so Nick didn't have to hide behind a therapist's mask of neutrality.

Andre gave a grunt. "Jenna's idea. Now that I know the truth about Morgan, makes me wonder if it wasn't her way of getting rid of her—I don't think she would have minded if Morgan never came back out."

He paused. They both knew a place like ReNew couldn't hold a girl like Morgan. "I've never seen Jenna act the way she does around Morgan. Not angry, more like vindictive, resentful. Before I knew the truth, I was the one defending Morgan, reminding Jenna that Morgan saved her life."

"Exactly why she deserves a chance. How many stone-cold killers do you know who would have risked their lives like that?" Nick asked, proving his point.

Andre jerked his chin, not actually agreeing, but at least considering. "Jenna called her a psychopath. Thought there was no cure for that? So why'd she do it, save Jenna from the Zapatas?"

"Sociopaths make up one to four percent of the population. Not all of them are violent or even criminal. They do what serves their needs and wants, often are impulsive, and require increasing levels of stimulation. But they can also be extremely driven and focused, single-minded. Think CEOs and neurosurgeons, prosecutors, politicians."

"If Morgan is focused on staying out of jail, not hurting people, she'll most likely be able to succeed?" Andre's voice held a tinge of skepticism, and Nick didn't blame him.

"No one can predict anyone's success in this world, and Morgan has more to deal with than her sociopathic tendencies—being exposed to her father's depravity at such a young age caused her lasting damage."

"Cut the clinical BS. Is she dangerous or not?"

"Morgan is smart enough to know that between you, Jenna, myself, and Lucy, if she steps out of line, she's going to prison. She'll avoid that at all costs."

"She steps out anywhere near me, and it won't be prison she has to worry about."

"Then maybe you and Jenna shouldn't be putting her in situations where she has no control. Like sending her into that detention center all alone. Do you know what those places are like?" Nick knew he did. Andre had been sent to a juvenile facility when he was seventeen. At least he'd been given a choice between serving his time in prison or joining the marines.

"It was Jenna's idea," Andre repeated. "But, we might still need to go through with it. If we don't find anything else to point to a reason why Bree killed herself." He paused, waiting for Nick to protest. Nick in turn waited for Andre to ask the question he needed to ask. "Unless . . . is Morgan dangerous? To someone else, like those kids?"

"You know the answer to that," Nick said in a low voice. "We're all dangerous, given the right circumstances."

"Stop splitting hairs, Nick. If we sent her into a place like ReNew, would we be putting the other kids in danger?"

"The fact that you're even asking the question proves my point. If you truly thought Morgan couldn't control herself, you wouldn't even be considering that option. Which means you believe she can change."

"This isn't about what I believe—"

"No. It's about innocent kids. If Morgan is their best chance, if something is going on at ReNew, then how can you not send her?"

"I thought for sure you'd say no."

Funny, Nick had as well. But somehow, despite all he knew about her—more than Andre, more than Jenna, even—he had faith in Morgan. Especially after yesterday's session when she'd shown a glimmer of empathy for BreeAnna. "One thing I've learned about Morgan. When she wants something as badly as she wants to shut down ReNew and find the truth behind BreeAnna's death, nothing is going to stop her."

"Lot like Jenna that way."

It was Nick's turn to grunt. "How are things between you two?"

"Sometimes great, sometimes I dunno."

"As if she's holding back?" Nick had noticed the same thing in his sessions with Jenna. It was the most Nick could say without violating privilege. But it was more than enough to let Andre know he was worried about Jenna. Obviously Andre was as well.

But as always with Jenna, there were no easy answers.

"Where is she now?"

"She and Greene are at ReNew, getting eyes on the situation."

"But you think you'll still need to send Morgan inside."

"I hope not. You know Jenna, though. Once she decides she wants something, she doesn't stop until she gets it."

Nick wondered why Jenna was so obsessed with this case. Did she see some reflection of her own past traumas in BreeAnna's life? He still didn't know everything that had happened to Jenna when she was a child, but there were obvious parallels between Jenna's wealthy yet emotionally distant family and the Greenes.

They turned into the Greenes' driveway, and Nick gave himself a mental shake, reminding himself that he wasn't here to judge but rather to observe. This wasn't about Jenna; it was about BreeAnna.

It was just past noon. The March sun was angled behind the mansion, creating an abrupt demarcation between light and dark as he pulled the car to a stop at the front steps. He sat for a moment, clearing his mind, trying to become a blank slate, but somehow couldn't shake the urge to put the car back in gear and drive away.

He stared at the building crowding out the sun, his face turned up to the windows on the top floor. BreeAnna's bedroom, Nick remembered from the floor plan. Her room on the northeast corner would be shrouded in shadow most of the day.

"Know what I think?" Andre said. "I think the kid left one prison only to get locked up in another."

CHAPTER 20

Morgan was relieved to leave Caren passed out on her sofa and escape the oppressive atmosphere of the Greenes' mansion. Not like the woman would be alone for long—the housekeeper was there, and Andre and Nick were due to arrive at noon to start Bree's psychological autopsy. Morgan thought it was best to give Andre a little more breathing room after their earlier confrontation, so she'd returned to the empty Galloway and Stone offices.

She could have gone to her current crash pad—the house she'd temporarily liberated along with the Audi. But Fred and Marge, the anniversary couple, lived all the way out in Fox Chapel, and the empty house was more boring than hanging out in the office. Usually she enjoyed ferreting out the secrets of her clueless hosts, but as far as she could tell the only secret Fred and Marge had was a four-year-old untouched tube of lubricant.

Jenna's laptop beckoned from the reception desk. Morgan logged on—she'd long ago installed backdoors to all of Jenna's and Andre's electronics—and examined Jenna's analysis of Bree's iPad, laptop, and phone. The police had given BreeAnna's electronics a cursory examination, and she could see why they didn't bother to dig deeper, not when everything supported the medical examiner's ruling of suicide.

But they also hadn't been armed with the information Morgan had about what really happened to Bree at that party. True, it was nothing actionable in a court of law, but she'd pieced a pretty good picture together from the postings on the other partygoers' social media. From the police report, they had no clue that Bree had been assaulted before she was sent to ReNew—Caren and Robert had painted Bree as just another mixed-up kid who was drinking, smoking, and acting out. Same story they'd given Jenna, Morgan, and Andre.

Couple Bree's assault at the party with Caren's confession and Robert's insistence that he be the one to go with Morgan to ReNew and it added up to a lot more going on than either Greene had admitted to. Morgan smiled as she carried the laptop up to Jenna's loft. Nothing more fun than digging up secrets.

After raiding Jenna's fridge, she started with Greene Energy, hacking into their corporate servers and company financials. Then she went after Greene's e-mail—his had a level of encryption beyond what she could easily bypass. But Caren's was laughably easy to gain access to. And it was there that she hit pay dirt: e-mails from ReNew with messages from Bree to her parents.

By the time she'd finished, a completely different picture behind Bree's discharge from ReNew was beginning to take shape.

Robert Greene had a lot to explain.

✦

"What did you and the Reverend talk about while I was gone?" Jenna asked once she and Greene were back in his Lexus headed away from ReNew. She was surprised he wasn't upset that they'd never gotten inside the youth facility. Instead he was relaxed, a smile on his face as if he'd just been dealt a winning hand.

"Financials. I set up a wire transfer, and we can bring Morgan back whenever we're ready. All I need to do is give them a call."

Really? She twisted in her seat to face him. "I think we might better spend our time and energy investigating other avenues."

"Well, then, it's a good thing I'm the client and it's my resources paying for your time. I want Benjamin and his staff, hell, his entire operation, turned inside out. He's behind all this, I'm certain of it."

"Funny. You two seemed so simpatico."

"Honey, you may have been some kind of hotshot federal agent, but you have no clue how to assess an opponent prior to a critical negotiation." His tone dripped with disdain. "Don't tell me you actually fell for their act? The man's a total fraud."

Takes one to know one. The thought raced through her mind even though she wasn't sure what Greene was hiding. But he was hiding something behind that grieving-father facade.

She decided to push him. "Exactly why I don't think there's anything going on inside ReNew. The students there are all spoiled rich kids, most of them girls brought by country club mothers who don't want to be bothered raising a kid once they're old enough to talk back." If Greene saw any resemblance to his own wife and family, he didn't take the bait. "There's no way in hell Benjamin would risk all those hefty tuitions by doing anything the kids might go home and tattle about."

He gave a grunt. Not in agreement. More like she'd totally missed the point and he wasn't about to clue her in. Jenna sat back in frustration. Greene pulled into his reserved spot at his corporate headquarters and got out of the SUV.

She hopped out and began to follow him inside the building, but he stopped her with a gesture. "I have work to catch up on. I expect Morgan ready to enter ReNew first thing tomorrow. In the meantime, I want you to dig deeper into Benjamin and his administrator, that Chapman fellow."

He spun on his heel and entered the building, leaving her behind, his posture one of command and confidence—no signs of worry. Certain she'd obey his command.

Asshole. Jenna got into her Tahoe and drove to an Eat'n Park down the road. She grabbed clothes from her go-bag and changed in the restaurant's bathroom. As she glanced in the mirror she adjusted her smile. She'd exchanged the frumpy dress for jeans, a silk blouse, and a leather blazer. Polished, kick-ass, and definitely not corporate. Exactly the vibe she was looking for.

Not to mention the surge of power that came from strapping her guns back on. One thing she'd learned from Nick's wife, Lucy, while they were chasing down Morgan's serial killer father, was that if one weapon was good, carrying two was better. Lucy called it her "one-plus" rule, and it was about the only rule Jenna followed.

She ordered lunch and called Andre for an update. He and Nick had just gotten started at the Greenes' house.

"Anything at ReNew?" he asked.

"Yes and no. Nothing concrete, more questions than answers. Greene still insists on Morgan going in undercover."

"You know my feelings about that."

"Did you ask Nick?"

He paused. "Yeah. He said he thought Morgan would be okay. Still—"

"Look. I met the staff, saw some of the kids." Well, Deidre had said the kids on the video were students, even if Jenna had her doubts. "They're a bunch of spoiled brats. They won't give Morgan any trouble. Or any reason for her to mess with them. I'll bet her main problem will be being bored out of her skull."

"If you say so." He still didn't sound convinced. "I'll call you if we find anything."

He hung up. She'd barely finished her bacon cheeseburger when Morgan called. "Are you still with Greene?"

"Just left him at his office. Why?"

"Wait until you hear what I dug up. A link between Greene Energy, a federal judge, lawsuits worth millions, and BreeAnna."

CHAPTER 21

Andre hung up from Jenna and rang the Greenes' doorbell. This time it was opened by a maid. She was a woman not much younger than his Grams, Hispanic appearance, looking more than a bit ridiculous in her pale-blue dress, apron, and frilly piece of lace pinned to her hair. Her resigned smile as she greeted them revealed the price exchanged for a steady paycheck.

"I'm Andre Stone from Galloway and Stone. This is Dr. Nick Callahan. Mrs. Greene is expecting us."

"*Sí, sí.* She says to tell you she's not feeling well. I should take you up to Miss BreeAnna's rooms myself."

Andre glanced at Nick, raised an eyebrow. Caren Greene had avoided answering any questions yesterday as well. It was just past noon. Could she be drunk already?

Nick didn't seem to notice. He was craning his neck to look up, comparing the view of the foyer with the photos from the police investigation on his phone. He swiveled his head, scanning the length of the third-floor balcony that circled the three interior walls of the foyer. He stopped, his gaze fixed on a place directly over the center of the grand staircase. The place where BreeAnna had hung herself.

The maid didn't seem to notice; she'd already begun trudging up the steps of the grand staircase. Andre caught up with her. "I'm sorry, we didn't meet yesterday."

"I do the shopping."

"You are?"

"Juanita. I take care of Mrs. Greene, Miss BreeAnna." She touched her fingers to her heart at BreeAnna's name, almost but not quite making the sign of the cross.

"Tell me about BreeAnna," Andre said as Nick joined them, hanging behind, listening. "Was she a difficult child?"

"No. Not difficult." They reached the top of the steps and paused directly beneath the third-floor banister. Juanita glanced up without raising her head, then looked away. She led them to the right, past Robert's suite of rooms to one of the two staircases leading to the third floor. Their footsteps sounded too bright against the hardwood floors—Andre found himself slowing, placing his weight on the ball of his foot first, as if moving through a minefield.

"Miss BreeAnna, she was a good girl," Juanita continued, her back to them. "Until she went to that party. Those kids, they hurt her, made her so sad. She stop playing her music, stop eating, stop smiling. Then she was sent away." Her tone made it clear that she disapproved of Caren's decision.

"Did you see her the day she came back?"

She shook her head. "No. Mrs. Greene, she send me home. Said family only."

"You don't live here?"

"No. Just cook and shop and clean. Mr. Greene, he's gone most of the time, and Mrs. Greene, she—" Juanita hesitated. "She live her own life. Not here much."

"BreeAnna must have spent a lot of time here alone, then?"

She sighed and nodded, gripping the banister tight as they climbed to the third floor. She led them to BreeAnna's music room. It was on the southeast corner of the house. Sunlight bathed the baby grand in a soft wave of gold. Juanita stopped outside the door, not crossing the threshold. "You find who made Miss BreeAnna so sad, made her do this awful thing. You make it right for her."

Then she left. Andre turned to Nick. "What do you think?"

Nick had turned to walk the length of hallway that opened onto the foyer below. He was examining the banister where BreeAnna attached the bathrobe belt that she used to hang herself. He leaned over, looking down onto the marble floor two stories below.

"I don't think anything yet," Nick answered. "I try to keep an open mind. But I can tell you one thing. Statistically speaking, it's pretty unusual for a teenage girl to kill herself the way BreeAnna did."

Andre reluctantly joined him at the banister, standing back so he didn't brush the wood that would have been the last thing BreeAnna touched. He'd seen the crime scene photos of her dangling, a simple slipknot securing the length of silk around her neck.

The medical examiner had said it was the worst way to hang yourself: even with the fall from a height, the knot wasn't positioned where it would cause a broken neck and quick, painless death. Instead he'd estimated that it would have taken several minutes for BreeAnna to suffocate. An agonizingly long time. With her parents asleep mere feet away.

Andre closed his eyes briefly, trying to banish the autopsy photos that revealed the scratch marks where BreeAnna had tried to claw her way free of the makeshift noose.

"Teenage girls don't hang themselves?" he asked Nick.

"Older teens, yes. Although males far outnumber females even then." Nick's tone was clinical, detached. "She was how tall?"

"Four eleven."

Nick raised and lowered his hand, palm flat as if measuring. "An awkward climb over the banister for someone so short." He put his back to the open space and reached for the banister. "I didn't see any mention of fingerprints in the police report. She would have held on, this way." He squeezed his hands, fingers facing in toward Andre. "Until she finally got the courage to let go." He opened his hands, tilting his body back, mimicking a fall.

Andre visualized BreeAnna's final minutes. Sliding the belt free from her bathrobe. Tying one end to the banister. Looping the other around her throat. Climbing over. He looked down. It was almost thirty feet to the cold marble floor of the foyer.

And then. Falling. Jerking to a stop. Twisting, spinning, unable to breathe or scream for help. His stomach dropped at the thought of a kid like BreeAnna thinking this was her best option. "Someone decides to kill themselves this way—they know there's no second chances. Not like pills or slitting your wrists. How's a kid get to that point?"

Nick straightened, his eyes narrowing as he followed Andre's gaze out over the banister to the open space of the foyer. A stray beam of sunlight found its way past the shadows at the front of the house to shimmer through the chandelier above them. "That's what we're here to try to find out. But I can tell you one thing. Doing it this way, right above where her parents were sleeping on the second floor, where she'd be the first thing they saw the next morning—"

"She was sending a message," Andre finished for him. One hell of a message. He wasn't afraid of heights and sure as hell didn't believe in ghosts, but suddenly goose bumps marched up his arms.

◆

Armed with Morgan's new intel, Jenna finished lunch and returned to the Greene Energy headquarters. Greene's Lexus was parked just where he'd left it. Remembering what Andre said about executives not carrying anything, she took only her phone, her weapons, and a business card as she entered the building.

Security at the front lobby was a joke. Two bored guards at a reception desk chatting about the Penguins-Devils game, surrounded by video monitors. Beyond them was a pair of glass doors controlled by key-card access. Jenna was certain she could have picked a random name from the company directory posted behind them and charmed her way past them easily, but there was no need. Another employee was coming out through the glass doors, so she simply held her business card in her hand as if getting ready to swipe the door and he kindly held it open for her.

"Thanks," she said.

"No problem."

And she was in. No key card needed for the elevator—unless she wanted to go to the third or fourth floors. Must be the labs where they developed the fracking recipes. She noted the make and model of the key-card reader. If she ever needed to prove a point, it would be child's play to return and breach that security as well.

Not today. All she needed right now was access to the top floor where Greene's office was. A simple push of a button and two minutes later she had arrived.

The decor was modern glass and steel. A receptionist was on the phone, and two more secretaries, busy typing on their computers, sat to one side. Past them was a glass-walled conference room and beside it a series of three offices, all with glass walls as well. Easy to spot Greene in the far corner office, leaning back in his oversized executive chair, talking on the phone.

Ignoring the sleek leather and chrome chairs of the reception area, Jenna strode past the receptionist and secretaries and headed straight for Greene's office.

"Wait," one of the women called from behind her. "You can't go back there."

Already have, Jenna thought as she pushed through the door into Greene's office.

"We need to talk," she told him as she took the chair in front of the desk and stretched her legs out, crossing her ankles, settling in. She was taking a huge risk, gambling on a few stray facts that Morgan had pieced together, no real evidence. But the payoff—gaining Greene Energy's business—was too large to ignore.

Greene glared at the woman who rushed in after her, told the person on the other end of the phone, "I'll call you back," then hung up. "Coffee for two, Tina."

Flustered, the woman bobbed her head. "Yes, Mr. Greene."

Jenna sat in silence while Greene made a show of clearing his desk. Neither said anything until after Tina had returned and served them each a cup of coffee.

"I usually don't tolerate melodrama," Greene told her, leaning back and sipping his coffee. His gaze was appraising, neutral. Waiting for her to show her hand before he passed judgment. "Nor do I appreciate your blurring the lines between my business and my personal life."

Jenna smiled over the rim of her cup. She'd expected heavy mugs with the company's logo, but instead the coffee was served in small china cups with a sleek, European design. It was good, too; Andre would have approved.

"I wasn't the one who blurred the lines or created the melodrama," she said, her tone matching his. "You did that, Mr. Greene. I know about what happened to BreeAnna before you sent her to ReNew—"

"That was Caren's decision, not mine," he interrupted her. "I had nothing to do with it."

She merely smiled. "Maybe not. In fact, I'll bet you hated the idea of BreeAnna leaving home, being outside of your control, didn't you?"

He stared at her in stony silence. She called his bluff.

"I know about the judge." His expression didn't change, but he shifted his weight and one hand touched his chin. Gotcha. "There are currently twenty-seven active lawsuits involving Greene Energy's fracking practices. Two weeks after BreeAnna went to that party, you suddenly had those lawsuits removed from the state court dockets to the federal district court. Where they'll conveniently all be heard by one judge: Judge Charles Fanton."

"Simple cost containment. It's all a matter of public record." He waved a hand in dismissal. "As is Greene Energy's record of successfully defending ourselves against these frivolous lawsuits in the past."

"You mean, drag out the court cases long enough that you finish grabbing all the natural gas, the damage is done, and you move on to the next field. Even the few cases that haven't gone your way, the cost of the damages is a small fraction of the profit you gain. And it's the people left in your wake who have to clean up the mess you leave behind."

"If you're so antifracking, then why did you take our business?" he asked, still no hint of emotion in his voice. But his eyes had narrowed—not in anger, rather with a wariness that confirmed her suspicions.

"I'm not antianything, I'm just stating facts. It's your business, and clearly as a business plan it works. But all those lawsuits are starting to add up, aren't they? Floodwaters building behind a dam, just waiting for someone to turn the release valve, send them pouring out." She finished her coffee and set the cup on the table beside her. Crossed her legs and leaned forward. "Only you're not worried, are you, Mr. Greene? Because you now control the man in charge of the release valve. You own Judge Fanton."

"I'm not sure where you—"

"That party where someone slipped BreeAnna the Ecstasy. All those pictures and videos of her. Funny how none of them show the face of the boy with her." She paused. His lips had tightened into a rigid line. "At least none of the pictures out there for anyone to see. Because I'm guessing you have the ones that count. The ones that show Judge Fanton's son raping your daughter."

CHAPTER 22

Micah must have passed out. Long enough for one of the Red Shirts to stretch his fingers and slide them into the space between the door hinges and the frame. Black splotches danced in his vision, and he thought he might pass out again. It was impossible to breathe, not with another Red Shirt sitting on his shoulders, pinning him facedown on the floor.

"You want to be an artist, right?" Nelson, the Red Shirt leader, said from where he stood in the doorway, ready to close the door on Micah's fingers. "Might need to rethink that."

The Red Shirts were Deidre's personal bully squad. Named for the coveted red polos they wore to mark them from the No Names, who wore featureless khaki tops and bottoms, they were handpicked for their unquestioning obedience to Deidre, ReNew's student leader.

Only problem? Deidre wasn't here right now to keep Nelson and his goons in check. Not that Micah could be certain that she would. In the past month, ever since Bree left—ever since Bree betrayed her, to use Deidre's words—Deidre had been growing more and more unpredictable. Her inability to control her own moods rippled through to the Red Shirts and down to the other ReNew students, creating a tension not unlike the subliminal rumblings of a volcano.

The Red Shirt on top of Micah shifted his weight enough so Micah could take a few shallow breaths, clear the spots from his eyes. They'd caught him outside the commons room, dragged him inside an unused classroom. He wasn't the one they were looking for, but Micah wasn't about to tell them that. The new kid, Tommy, he was only twelve. The Red Shirts would break him like a twig if they lost control.

And without Deidre, there was no one to keep them in control.

Nelson shifted suddenly, relaxing his hold on the door. He stepped inside the room, eyes lowered, as Deidre appeared.

Despite the fact that it was chilly—Reverend Benjamin was too cheap to pay to heat the place properly—Deidre always wore filmy dresses that swirled around her ankles like wildflowers in a field. Today's was pale grey with tiny flowers that matched the blue in her eyes. She walked as if she was dancing, head held high, spine straight, but not as if she was stiff, rather, she kind of . . . glided.

"What's going on here?" she asked Nelson.

He shifted weight, back forth, back forth, then looked up. "Someone stole bread from our table at lunch. This one," he nudged Micah with his foot, "is about to confess."

Deidre crouched down so she could meet Micah's gaze. "Is this true, Micah?" she asked in a voice dark with disappointment. "You stole?"

What made Deidre so frightening wasn't that she was the Red Shirts' leader or even that she'd been living the ReNew program since she herself was a troubled twelve-year-old, as she put it, striding down the devil's path.

No, she was dangerous because she was a true believer. In her mind, the ReNew way was the only way sinners like Micah could be saved.

For Deidre, a student's time at ReNew was a turning point in the war between Good and Evil. Something she took very, very seriously. Which was why she'd seen Bree's leaving early as a personal betrayal. Unforgivable.

Before Micah could answer, Nelson stepped forward. "We need to make an example of him. Especially since he's a short-timer. The others need to know that it doesn't matter how long you have before leaving, you must obey the rules."

"More than rules. You must learn to obey God. You should offer your talent to Him." Deidre caressed Micah's free hand. "He gave it to you. And He can take it away. Hard to create anything with your fingers crushed, Micah Chase."

She stretched her other hand back and closed the door. Not a hard slam that would have left evidence behind like a few broken fingers. Instead a slow leveraging that created pain without permanent damage.

"Confess, Micah," she whispered. "Confess and this all stops."

Micah tightened his lips and shook his head, unable to manage any sound without screaming in pain.

The guy sitting on top of Micah twisted his fingers in Micah's hair and yanked. Hard. Pain shrieked across his scalp, joining with the screaming from his arms and legs, but it was nothing to the choking sensation as the Red Shirt pulled Micah's head back so far that he couldn't breathe.

This is how people die, Micah thought. The overhead light stabbed his eyes, but he didn't have the spare energy to close them. Every ounce of strength went into sucking molecules of air into his straining lungs.

His heart was a thundering herd of wild horses, out of control and careening to a cliff. Micah liked horses, but he liked breathing even more. The weird thought and the sudden images of wild horses stampeding, out of control, distracted him from the pain.

Made him want to laugh. Of course, he couldn't, not with his air cut off, but even that realization felt hysterical.

Bright light, feeling of mirth, all he needed was the out-of-body part of the near-death experience, shed all this pain, leave it behind . . . where were those brain endorphins with their magic oblivion when you needed them?

He must have passed out again. A sharp pain slapped across his cheek. He blinked his eyes open. He was on his back now, one arm and both legs bent beneath his weight; damn it hurt, but at least he could breathe. He hauled in deep, hungry breaths, not sure how long the reprieve would last.

Deidre cradled his head in her lap, caressing his sweat-soaked hair away from his face. "The road to salvation, Micah," she crooned. "You can only walk it after you repent. Confess. Let me save you, Micah. Let me bring you into the light. This is your last chance."

He shook his head, his gaze never leaving hers. Maybe his brain finally released a few stray endorphins, because as he looked into Deidre's twisted expression with her angelic smile and devil's eyes, as he heard the laughter of the other Red Shirts behind her and saw the rest of the No Names gathered in the hallway, staring down at him, their expressions a mix of fear and hope, all he could think was, *my parents are shelling out good money for this freak show?*

✦

"BreeAnna's medical records show a visit to your wife's ob-gyn the day after the party," Jenna continued when Greene said nothing after her accusation. "Evidence collection? Kept safe, hidden by doctor-patient confidentiality until the day you might need it to persuade a federal judge?"

"The incident at the party happened weeks before BreeAnna's mother sent her to ReNew. What does any of this have to do with my daughter's death? Aren't you supposed to be investigating ReNew?"

"Maybe I'm wrong. Maybe *you* were behind her being sent to ReNew, not your wife. Figured you could hide her away? Out of the judge's reach. I'm sure you didn't know that most kids sent there spend an average of almost three years locked up inside. Or maybe you did. That's just about how long it will take for all those court cases to wind up, right?"

She pushed to her feet and leaned over his desk, forcing him to look up at her. "If that's so, then why did you bring her home again? Were you afraid she was going to tell the ReNew counselors what happened at the party?" She paused. "After all, BreeAnna was the weak link in your plan. If she talked, it would remove your leverage over the judge."

"How dare you! I hired you to find out why my daughter died, not to accuse me with outrageous suppositions—"

"Why did you hire us? Really? Because you and your wife are obsessed about BreeAnna's death? Finding justice for her? I don't think so. Not when her dying was the answer to your problems, might have saved your business. Twenty-seven lawsuits, if even a fraction were settled for the plaintiffs, you'd be bankrupt. But now, thanks to BreeAnna's death, thanks to her permanent silence, your company is safe."

"This has nothing to do with saving my company. Don't you understand? My daughter, my lovely, beautiful baby girl, she's gone—and I wasn't there to save her."

Jenna took a breath, translated the expression on his face: pure anguish. Maybe the first true emotion she'd seen from him since they met. She sank back into her chair, regrouped. "What do you mean, you weren't there?"

"Caren and I lied to the police. Told them we were asleep and didn't hear anything. Said I woke to get something to drink and that's when I found BreeAnna."

"What really happened?"

He pushed the chair out of his way and paced the area between his desk and the wall of windows. "We left her. Home. Alone."

"But why bring her home that day just to leave—"

"She's fourteen. It was only ten o'clock at night. It shouldn't have been a problem."

Jenna stared at him. Tried to imagine being a child isolated from friends and family for two months and then brought home only to be left alone again. No wonder the Greenes were driven to find someone else to blame for BreeAnna's suicide.

"Why?" she asked. She didn't need to know, not to do the job he'd hired her for. But she had to ask.

He leaned back in his chair, rubbed his face with his palm as if scrubbing himself clean of any guilt. "It was Caren's idea. She hadn't seen me in a month, thought we needed to rekindle the romance or some such crap she read in a magazine. So we took a drive out to the country, built a fire, drank wine, made love under the stars. Like we were kids again."

His voice trailed off. No need for either of them to fill in what happened next. Coming home to find their daughter hanging from the third-floor balcony.

Greene was still lying, but she wasn't sure what about. Which meant it might be better off if she didn't push him too hard. Not yet, anyway. Jenna stood and headed for the door.

"Wait," he called. "Where are you going?"

"To do my job. Find out why your daughter died." She paused, arching an eyebrow at him. "At least I assume that's still what you want."

He didn't meet her gaze. "I know you think me heartless, using what happened to my daughter to save my company. But I want— no, I need—to know what BreeAnna went through. Why she died. Someone drove her to her death, and I need to know who."

"Okay, then. Guess I have work to do."

"And since BreeAnna's death has nothing to do with my company, you have no need to reveal any proprietary information." Using big words to intimidate her. Did he really think that would work?

She whirled around. "If you'd like to hire my company to do more than simply investigate your daughter's death, we can negotiate a contract. I'd be happy to discuss our rates for a comprehensive corporate review. Lord knows, your company could use a professional handling things. Security around here is a joke."

Despite his scowl, he nodded in agreement. How could he not? Less than a day on the job and she already knew his greatest vulnerabilities. Not to mention the blackmail potential her knowledge brought with it.

Which she most definitely was not doing. This wasn't blackmail, she told herself. It was simply an audition.

"You've made your point, Ms. Galloway. Let's discuss terms."

Jenna beamed in triumph as she resumed her seat. "First, I'd like more coffee."

Greene came around his desk to stand over her. He leaned back, bracing his hands against the edge of the desk. "First, I'd like to come to an agreement. You have something I want, and I have something you want."

His gaze roamed her body, stopping on her breasts. She was surprised it'd taken him this long. From the way his secretary looked at him, it was obvious Greene enjoyed blurring the lines between business relationships and personal ones. Jenna was well acquainted with men like him. Her father and her grandfather both had had multiple affairs, treating the women in their lives as if they were so many flavors waiting to be sampled. She'd had coworkers and supervisors who'd also looked at her just like Greene was now.

In fact, most of the men in her life . . . until Andre. Maybe that's why he scared her so much. Lust, hunger, greed . . . she could handle. But true affection? She had no earthly idea what to do with that.

She shook herself. One troublesome man at a time.

Jenna stood, now mere inches away from Greene. His smile turned wolfish. "So tell me, Ms. Galloway, are you a natural red-head? No. Wait. Don't tell me."

He placed one hand on her hip. Jenna flattened her palm against his chest, giving him a pat like she would a little boy's head when he'd said something particularly charming.

Then she turned away. "I'm afraid you'll never have the chance to find out. I'll send over a contract for our security services. Good day, Mr. Greene."

She strode through the door. Because of the glass walls, she could see Greene watching her walk away. He didn't look upset, didn't look like a man who'd just had his deepest secret revealed and used as a threat against his company. Rather he gave her a nod—a man accepting a challenge.

Jenna kept going, noticing for the first time that Greene had staffed his office exclusively with young women. Right now the eyes of every one of them followed her with hateful jealousy.

She smiled. She'd arrived here with vague suspicions, hoping to turn them into a professional opportunity. She was leaving with those suspicions confirmed as well as more that might provide leverage in the future.

Only thing she didn't have was any useful information about BreeAnna's death. But that didn't stop her from humming along with the Muzak as she rode down in the elevator.

CHAPTER 23

Morgan turned from burrowing into the Greenes' social media to the judge's son. Idiot allowed geotagging on all his photos and videos, so it was easy to reconstruct his whereabouts on the night of the party. Also easy from the file names to discover there were a bunch he hadn't uploaded.

Then came the kicker. A few days after the party he posted from a new phone, complaining that his old one had been stolen by some "Homewood raghead."

She sat back, thought about the implications. Wondered how much it had cost Greene to steal the phone with everything he needed to send the judge's son to prison and have him labeled a sexual predator.

Pretty impressive maneuvering for a former coal miner with a GED. But Greene had left those humble beginnings far behind, clawed his way out of the mines to build his own energy empire. More than driven, he was obsessed with protecting the company that bore his name.

Even if the cost was his daughter's chance at justice? Could a father be so callous?

Morgan didn't need to think twice about that. She knew the answer all too well.

Her phone rang. Greene. Interesting. Why would he be calling her private cell instead of dealing with Jenna or Andre?

Curious, she answered, pretending it was a work number. "Galloway and Stone, how may I help you?"

"I know it was you," he said. "You can drop the act. You're more than just a receptionist."

Morgan considered. "I do whatever needs to be done. To solve our client's problem."

His chuckle was devoid of warmth. "I knew I was right. Jenna had no time to dig up that info on the judge, and Stone is just a muscleman."

"What can I do for you, Mr. Greene?" Morgan kept her tone professional.

"Did Jenna tell you we still need you to go undercover at ReNew?"

"She mentioned it."

"I'd like you to go in today. I'll make it worth your while. A private commission that Jenna doesn't need to know about. Can we meet to discuss it?"

Morgan considered it. She didn't trust Greene—even less now than when she'd first met him. But they were still no closer to understanding what happened to Bree, inside ReNew or after she'd gotten home. Maybe her parents really didn't care about the truth, but Morgan did. Bree deserved that much.

"Where?" she asked.

"There's an old gas station down the road from my office. Meet me behind it, say half an hour?"

She glanced at the clock. Ten after one. "I'll be there."

He hung up without saying good-bye.

Morgan grabbed the surveillance gear: glasses, pen, and small stack of pennies. She debated calling Jenna, decided against it.

Jenna would just tell her not to go—or worse, show up and ruin everything.

Greene was hiding something, and Morgan was determined to find out what.

Better that she handle Greene herself. Alone.

✦

The Red Shirts dragged Micah back into the commons room and threw him onto the floor. It took every ounce of his strength, but Micah heaved himself up onto his knees. He hauled in one breath, then another, his kaleidoscope vision slowly returning to normal.

Garish banners with ReNew's cheerful logo of a sunrise covered the walls of the windowless commons room, mocking him from above. "ReNew your Mind. ReNew your Body. ReNew your Spirit," they said. "ReNew your Faith. ReNew is your Path to Salvation. ReNew brings Redemption. ReNew is the Way!"

If he had the energy, he'd choke on the irony. He focused on the crowd before him. Khaki-clad No Names gathered, all kneeling in a semicircle facing him. Surrounding them were the Red Shirts. No one advanced to the upper levels of the ReNew program and earned the right to wear the coveted red polo top with its sunrise emblem embroidered over their heart unless they were a true believer, intent on doing whatever it took to help their fellow sinners walk the ReNew path to righteousness.

Deidre strode back and forth behind him. "That's right, Micah Chase. Kneel before your peers. Have you anything to say to make things right with them?"

Micah had only been at ReNew for three months—most of these kids had been here a year or more—but he knew better than to say anything. Words, twisted and turned back on her target, were Deidre's favorite ammunition.

He knelt in silence, trying not to let the pain racking his limbs show. He hated to give her even that small satisfaction. Slowly, cautiously, he flexed each of his fingers. They all still worked, just hurt like hell.

"Such a shame," Deidre said, stopping as if overcome with sorrow. But her tone was more gleeful than anything. "You'd made it all the way to Level Four. I'm sending you back. You walk the Path from Step Zero."

Whatever. Wasn't like they were going to let him ever advance to Level Seven—the first Red Shirt level. Hell, he wasn't even sure if they were ever going to let him out of this hellhole. The judge had sentenced him to ninety days, and those had been up over a week ago without any word from the outside world.

At night when he lay alone on his thin mattress in the boys' dorm, surrounded by muffled sniffles and loud snoring, sometimes Micah wondered if anyone at home even remembered he was still here. Had his mothers forgotten him? Abandoned him?

Did they even know he was alive?

Deidre clapped her hands and the crowd of No Names, fifty kids aged twelve to seventeen, began chanting his name. Not in a nice way, either.

She knelt beside Micah, whispered seductively in his ear. "Hear them? I can make them do anything I want. They're just a crowd, Micah. A mob. Rabble. Not worthy of your suffering. Tell me who really stole the bread, and I'll take care of you." She riffled her fingers through his hair—it'd grown long, three months without being cut.

No way was he ever going to betray Tommy. The kid was new here, one of the youngest among them. He didn't understand the rules; all he'd known was he was hungry and there was extra food on the Red Shirts' table.

"Told you," he muttered. "I stole your damn bread. Tasted real good, too."

Deidre twisted her fingers in his hair, yanked hard, hard enough to pull a clump from his scalp. He couldn't hide his wince of pain.

She stood, paced some more as the No Names continued yelling his name, now prodded by the Red Shirts. Then she waved them to silence.

"Micah Chase, you are accused of lying. What is the punishment for breaking a Commandment?" She pointed to a Level Two.

The girl cowered, not meeting Micah's gaze. "Cornering," she whispered.

Everyone hated Cornering. It wasn't the isolation of being forced to kneel, your forehead touching a corner of the cinder-block commons room, elbows stretched behind your head so they each touched a wall. Not the pain, either, although after an hour or so, your shoulders and knees screamed in agony.

It was the boredom. You saw nothing but grey wall, you didn't speak, and no one was allowed to speak to you. If you fell asleep or even closed your eyes, the Red Shirts guarding you would prod you back into position and another hour would be added to your sentence.

"Eight hours in the corner," Deidre pronounced sentence.

The No Names gasped in dismay. The Red Shirts grinned. They knew Micah would never make it that long—no one had. And each of them wanted to be the one guarding him when he failed.

Micah grinned right back at them. He didn't like Cornering, but he had a secret weapon: his art. As he imagined covering wide open stretches with color and shapes, it kept him focused on something other than pain and exhaustion. They hadn't broken him yet; he wasn't about to give Deidre the satisfaction of breaking him now.

Not when he was getting out of here. Any day his mothers would be coming for him. He had to believe that, hold on to that.

And when they did, when they heard about what went on in here—talk about divine retribution. ReNew had no idea who they were dealing with. His mothers would take this *Lord of the Flies* hellhole and tear it down brick by brick.

Deidre sensed his rebellion. She stood in front of him, hands on her hips. "And eight more hours for stealing," she said with a sneer. She whipped around, facing the cowering No Names. "Unless someone wants to come forward and confess their crime." She softened her tone. "It's all right. If you confess, you'll set Micah free and your only penance will be Gifting a meal."

Ha. Gifting a meal translated to watching Red Shirts eat your food while you went hungry.

"No one?" She scanned the crowd in their khaki pants and shirts. Silence thudded as everyone's gaze hit the floor. Deidre glowered down at Micah once more. "Last chance, Micah Chase."

He smiled up at her. Show no fear; that was the best way to handle Deidre when she was in a rage like this. Times like this he missed Bree. She'd been a calming influence on Deidre, on them all.

"Fine." She whirled back to the No Names. "The sixteen hours that Micah Chase is in the corner will be sixteen hours of fasting and prayer for all of you. No one sleeps, no one eats, no one leaves this room until Micah Chase has served his sentence or someone comes forward, confesses, and begs for repentance."

She nodded to the Red Shirts. They dragged Micah to the corner and positioned him. Stress position the army called it, Micah remembered from reading about Guantánamo and Abu Ghraib. Used to break down enemy combatants, get them to confess anything.

He risked a glance over his shoulders at the terrified No Names watching. Gave them a smile of encouragement: *I'm not breaking, don't any of you.*

A Red Shirt punched him in the spine and forced him to face the grey, featureless corner. Then he rammed a broomstick down the back of Micah's shirt, adjusting it to keep Micah's spine rigid, no chance of relaxing.

Only sixteen hours to go, Micah thought, creating a fresh canvas in his mind. Easy time.

CHAPTER 24

It was a struggle for Nick to remain clinical as he re-created BreeAnna Greene's death. His own daughter's face kept flashing in his vision.

He imagined the parents, waking to find BreeAnna. The howl of anguish, the horrified screams, thundering footsteps racing to reach their child, even though by the time they arrived it would have been obvious it was too late.

He shook himself, covered by glancing once more at the autopsy report. The ME hadn't been able to pinpoint the time of death beyond the window of time between when BreeAnna had said good night to her parents, around 10:00 p.m., and when her father woke and found her at 1:24 the next morning.

"No note?" he asked Andre even though he knew one hadn't been found.

"Not unless the parents are holding out on us."

Nick looked up at Andre's tone. The former marine was an excellent judge of people. "You think that might be the case?"

Andre shrugged. "They're both lying to us. Just haven't figured out what about. Yet."

"Let's take a look at BreeAnna's rooms, and maybe we can find a clue." Of the three rooms that made up BreeAnna's suite, Nick decided that the music room would best reveal her personality, so he started there while Andre began next door in her study.

Despite its owner being gone so long, the piano and recording equipment had been well cared for. Juanita simply doing her job? Or was she paying homage to the girl she hadn't been able to help? Nick raised the lid on the piano. Nothing concealed there. Sheet music was on the stand, turned to a section in the center as if left half-played.

He flipped to the front cover. Liszt's Sonata in B Minor. A difficult piece. There were notations in two different handwritings. BreeAnna must have been working with an instructor. He added it to his list of people to contact, then flipped through the sheets of music, searching for any messages that weren't related to performance. Nothing there or in any of the musical arrangements neatly stacked inside the piano seat.

Nick trailed his fingers along the keys, releasing a stream of notes. With the doors closed and the window shut, the acoustics of the room felt solid. Not quite soundproof, but definitely private.

He glanced at the computerized keyboard and recording equipment. If the piano was for work, maybe the keyboard was for play?

The chair in front of the keyboard was a simple office chair, adjusted to BreeAnna's height. He imagined her sitting, feet propped up on the lower bar so they didn't dangle, headphones on, her world collapsed to the sounds of her music—a world she could create, bend to her will. That would be comforting to someone who didn't feel in control of anything else in her life.

He tried on her headset, feeling as if he was trespassing—a feeling that came with the job of prying into the private lives of his patients, exposing secrets they didn't even know they kept from themselves. A flick of the switch labeled "Playback" and music filled his ears.

Definitely not Liszt. This music was wild, imaginative, soaring yet also echoing with tones of despair. The composition was a bit clumsy, but he had a feeling that had more to do with BreeAnna's lack of talent as a musician than anything else. It was clear she'd had a rich future as a composer. Despite the limitations of the keyboard, he could easily visualize the piece played by a full orchestra.

He listened, sorrow weighing him down. What a waste. To lose such a talent, so young. Then the music stopped, the silence so jarring that Nick jerked upright.

"Damn it." BreeAnna's voice came through clearly. There was the sound of her picking out a passage on the keyboard, trying different variations, then a discordant smashing of notes. "It was all so clear while I was there, why can't I remember it? Maybe in the morning after I get some sleep. I need to practice what I'm going to tell Dad—I don't understand why he wouldn't listen to me tonight when I told him what was going on. I have to make him understand."

Deep, ominous chords punctuated her words. "It's like they think because I was in there, I must be crazy and mixed-up. Even Mom—and she of all people knows that's not true."

Nick hit the "Pause" button. Rewound and listened again. This was recorded the night BreeAnna died.

"Everyone's so afraid all the time," she went on. "Mom's afraid I'll tell her secret. Dad worries about the business and all those lawsuits. It's weird. I used to be afraid, too. Of the kids at school, of letting everyone down, not being good enough, but now—now I know what needs to be done, and for the first time that I can remember, I'm not afraid."

A sigh. "I hope Micah's okay. I can't wait to see his face when we get him and the others out of there. And Deidre, poor Deidre. I know she hates me for what I've done. She needs help. Tomorrow."

Her tone was one of determination. "Tomorrow, I'll make Daddy listen. He knows judges, people who can make things happen."

More notes picked out, this time a whimsical version of "Over the Rainbow."

"Micah and the others will be back home where they belong. And then I can—"

A faint sound interrupted her. There was a pause.

"Who could that be?" she asked. There was the clatter of the headphones being set down.

The sound quality changed as BreeAnna opened the music room's door. A doorbell echoed through the foyer beyond. Followed by running footsteps as she raced down the hardwood stairs in her bare feet.

Nick leaned forward, listening intently. Voices, unintelligible by the time they reverberated through the empty foyer to reach the microphone, but definitely there. Then silence for another minute until the sound-activated mic clicked off.

There was nothing else recorded. He fiddled with the controls and was able to pull up a list of recordings. The last one, the only one from the date BreeAnna came home from ReNew, was listed as 10:21 p.m. Hours, maybe minutes, before she died.

He removed the headset, stood, and walked to the window, squinting in the bright sun now aimed directly at him. BreeAnna hadn't sounded suicidal nor had she exhibited the relaxation that some patients felt once they'd made up their mind to kill themselves.

Instead she'd sounded determined. She had a mission—something to help the other kids at ReNew. Something she wanted her parents to help with.

He turned and put his back to the sun, his shadow stretching out across the polished surface of the piano. Suddenly he had more questions than answers.

Why had BreeAnna answered the door that night and not one of her parents?

Who had she let into her house?

Did she kill herself? Or was she murdered?

◆

Jenna sat in the empty Galloway and Stone offices surrounded by electronics: her two-screen desktop computer along with BreeAnna's phone, laptop, and iPad. Morgan, as usual, was nowhere to be found now that Jenna could actually use her help and cyber expertise. So typical.

She had verified most of Morgan's information but still needed more, so she worked on correlating texts, e-mails, voice messages, and social media posts to and from BreeAnna with online postings from the people BreeAnna knew.

Painting a portrait with data. Much better than the type of portrait Nick and Andre were trying to create by talking to Caren and the housekeeper. People lied, data didn't.

When she was a federal agent, Jenna hadn't minded the fact that almost everyone she interviewed lied to her. Lying to a federal agent was against the law—a law she didn't hesitate to use if the occasion warranted. Their lies became her weapons to get what she wanted.

But this private sector stuff, being forced to make nice with the clients even as they lied to Jenna's face? Not as much fun.

At least not until she figured out a way to use those lies to her advantage, like with Greene earlier. She felt a flush of triumph at the memory of the way he'd given in to her demands. All that was left was deciding exactly how much it was going to cost him.

Her phone rang. Andre.

Jenna leaned back and sipped at her Diet Dr Pepper as she answered. "What's up?"

"We found something. Several somethings. Wanted to fill you in."

"Go ahead."

Nick's voice came over the speaker. "BreeAnna was recording herself playing the piano on the night she died. The microphone caught the sound of a doorbell ringing and her going to answer it."

"At ten twenty-one," Andre put in. "Just after the time her parents said they told her good night. Jenna, she was home alone. Her parents weren't here."

Jenna straightened. Should she protect Greene, hide his lie? No. Andre and Nick were too smart; they'd already figured out most of it anyway.

"They lied," Andre continued. "To us and the police."

"Did you talk to the mom yet?" Jenna asked, wondering if Caren's story would support what Greene had told her about where they'd been.

"No. We wanted to see how you wanted to handle it. Should we confront her ourselves? Talk to the police?"

"The police? Why get them involved?"

"Don't they need to know? Maybe reopen her case?"

Andre had many useful skills, but he had no idea what really went on behind the scenes of a police investigation—not to mention how little in the way of time and resources local police had to devote to any one case. "You've been watching too much TV. In the real world, the police won't open a closed investigation and overrule the medical examiner unless there's hard evidence. More than a doorbell ringing."

"Nick says he hasn't found any indication that BreeAnna was suicidal. And if the parents are lying to us and they weren't home but someone else was here with her—"

"You think she was murdered?" Jenna glanced at her computer and the evidence she'd gathered. Evidence that might insure Galloway and Stone's future if she played her cards right. But only if Robert Greene stayed out of prison and his company remained successful.

"Maybe." Andre didn't sound as certain as he had a few moments ago. "Don't you?"

"No. There are too many unanswered questions. It could have been a prank, or she might not have even answered the door, just went to see who it was and went back to whatever she was doing. Or, who knows, maybe BreeAnna's late-night visitor told her something that made her kill herself."

Nick's voice came. "If the parents weren't home, that explains why they're so desperate to assuage their guilt by blaming ReNew—because they weren't there to stop her."

"Right." Jenna hedged, not sure if she should reveal Greene's admission about where he and his wife had been the night BreeAnna died. Instead she sidestepped the issue. "There's nothing here for the police, not yet. We need more answers."

"Okay," Andre said. "We'll talk to the mom, ask her where she and Greene really were the night BreeAnna died."

"No." She thought fast. She needed to control this, make sure Caren didn't reveal anything that might destroy her newly forged relationship with Greene's company. "Finish going through her things, talking to the staff. Then we'll talk to Caren together."

Jenna gulped down the rest of her soda, enjoying the fizzle of the bubbles against her throat. She tossed the empty can into the garbage. "Upload the audio file for me—and any files from the week of that party before she went into ReNew. If BreeAnna was in the habit of recording her thoughts, there might be something useful there as well. I can listen in the car on my way there."

"Will do. Is Morgan coming as well?"

"No idea where she is, she was gone when I got back to the office."

"Maybe now we won't have to send her undercover."

"Too early to say. This phantom visitor of yours could still be linked to ReNew. It's only the kids locked up; the staff is free to come and go."

"Why would they go to the Greenes' house in the middle of the night after they'd just released her?"

"Exactly. If someone from ReNew was there, it wasn't for anything legit." She stood. "I'll be there soon."

CHAPTER 25

When Morgan arrived for their meeting, Greene was already there, waiting. The gas station was abandoned but in sight of the highway, and it was midafternoon, bright sunlight, nothing to be worried about. At least that's how most people might feel.

There was no good reason for Greene to do her harm—she'd already exposed his secrets and shared them with Jenna. Silencing her would accomplish nothing. But still, Morgan kept her blade close to hand beneath the sleeve of her jacket. She also had a stun gun and a .38 in her purse. "Be prepared," that was her motto.

He opened her car door for her and held her elbow as he helped her into his Lexus SUV. "It's quieter," he explained, nodding to the busy highway.

She said nothing, waiting for him to take the lead.

"How old are you, anyway?" he asked once he'd settled into the driver's seat, sliding a glance in her direction. "Twenty-one, twenty-two, right?"

"Why?" Morgan asked.

"I just can't get over how different you look. It's more than the clothes—"

Duh. That's why they called it undercover. But then his hand fell off the steering wheel and brushed her thigh as he reached for his travel mug in the center console. Hell no. She wasn't getting paid enough for *that*. Her fingers tightened on her knife, ready to slip it free. His jugular was in easy reach. Ten seconds, maybe less, and it'd all be over.

"I'm sorry if my looking like this reminds you of your daughter," she said in a mournful tone, reminding him he was a grieving father.

He covered a flash of annoyance with a sip of his coffee. "You're nothing like BreeAnna." He paused. "I need you to help me out with something."

Uh-huh. She had a feeling there'd be a "something." The way he'd pushed to be the one to take her to ReNew, it had to be about more than not wanting to wait for them to hire an actor. She sat up straight, turning to face him, which also put distance between them. "What can I do for you, Mr. Greene?"

"Well . . ." He took his time replacing the mug as if the simple act required all his concentration. "Part of the ReNew program is counseling sessions with a therapist."

Right. They'd been over all this. Caren had raved about the ReNew program—how she didn't know what had gone wrong, it was so comprehensive. An on-site therapist. Excellent security. Even a state-of-the-art computer lab and classrooms. All according to the brochure—since after the night when she'd called the ReNew goons to kidnap her daughter, she'd never actually set foot back into the place. No visits for the first thirty days, she'd said. Part of their acclimation policy.

No one bothered with an excuse as to why Bree's second month had also passed without a visit from her parents.

"You're worried about something Bree told this doctor?" Morgan guessed. "Maybe something about the judge's son and that party?"

Greene's face tightened slightly. Most honest emotion she'd seen from him. "Apparently this therapist tapes the sessions. Keeps the recordings on a computer."

"You want me to try to retrieve them?" She frowned. This job was going to be hard enough, going in naked—literally—without adding on extras.

"Destroying them would be fine. I've access to a DOD program guaranteed to scrub files beyond retrieval. I can load it to the USB drive in your glasses. You get access to the computer, and it won't take but two minutes tops to finish the job."

Morgan stared at him. He either thought she was some kind of superspy or he thought her an idiot. Didn't he realize that if she was caught, it would ruin everything he and his wife had hired them for?

Obviously protecting his company was more important to Robert Greene than discovering the truth behind his daughter's death. Not to Morgan. But he didn't have to know that.

"You know there will be hard copies," she told him. "A paper trail. Not to mention the counselor."

"Leave them to me." He jerked his chin as if making an affirmation. "You need to understand one thing about me, Ms. Ames. There is nothing I won't do to protect my family and their interests. Are you going to help me or not?"

"Why should I?"

"I'll pay you cash," he answered. "Just you. Your bosses don't need to know about it."

"How much?" she asked, more out of curiosity than anything.

"Twenty thousand."

Shit. Whatever Bree had told the shrink, it was incendiary. If it was worth twenty grand, no way in hell was she destroying the evidence.

"That's a lot of money," she told Greene.

"So you'll do it?" He turned to her with a smile that would have made a crocodile proud.

She mirrored it right back at him. "Of course. Anything to help."

While Greene uploaded the program to the small hard drive in her glasses, Morgan licked her lips, surprised they were dry, and asked the question that had been nagging at her since yesterday.

"You could have gone to get her from ReNew yourself. Why send Caren alone?"

Irritation flashed across his face, but it was chased by another emotion. Smugness. He turned to her, placing the fake eyeglasses on her face himself and adjusting their fit. "Perfect."

"You didn't answer my question."

He regarded her for a long moment, one hand on her arm. Not restraining her. Not yet. "ReNew has a policy where only the custodial parent who signed the child into the program can remove them—forfeiting the full tuition, of course. Guess they don't want to get caught in custodial disputes, give a kid back to the wrong parent."

Damn, she'd been worried there was another wrinkle in this plan . . . but now she understood his game.

He smiled at her, slid his hand along her arm, reassuring her. "I'll do the same for you—as soon as I'm certain those files are destroyed."

A white paneled van pulled off the highway and into the gas station. The knife was in her hand, although Greene didn't notice it.

"Good. They're right on time," he said, turning away from her to look out the window. "I hope you appreciate that I paid extra for this. But it was the fastest way to get you in—and I want you to record everything my daughter went through."

"That wasn't part of the bargain." But she'd already decided. He and the men in the van would live. She dropped the knife into her bag, knowing she wouldn't be using it.

Greene turned back to her and raised a hand to caress her cheek. "It is now." He clicked the "Record" button on her glasses. "I know you think I'm awful, that I don't care. But that bastard Benjamin is responsible for my daughter's death, not me. I need to know what happened to her, what he did." He leaned forward until their foreheads touched. "Everything."

Morgan pretended to surrender, noting the men leaving the van and heading their way. Playing her role. But still . . . she hated that she might have to depend on this man, a stranger with motives she didn't fully understand, to set her free after she entered ReNew. "Okay. But promise me, you'll come when I call."

He flashed a smile at her. "Don't worry, Morgan. You can trust me."

Finally his mask slipped, and Morgan realized Greene wasn't a Norm, not at all. Another wolf. Lazy, relying on cunning rather than violence, but that didn't make him any less dangerous.

She nodded and looked away. Let him think he was in control—just like she'd learned to do with her father. Better he didn't see past her own mask.

Because Robert Greene had no idea that he'd just given her exactly what she wanted—a way to answer the question she'd been asking since she'd heard of this case.

What happened inside ReNew that drove Bree to kill herself?

The men rushed Morgan's side of the car and yanked the door open, pulling her out by both arms.

"Daddy!" she screamed, sending her voice into an ear-piercing screech. "Please, don't!"

Too late. The bag was over her head, arms zip-tied behind her back, and she was shoved onto the floor of the van. Two men climbed in with her, one kneeling on her back to keep her still, the other catching her flailing legs and restraining them.

The door slammed shut, and the van rumbled over the broken pavement and back onto the highway. No one said a word. They didn't need to. Morgan was helpless.

A prisoner. Totally powerless for the first time in her life.

CHAPTER 26

Andre spoke with the housekeeper while Nick finished going through BreeAnna's personal belongings. Jenna still hadn't arrived, neither had Robert Greene.

Then the housekeeper ushered them to Caren's "sewing room" where they waited for BreeAnna's mother to dredge up enough energy to join them and discuss her daughter's life. The room sat below BreeAnna's music room. Two walls had windows filled with midafternoon sunshine filtered through lace curtains framed by heavy drapes that looked like a child had drawn the same ugly pattern over and over again. Toile, Andre's Grams had called that kind of material. There were two chairs and a love seat, all stiff-backed, with too little padding and skinny legs that made Andre afraid to sit down anywhere.

Finally the door to Caren's inner sanctum opened and the lady of the house made her appearance. Despite the fact that it was after two in the afternoon, she wore silk pajamas that reminded Andre of an old Doris Day movie his Grams loved and a brocade robe that probably cost more than his car. Rich white people, did they ever get tired of obsessing about impressions?

Although she'd made an obvious effort to put on makeup, her color was pale and the skin around her mouth sagged, making her appear older than she was. She swirled into the room, settling herself on the love seat like a moth perching on the edge of a candle, not sure if it would remain, wary of having its wings singed.

Maybe she wasn't so oblivious after all. Because Andre had a feeling she wouldn't be too happy with what they had to discuss.

"Thank you for seeing us," Nick said, leaning forward in one of the dainty chairs Andre had avoided and focusing on Caren. "I know how difficult this must be."

Andre sidled to the far side of the room, staying out of Caren's peripheral vision so he could watch without her noticing. She nodded graciously at Nick. "You said you had a few questions?"

"I understand BreeAnna began acting out after her experiences at the party where she was given Ecstasy." Nick made it a statement not a question. "You mentioned that she'd begun shoplifting and going out without permission, even using drugs and alcohol with her friends?"

Caren released a sigh. Gave it time to circle the room before answering. "Yes. That's right. She became volatile, unreasonable, out of control. Even violent."

Nick nodded as he adjusted his posture to mirror hers. It wasn't often that Andre had the chance to observe him in full-on therapist mode; it was interesting to see the subtle techniques he employed. "That must have been terrifying. Your own daughter turning into a total stranger."

"Yes. Yes, it was."

"Tell me about her friends."

Caren stiffened. "Friends?"

"Yes. This bad crowd she'd fallen in with. The ones she went to the mall with and drank and smoked marijuana with. Could you give us their names?"

"I'm not sure I ever knew them. She was extremely uncommunicative. Whenever I asked, she'd fly into a rage." Somehow Caren became the victim in all of this.

Nick kept his posture open and waited. The silence grew. And then Caren began to fill it. "Of course, BreeAnna had many friends from good families—the ones who took her to that party, in fact. Son and daughter of a federal judge. I'm not sure why she couldn't continue socializing with that crowd. Part of rebelling against her father, I suppose. He puts great stock in that sort of thing."

As if Caren didn't care who her daughter socialized with? Or implying that Robert was fine with his daughter being friends with kids who gave her drugs and sexually assaulted her as long as their father was a judge?

"Tell me about some of the trouble BreeAnna's new friends got her into," Nick suggested. "I'm sure that must have been a difficult time for you."

Caren grabbed on to that as if he'd thrown her a lifeline. She began telling Nick about middle-of-the-night trips from the house, finding expensive items in BreeAnna's room, the pregnancy scare. The more Caren talked, the more she dug herself into a hole.

And through it all, she never once called her daughter by name, Andre noticed. Worst thing was, he had the feeling she'd fed herself her own lies for so long that she actually believed them.

Finally she wound down. "So you can see, I had to do something."

"Just a few more questions, Mrs. Greene," Nick continued in the same friendly tone.

"Of course, anything."

"How did BreeAnna get to the mall on all those occasions?"

Caren blinked, looked down to adjust the belt of her robe. "I suppose her friends picked her up."

"Here at the house?"

"Or from school." She perked up. "Maybe she took a bus from school."

"Then how did she get home again?"

She didn't answer, but her shoulders hunched. Indignation flashed over her face, and she opened her mouth, but Nick interrupted her before she could make a sound.

"BreeAnna never went to the mall, did she, Caren? She never left in the middle of the night, she never made new friends. In fact, she never had any friends after that party. All she did was go to school and come home. That was it, her entire life until you sent her away."

Caren stood up, halfway, then dropped back down again. "You spoke with Juanita."

"We spoke with Juanita," Nick confirmed, his tone still gentle. "And we checked BreeAnna's social media accounts—a great way to build a map of someone's movements. So tell me, Caren. Why did you send BreeAnna to ReNew? What really happened?"

Caren blinked, opened her mouth, blinked again, and closed it. Then she began to sob. More than sob, blubber. Andre moved forward to comfort her, but Nick waved him back. Finally she choked down her tears long enough to say, "You think it's all my fault. You think she's dead because of me. You think I killed my baby."

Andre turned away. Caren's act was becoming all too familiar, and he couldn't stand any more lies. This was supposed to be about BreeAnna, not about assuaging Caren's guilt or defending the Greene family's honor.

Nick joined Caren on the love seat. He didn't offer any physical comfort, instead merely spoke to her in a soothing tone. "It's okay, Caren. No one is judging you here. But your daughter deserves the truth, doesn't she?"

The truth? Did these people even know what that was? If this was what it was going to be like working with rich clients, Andre thought he might be better off finding another job. Something honest. Like digging ditches or hauling garbage.

"That fancy lingerie you said BreeAnna stole," Nick continued. "She didn't shoplift it. You bought it, didn't you?"

Face buried in her hands, Caren nodded.

"And that pregnancy test. That was yours as well?"

Caren's shoulders tightened as if she was trying to avoid Nick's words, but finally she relaxed them and raised her head. "Yes. BreeAnna found it. Knew her father had had a vasectomy. She was so angry—so very disappointed. Judgmental. She just has no idea what it's like being trapped in a marriage, no escape. She threatened to tell Robert."

She flung herself into Nick's arms. Nick gently but firmly untangled himself from her embrace and moved back to the chair opposite her.

"You have to understand. I signed a prenup. He can have all the affairs he wants—and believe me, he does—but I, one tiny mistake, a single moment of happiness, and I lose everything."

"What happened with BreeAnna?" Nick steered her back on track.

"She'd been moping around for weeks. Ever since that damn party. Talking back, or worse, not talking at all, giving me the silent treatment. Of course, she acted just fine around Robert the few times he was home. Daddy's little angel. Then she found out about Tyler. He's no one, really. Just a waiter over at the clubhouse. But he knew how to make me laugh and feel young again. That's all I wanted. Is that so awful? To want to feel happy and not feel like a prisoner in my own damn house?"

"So you and BreeAnna had a fight?"

"Had several fights. I kept her home from school that day, didn't want to give her a chance to call her father. First, she was angry, said I betrayed Robert. Then she turned nasty, tried to blackmail me, said if I let her change schools, she wouldn't say anything."

She straightened, indignant. "I'm not going to take that kind of treatment, not from my own daughter. A friend had told me about ReNew, about how they'd come day or night to pick up a kid. Said they really turned her daughter around—she'd been drinking and doing drugs and came back a year and a half later clean and sober. The tuition was outrageous, but I didn't care. Figured it was the least Robert could do for his little angel."

"So you made the call."

Shoulders back, Caren faced Nick. Flashed him a triumphant smile. Andre thought it was the first time he was seeing the real woman. "So I made the call. Those two months she was gone were the happiest I've had since I got married."

CHAPTER 27

Once she quieted and stopped fighting back, the men in the van left Morgan alone. That didn't make her feel any better. Instead it demonstrated exactly what little control she had.

Fear chilled her. Was this how Bree had felt? she wondered. Probably not, but it was as close as Morgan was ever going to get.

The Norms had it all wrong—they said people like her didn't feel emotion. Bullshit. Morgan had plenty of emotions; she just usually wasn't guided by them, could keep them tamped down, focus on what *she* wanted instead of what silly neurochemicals and hormones urged her to do.

No, she felt. Sometimes much, much more than Norms ever could. Because when Morgan's emotions were unleashed—the strong ones like fear, anger, maybe love, she wouldn't know—they crescendoed into a wave that consumed her, lifting her higher, far above to lofty heights where she could do anything, where there were no rules, no limitations, no reason why she couldn't be a god.

Whoever said, "The only thing we have to fear is fear itself," was so very right—for the wrong reasons. He meant to forget fear, just carry on, stiff upper lip. Typical sheep reasoning. Gather together and huddle into one big fat target for the wolf to devour.

Norms didn't understand the power of emotions. If you embraced them, allowed them to escape from Pandora's box and sweep you up, they were like riding a tsunami. Her father had tasted that power at an early age. He'd lived his life seeking more, more, more until his addiction had crashed him back down to earth. He'd fallen hard and now paid the price.

Yes, Morgan felt. But she had none of the paralysis, deer-in-the-headlights freezing that many Norms exhibited. Instead she would become deathly still just long enough to coldly analyze the situation before springing into action. Instead of the tunnel vision and sound dampening that Nick's soldier patients reported during their traumatic combat experiences, Morgan's vision expanded to the point where she only needed to move her eyes but the slightest fraction to see everything around her. Her hearing became preternatural as well.

And instead of fear or anger driving her into a fog of action later poorly remembered—as if Norms' brains tried to protect them from the repercussions of any heightened emotional state—Morgan would remember everything in precise, intimate detail.

Something else her father reveled in. Reliving each moment of every heinous crime over and over—but it was only by committing another atrocity, bigger, badder, bolder, that he could truly achieve the stimulation he sought. For him, there was no end, only an infinite compulsion for more, more, more.

When Morgan felt fear she harnessed it. Like now. Assessing her options and her weapons. Even wryly observing that she'd brought this on herself—and wasn't this exactly what she'd asked for? An intimate understanding of what Bree had gone through?

Although Bree didn't have what Morgan had. Namely, two transmitters, one audio/visual recorder, and a pair of hidden lock picks that not even Jenna knew about.

Jenna. Did she know what Greene had planned? Maybe. She'd been excited by the possibility of what Morgan could learn inside ReNew. Clever of Greene to outmaneuver Jenna so he could be alone with Morgan long enough to ask her to also get his precious files.

She couldn't trust either of them. Fine with Morgan. She was better off trusting herself anyway.

The van made a sharp right-hand turn and rocked as it traveled over a gravel or dirt road. Finally it came to a stop.

What would a fish do? Morgan didn't have to imagine, all she had to do was remember her father's victims.

"Where are we?" she cried out. The van door slid open and hands lifted her out, feet on the ground. "Daddy! Daddy, are you there?"

"I'm here, sweetheart," came Greene's voice. "Just do what they tell you to. Everything's going to be okay."

One man held her in place while the other cut the restraints circling her ankles. Then they removed the hood. She blinked in the sunlight. They were in the parking lot in front of the main doors leading into the ReNew facility.

Not even dinnertime. Guess she was stuck here for at least the night. Hopefully not longer.

She didn't look at Greene or her captors, rather she stared at the featureless concrete block wall beyond them. Took a deep breath, focusing on what she wanted rather than the adrenaline jackhammering through her, just like Nick had taught her. She wasn't nervous or afraid; she simply did not want to be here—and it wasn't often that Morgan did anything she didn't want to do.

"Daddy?" she turned it into a plaintive wail, edged with desperation.

Greene stepped in front of her. "It's for your own good, sweetheart. Really."

"You sonofabitch!" she screamed at him, falling into her character, struggling against her bonds. The men effortlessly held her in place.

"Lower your voice," Greene shouted back. "Haven't you caused me enough problems already?"

One of the guards interceded. "You can come peacefully, and we'll let your hands free," he said in a bored tone that indicated he really didn't care what she did. "Or we can carry you in and sedate you."

She scowled at him but nodded and stopped struggling. "Okay, okay. You win."

"Good girl." He cut her wrists free. She shoved both hands deep into her jacket pockets, hunching her shoulders up around her ears, a turtle withdrawing into its shell. Greene took her elbow and led her to the door.

The guard opened the door and held it for them. "Director Chapman is waiting for you. Right this way, please."

Morgan couldn't help but note how quickly she was relegated to nonentity, being ushered through the corridor as if she was a piece of luggage. All attention was on Greene—a.k.a. James Renshaw. Fine with her, it gave her a chance to assess the situation.

Inside, the building continued its pleasant elementary school facade. The front doors were solid wood with sidelights on either side, the lock nothing Morgan couldn't handle. No alarm system— at least nothing obvious, not out here in the public area.

The guard led them down the hall to what would have been the principal's office if this really were a school. Despite the expensive "tuition" ReNew charged, the decor was low-key, businesslike, designed to underwhelm. Made sense. They weren't selling a posh prep school experience; they were selling the illusion of serious people seriously interested in helping children.

Sean Chapman, the program's director, waited behind a plain oak desk clear of everything except a single file folder and a phone.

She was surprised to see that he was only in his midtwenties, although he wore glasses and a formal suit designed to make him appear older.

"Mr. Renshaw," he said, standing to shake Greene's hand. "It's good to see you again. Sorry it has to be under these circumstances."

Chapman's office had two walls lined with floor-to-ceiling bookcases. The wall opposite the door was filled with windows adorned with the omnipresent ReNew sunrise graphic done in a film that allowed the real sunlight to stream through the colors, giving it the impression of stained glass. The only other adornment was a simple cross on the wall beside the door.

There were two leather chairs in front of the desk. Chapman smiled at Greene and nodded him to one. He, like the guard, didn't acknowledge Morgan's presence. She played along, acting her role of disgruntled teen, by slouching in the corner, her back to a bookshelf.

Director Chapman and Greene talked particulars about Morgan's "personalized curriculum." It sounded like pretty non-personalized rules to her: no visitation for the first thirty days and after that only once she completed Step Five, whatever the hell that was; staff wasn't allowed to administer any corporal punishment but could restrain students for their safety and the safety of others if a student grew agitated and out of control; students slept in a same-sex dorm room to facilitate socialization, but if they were disruptive, they were moved to an isolation room; periodic searches for contraband were required for the safety of all; and, of course, ReNew and their employees were not liable for anything that happened to the children left in their care. Sign here and here.

Yada yada . . . their words faded as Morgan focused on slipping the pen-recorder on top of the books on one of the lower shelves, where it wouldn't be seen. Mission accomplished, she began pacing behind Greene, head down, hair covering her face to hide her gaze as she focused on the door. A Schlage lock—good quality, but she could handle it. She pretended to examine the other bookcase, all books on religion and spirituality and self-help crap.

No signs of a hidden safe, no signs of any file cabinets, no computers, and she hadn't seen any in the waiting area out front. The files must be kept somewhere else.

She tuned back into their conversation just as Chapman was asking about her medical history. So far Greene had done a good job establishing their cover.

"Any surgeries?" Chapman asked, his pen hovering over a checklist.

"No," Greene answered.

Morgan didn't turn to face them but said over her shoulder, "Don't forget my appendix." Then she whirled to Chapman, leaning over him and pulling up her shirt to expose her belly button. "Wanna see my scar?"

He dropped his pen and for the first time looked her in the eye. "It is rude to interrupt your elders, young lady. I think it's time for you to leave." He focused on Greene once more. "Given the extreme nature of your situation, the good Reverend Doctor Benjamin has come in person to do your daughter's intake evaluation."

His tone was one of awe, as if the good Reverend Doctor was granting them a royal boon. Greene played along, nodding eagerly as he juggled the stack of forms in front of him.

The guards must have been right outside because the door opened and before Morgan could blink, they were hustling her out, her toes barely touching the ground, one guard on each elbow.

Staying in role, she twisted her head and glanced back over her shoulder and cried out in a plaintive wail, "Daddy!"

CHAPTER 28

The guards ushered Morgan to a second office around the corner from Chapman's. Just before they shoved her over the threshold, she got a glimpse of a third room across the hallway from the counselor's office. It was labeled "Intake." The floor was covered with gym mats, and on the wall across from the open door was a set of two solid metal doors.

Beyond them would be her home for the next few days.

First, she had to make it past the good Reverend Doctor. The guards wheeled her around, and before she knew it she was sitting in a plastic chair—the kind that would blow away in a strong breeze if you left it out on the patio—across from a middle-aged man who lounged in his executive leather chair as if he owned the world.

Which she guessed he pretty much did. At least the world of ReNew.

The good Reverend Doctor Amos Benjamin. His grey suit had a subtle shimmer to it, as if it was made of Teflon. Beneath it he wore a royal-blue shirt with a clerical collar. Jenna hadn't been able to trace any aliases or find any hint of wrongdoing in

Benjamin's past. Neither had Morgan—which made her all the more suspicious.

The man was either a master manipulator, walking away clean, leaving others to take the fall, or he was exactly what he appeared to be: a God-fearing man of the cloth, working passionately to save troubled children fallen from grace.

There was no mistaking the power Benjamin exuded. A certainty that he was absolutely correct in whatever he did. That he was the one in control, the one with a direct line to the Almighty. "Ms. Renshaw. You've caused your poor parents quite a lot of pain and suffering. What do you have to say for yourself?"

The guards didn't leave, instead stood behind Morgan as if waiting for her to do something. More than waiting . . . wanting. As if they lived and died for the chance to forcibly restrain a skinny teenage girl.

Of course, they did, Morgan realized. What better way to convince parents they'd come to the right place while also relieving any guilt or misgivings they might have? She glanced up and saw cameras overhead in two of the corners. No books here—too easy to use as weapons.

No furniture besides the two chairs. The wall beside the door was lined with large important-looking diplomas in expensive frames. Their writing was in Latin, so it was impossible to read much except the institution name and Benjamin's. Maybe she could hide the bug on top of one of the frames? Because clearly this was the room where all the good stuff happened.

She eyed the cameras. They had to be feeding into a computer somewhere in a back room not visible to the public. Hopefully on-site. If not, she'd be returning to Greene empty-handed.

"Ms. Renshaw." Benjamin's voice cracked across the space between them, although his posture remained relaxed. "Please do me the courtesy of answering me when I speak to you. I asked what you have to say for yourself."

"About what?" Morgan replied. Benjamin was deliberately baiting her, she was certain.

He steepled his fingers and gazed above her as if reading something only he could see. "I understand your parents have caught you stealing liquor from them. Is that true?"

Morgan shrugged in answer. Benjamin glared at her. "I couldn't hear you. Is it true, did you steal from your parents?"

"Yeah, I snuck a few beers. So what?"

"So you're a thief and an alcoholic." Benjamin nodded in satisfaction.

"A few beers doesn't make me an alcoholic," Morgan protested.

"Denial is a common response, Ms. Renshaw. No worries, we'll deal with all that in good time. I see that you've also used drugs? Which ones?"

Morgan slouched in her chair, arms crossed over her chest. "I've never used drugs."

Benjamin jerked a chin at the guards. One of them wrapped his fist around Morgan's jacket collar, jerking her upright so hard and fast that the denim cut into her armpits, while the other emptied her pockets. There went her lighter, a pack of cigarettes, lipstick, comb, cash. And the small stack of pennies with the hidden microphone. It rolled to the far side of the desk and fell to the floor.

The guards and Benjamin didn't even notice. Instead Benjamin nodded at the cigarettes. "Tobacco is a drug and against the law for someone your age to possess." He made a dramatic sound, not a sigh, rather a reluctant inhalation. "So now we have lying, thieving, drinking, and drug use." He squinted at Morgan. "I assume we can add sex to that as well?"

The guards dumped Morgan back into her chair. She glanced at one of the cameras, giving a show of being flustered. But secretly she was thrilled—both bugs planted without any problem. "None of your business."

"Your parents found you along with a girlfriend in the company of three older men. Two eighteen-year-olds and"—Benjamin raised an eyebrow—"a twenty-three-year-old? That's statutory rape. Oh, and your friend is a year younger than you, only fourteen? That makes you an accomplice. You could be labeled a sexual predator if we took this to the police."

He leaned back once more and smiled at the guards, shaking his head sadly. "Can you imagine that? Fifteen and already a sexual predator facing felony time. And in Pennsylvania, a fifteen-year-old can be prosecuted as an adult, which means real prison." Benjamin leered at Morgan. "You ever hear of Rockview, the state penitentiary? It's where they keep the electric chair."

Morgan had to fight her laughter, twisting it into a sound of dismay and fear. Last thing she needed was for Benjamin to know she'd visited Rockview only yesterday when she went to see her father.

Her father. If he could see her now. Lord, how he would be howling with delight at the sheer irony. Morgan trapped as good as any fish. Forced to play the victim.

"What do you want?" she finally whispered. This was the real reason why Benjamin took the time to do his intake interview. To learn where his new prisoners were most vulnerable, assess their breaking point.

That and the ridiculous extra fee he charged for his personal attention.

"We're here to help," Benjamin crooned as if leading a prayer. "All we want is to redirect you onto the right path, to help you ReNew your life. You work the steps, do as you're told, stay out of trouble, and we'll get along just fine. If you relapse into your old, criminal, drug-addict, sexual-predator ways, well, then, we'll just have to work harder, won't we? So you see, there's an easy way to spend your time with us and a difficult way. Which would you prefer?"

The guards edged closer, looming over Morgan. Benjamin's stare was more intimidating than their physical bulk. Because he looked like he wanted Morgan to pick door number two, to test the limits of his power—a test he would enjoy winning.

"The easy way," Morgan muttered, chin down on her chest.

"Look at me when you speak. What did you say?"

Morgan jerked her chin up. "The easy way. Anything to get out of this hellhole as fast as possible."

Benjamin stood, the light coming in through the window with its ReNew sunrise logo haloing him in color as he cast his shadow over her. "Well then, you're off to a poor start of it."

CHAPTER 29

Nick's jaw clenched, and he had to work hard to not allow his emotions to make it to his face. What kind of mother used her child to cover up her affair? Exiled her to protect her secret? Then abandoned her once again when she no longer needed her silence?

This was why he didn't do family therapy. First responders and military personnel suffering from PTSD and the aftereffects of trauma, that he understood. That he could help heal.

This woman clearly had an Axis II diagnosis, probably borderline personality disorder. Creating a world, part fantasy, part reality, all revolving around her and her petty need for attention. And the husband? Nick hadn't met him yet, but he sounded as if he had some pathology himself. Narcissist, maybe.

BreeAnna, poor kid, hadn't stood a chance. Not with these two. And yet, she hadn't ended her own life; he was certain of it. Someone else had.

As a therapist, he was good at closeting his emotions, focusing on the needs of his clients. But BreeAnna was his client, and she was dead. And right now he felt a surge of anger at that fact. He wanted her truth to be told, not the warped lies her parents would spin to fit their own needs.

He wanted justice. But what he had was this poor excuse of a mother before him. He glanced over to Andre who had turned to stare out the window, his body tension proclaiming his own disgust at Caren's admission.

Caren huddled in the corner of the love seat, hands playing with the knot on her robe. "I know you think I'm awful," she said. Nick remained silent, too upset to trust his voice. "But I didn't just abandon my daughter in that place. I did try to visit her."

That caught his attention. Why hadn't she mentioned it before? Maybe she'd seen something that might lead to BreeAnna's killer. "You were there? At ReNew?"

She shook her head. "Not the treatment center. The church."

"What happened?"

"They'd said BreeAnna was able to have visitors after the first month. So I called and called, and that administrator, Mr. Chapman, kept putting me off. Finally I called Reverend Benjamin himself. He was so understanding. Explained that BreeAnna was having a difficult time adjusting to life without drugs or alcohol."

No matter that BreeAnna's drug and alcohol use had been fabricated by Caren in the first place. But Nick remained silent, not challenging her delusions.

"He invited me for a special visit on a Sunday. We met at his office in the church where he was preparing his sermon. Such a charming man—and despite the fact that he has no children of his own, he truly understood how difficult raising a girl like BreeAnna could be. I can't tell you how helpful it was, knowing that someone appreciated everything I'd gone through."

Caren leaned back, waiting for Nick to say something sympathetic. When he didn't, she continued, "I attended services at ReNew. Lovely place and the congregation is so supportive. The student leader, Deidre, came and gave testimony about how the treatment program had saved her. The Reverend gave a beautiful sermon about the power of forgiveness and how first we need to forgive ourselves. And then—"

To Nick's surprise, she broke off to fish a tissue from the pocket of her robe. She sniffed into it, blinking fast as if holding back tears.

The tears weren't for BreeAnna. They were for Caren.

The chime of the doorbell sounded, carrying clearly through the closed doors to the suite. Andre met Nick's eyes. Guess that answered the question of whether Caren or Robert somehow hadn't heard the doorbell ringing the night BreeAnna died.

A few minutes later there was a knock and Jenna entered. She took the chair beside Nick and gave Andre a quick nod.

"Caren was just walking us through the time she went to visit BreeAnna at ReNew," Nick told her. "Reverend Benjamin invited her to a church service."

"Good," Jenna said. "Don't let me interrupt."

"And then," Caren resumed her story, glancing from Jenna to Nick, obviously delighted to have all eyes on her, "he showed a video to the congregation. Deidre and my BreeAnna, singing together. 'This Little Light of Mine.'" She cleared her throat. "It was so beautiful—I was overwhelmed. To see BreeAnna smile like that. Well, I knew she was in the right place."

"Did you see her? Inside the treatment facility?" Jenna asked.

She shook her head. "No. After the service, I spoke with the Reverend—he's so easy to talk to. I felt I could tell him anything. Together we decided that we needed to give BreeAnna more time to adjust—although I told him, she was already so much better than what I'd seen from her at home. It'd been weeks and weeks since I'd seen her smile, much less heard her sing."

"Since the party?" Jenna leaned forward anxiously. Nick caught her eye, shook his head. Too many interruptions and Caren might withdraw, throw one of her fits before they got any answers. Jenna gave him a nod and relaxed back in her chair.

"Why does everyone keep bringing up that damn party? Kids are kids." She seemed irritated that Jenna had deflected attention away from her spiritual awakening back to BreeAnna. "Anyway, the Reverend e-mailed me and Robert a video of BreeAnna singing and a note from her. It inspired me to tell Robert the truth about Tyler."

"That must have been difficult," Nick said.

She sat up straight, eyes wide, focusing on him. "Oh, it was. I was terrified. But BreeAnna and that student leader and the Reverend, they made me see that my secrets were destroying my marriage. And I was the only one who could heal it."

"How did Robert take it?"

"Furious. Of course. That's why I told him over the phone while he was out of town. Then I made sure BreeAnna was home by the time he got home. So he could see how important keeping our family together was." She sounded almost proud of herself, using BreeAnna as a hostage to her husband's affection.

Nick tried to push Caren's focus back to BreeAnna. "Can we see that video? And the message the Reverend sent you?"

She thought about it for a moment, then stood, leading him to a small hutch in the corner. Andre remained at the window, but Jenna crowded in, peering over his shoulder. The hutch appeared to be a delicate antique, but when the doors opened the interior was set up as a modern computer desk. She hit a few keys, and the Reverend's e-mail appeared. Caren clicked on the video, filling the room with two girls' voices, sweet and innocent.

BreeAnna played an upright piano, sunlight streaming in through windows behind her, as another girl, a blonde, stood beside her, swaying to the tune, her eyes closed as she sang.

"Who's the other girl with BreeAnna?" Nick asked.

"That's Deidre. The ReNew student leader."

BreeAnna must have known the song by heart because her gaze never left the second girl, Deidre. She seemed enraptured by the older girl, smiling not with the tune but rather in response to Deidre's expression.

It appeared as if, after being let down by the adults in her life, BreeAnna had finally found a hero.

And hero worship could be dangerous, Nick knew. Especially to someone as isolated as BreeAnna.

The song ended, and Caren clicked the video off. Nick read the message, supposedly from BreeAnna, that Reverend Benjamin had included in the body of the e-mail.

I'm so thankful for the guidance I'm receiving here at ReNew. I have so much to learn and have only just begun my journey.

I now understand the destructive power of the secrets I've been keeping. We must seek the light, shun the dark. So I must embrace the truth.

"Isn't it beautiful?" Caren gushed. "Embrace the truth. So simple, yet so wise. I always knew BreeAnna had hidden depths—her music teachers were constantly telling us that she had more talent, if she'd only apply herself, break free of her insecurities."

"Does that message sound like BreeAnna to you?" Nick asked. His own daughter was thirteen, just a year younger than BreeAnna, and she'd never write anything like this.

"Well, BreeAnna is mature for her age, you know. Gets that from me."

Right. "And this message is what caused you to tell your husband about your affair?"

"It was pretty much over, anyway. But, yes, after getting this, I decided to tell Robert the truth. He needed to know how much pain I was in, that I'd resort to something like that. We needed to heal our marriage—and we couldn't do that with secrets between us."

Nick read the message once more. Noted that it was sent to two separate e-mails: Caren's and Robert's. As if the sender wanted to make certain both parents saw it, without relying on Caren sharing it with Robert.

Which made Robert the true target. Because to Nick, the message didn't read like a note from a fourteen-year-old girl. It read like a veiled threat of exposure.

Made him wonder what secrets Robert Greene was keeping. And how far he'd go to keep them buried.

CHAPTER 30

Benjamin and the guards escorted Morgan back to Director Chapman's office. They passed an empty classroom, desks filled with computer equipment, bright sunshine streaming in through a wall of windows, bouncing off whiteboards brimming with hope. Morgan had the suspicion that the room had never been used—except maybe for the occasional parents' night. It had the air of a theatrical set piece rather than an actual place of learning.

Facades upon facades, that was ReNew. Glittery rhetoric, promises parents frustrated beyond belief were ready to believe—and pay for. All the parents wanted was guilt-free release from the burden their children represented. ReNew provided that, but Morgan sincerely doubted they did it via any kind of rehabilitation or reeducation, much less actual treatment.

She'd assumed ReNew was like any other prison, basically a warehouse behind locked doors, troubled kids kept safely out of sight and out of mind. But after meeting the good Reverend Doctor, she realized she was wrong.

ReNew wasn't about locking kids up. It was about breaking them down.

Given what Greene had implied about being blackmailed by Benjamin and Chapman, it made sense. Break a kid, get them to talk—even if they were simply saying what Benjamin wanted to hear—use that against both them and their parents.

No wonder no one had ever followed up on any complaints against ReNew. What kid would testify, knowing their most humiliating moments were on record, just waiting for the chance to expose their darkest secrets to the world?

The guards pivoted her and held her at attention in the doorway to Chapman's office. Benjamin strode behind Chapman's desk, dwarfing the director.

He shook his head in sympathy. "I'm so glad you brought Morgan to us, Mr. Renshaw. I'm afraid it's worse than you ever imagined. She disclosed to me drug use, stealing, even predatory sexual acts."

Greene played his role, eyes going wide, lips pursed in shock as he looked from Benjamin to Chapman and finally over his shoulder to where Morgan stood suspended in place by the two guards who held her by the elbows.

"I never imagined—" He focused on Benjamin. "Can you help her? Can you bring me back my sweet little girl?"

Damn, he was good. Benjamin and Chapman ate it up, Chapman standing and meeting Benjamin's gaze as if taking on a particularly difficult duty. Greene stood as well, and Benjamin came around from behind the desk to take his hand, clasping it with the earnest grip of someone swearing a blood oath.

"Of course, Mr. Renshaw. We'll do everything in our power. I promise you that. Would you like to say good-bye to your daughter now so we can get started?"

Greene turned to Morgan, the width of the office still between them as the guards held her at the doorway. "I just hope—" He trailed off, shoulders trembling as if holding back tears. "Please, baby, try. That's all your mom and I ask. Try to get better. We'll be here for you."

Morgan figured this would be the time a normal girl would panic. She struggled in the guards' arms, trying to break free and run to Greene. "No!" she cried. "Daddy! Don't leave me! I'll be good, I promise. I'll do anything you want."

Benjamin placed an arm around Greene's shoulders and turned him away as the guards dragged Morgan down the hall and around the corner. She struggled and fought, forcing actual tears and blubbering, but it was all for naught. They tossed her through the door of the intake room and closed it behind her.

Leaving her alone in the dark. Morgan spun on her knees, the gym mats lining the floors rustling with her movement. She pounded on the door with one hand, wailing.

Finally after she'd slumped exhausted against the wall, the doors on the opposite side of the room banged open, spilling blinding light into the small, dark room. Morgan turned around, still on her knees. Several figures crowded through the doorway, fanning out on either side, leaving one standing alone in the center. A dark silhouette surrounded by a halo of light. A girl in a long, flowing dress.

Morgan blinked, playing her role despite the fact that every instinct in her told her to charge the girl—obviously the leader—and take her down, hard and fast and dirty.

Instead she knelt there, role-playing a quivering mass of uncertainty. Someone flicked the lights on, and she saw that these weren't staff members, despite their red shirts with the ReNew sunrise embroidered over their hearts. These were all kids. Kids drunk with power from the way they bounced on their heels, anxious for action.

Five boys, aged fifteen to eighteen, she guessed. Two girls, maybe sixteen or seventeen. And the leader in the center: a girl, long blonde hair cascading down past her shoulders in contrast to the other girls who had short, raggedy haircuts. She was like Morgan—could have passed for anywhere from fourteen to midtwenties with her beatific smile and placid, imperturbable expression. She stared at Morgan with dull blue eyes—the only part of her that seemed lifeless.

Morgan studied her from beneath heavy lids, her face shielded by her own long hair. She could have been looking into a mirror. Not their physical features, she had nothing in common with this blonde beauty. No, it was what lay beneath the mask. She'd met the wolf—but Morgan's job was to play a sheep, hide her own true nature.

The leader gave some unseen signal and a boy and girl, both tall and muscular, bigger than Morgan, approached from either side. Morgan huddled back against the door.

"Welcome to ReNew," the leader said, her voice a cheerful singsong. "I'm Deidre, the student leader. You're only at Step Zero, not even a Level One, so you will not look at me or address anyone unless you are addressed. You will not speak unless spoken to. You will do exactly as any Level Seven or above—the ones in the red shirts—tells you, without question. Do you understand?"

Morgan nodded, more of her dark curls falling in front of her face. Deidre arched an eyebrow, and the girl on Morgan's right side grabbed a fistful of Morgan's hair, yanking so hard that Morgan's head hit the door behind her.

"You will speak when spoken to," Deidre repeated, the spark in her voice honed by impatience. "I can't hear a nod. Do you understand?"

"Yes." The syllable tore past Morgan's lips with a shudder that shook her body.

"Very well. Stand and take off your clothes."

Morgan must have hesitated a moment too long because before she could move, the girl hauled her to her feet by her hair and the boy was tearing off her jacket, hurling it to the floor. As soon as he had it clear, the girl had Morgan's tee off, and within moments she stood in her underwear, all eyes on her.

"All of it," Deidre snapped.

The boy and girl stepped back, giving Morgan time to finish stripping. She knew what they were doing: first, taking control, then coercing her into cooperating in her own humiliation. Effective combination—she wondered if they were self-taught. Leave it to adolescents to figure out how to best torture their peers.

As she removed her bra and panties, she couldn't help but think that her father would have approved of Deidre—and would have been disgusted by Morgan playing the sheep.

She'd come here thinking the adults were the problem, that she could record enough abuses to shut down ReNew for good, free the kids, and find some justice for Bree. But now she doubted it would be that simple.

"Squat," Deidre ordered. The girl pushed Morgan down while the boy donned vinyl gloves and spread her butt cheeks apart. "Cough. Harder."

"She's clean," the boy said, his hands and fingers probing Morgan longer than necessary.

The girl released Morgan and grabbed a stack of khaki-colored clothing from a random cubbyhole. There were flip-flops, plain white cotton underwear and a sports bra, a pair of pants with an elastic waist, and a top like the scrubs nurses and surgeons wore. All hopelessly too big.

"Get dressed. Faster!" They all laughed when Morgan, in her rush, got her foot caught in the too-long pants leg and fell face-first onto the mat.

The boy and girl roughly finished dressing her, then the boy hauled her to her feet by wrapping the waistband of her pants into a fist planted at the small of her back—creating a combination of a superwedgie and a painful punch to the spine that made her gasp.

Another laugh as he pulled her up to her tiptoes, inches of the pants legs extending past her bare feet protected only by the flip-flops, her groin burning with the pressure of her weight suspended on the crotch seam of the pants. She flailed, totally off balance, trying to relieve the pain, but he propelled her forward, not giving her a chance. Her feet pedaled, like a cartoon character's searching for firm ground after running off a cliff.

Her father's laughter rang through her mind as she realized she was as helpless in the boy's grasp as any of her father's victims had been in his. Deidre leaned forward. The two guards lifted Morgan higher so that Morgan's face was opposite Deidre's despite Morgan's shorter stature.

"I met your parents this morning," Deidre said. Morgan forced herself not to look her in the eyes. "They said you were rotten. No good. Out of control."

She shoved her palm into Morgan's breastbone, hard enough to make Morgan gasp as the breath rushed out of her body. Pinioned by the guards hoisting her by her elbows and the balled-up waistband of her pants, she had no choice but to absorb the energy of the blow rather than deflect it.

"Funny. Looks to me like we're the ones in control." Deidre clapped her palm against Morgan's cheekbone. "Remember that and you'll do fine."

Morgan's blood burned ice-cold. But she wasn't here to kill. She was here to observe. Which meant either bowing to the will of the bully in charge—Deidre—or giving the bully a reason to do what they really wanted: to prove themselves the most powerful. *King of the hill*, her dad called it.

Either way, Morgan would be the one paying the price. She calculated the odds, gauged the guards—of the seven, two didn't seem cowed at all by Deidre. Was the student leader embroiled in a power struggle? If so, then a show of dominance might help both Deidre and Morgan get what they wanted.

Morgan tilted her chin up, pursed her lips, and spat a wad of mucus into Deidre's face.

Deidre gasped and jumped back. Both of the guards that Morgan had pegged as possible trouble laughed, proving her right. As did the two guards holding her. She didn't get a chance to notice much more, not after Deidre stepped forward and slapped her so hard her jaw threatened to slip out of joint and her glasses went crooked on her nose.

"Bring her," Deidre ordered, glaring at the two guards who had dared laugh. "I believe a lesson in humility is in order."

The guards hauled her across the threshold, leaving the intake room. Morgan didn't need to fake her cringe when the heavy metal door slammed shut behind her.

They entered a large room. No windows, cinder-block walls. In a real school it would have been the gymnasium or cafeteria. Plastic tables lined the back wall, surrounded by chairs made of the same lightweight material. In front of them five rows of kids dressed in khaki knelt on the linoleum, facing Morgan. Their silence was as painful as the look of abject dejection in their eyes. Not one of them with a spark of defiance—in fact, the youngest, a boy who couldn't be more than twelve and who knelt all alone in the front row except for the Red Shirt standing behind him, hands on the boy's shoulders pinning him down, was crying.

"This is our new Step Zero," Deidre announced, not bothering with Morgan's name. As if she no longer had one—or an identity to go with it. "She already has two demerits, one for lying and one for disrespecting the good Reverend Doctor. What does she need?"

"ReNew," a ragged murmur came from the kneeling kids. Their voices were soft, all emotion exhausted.

"I can't hear you!" Deidre screamed like a cheerleader in the fourth quarter of the big game.

"ReNew, ReNew, ReNew!" The Red Shirts, except the two flanking Morgan, still dangling from the wedgie to end all wedgies, spread around the room, hands pumping up and down, encouraging the kneeling kids into a chant that gained in volume and enthusiasm.

"And what path leads to ReNewal?" Deidre shouted. "Shall we purge her of sin?"

There was a sudden silence followed by a gasp. Several of the students glanced at each other in confusion until the Red Shirts began chanting, "Purge! Purge! Purge!"

Soon they were all screaming the word, waving their arms, their bodies gyrating, feet knocking against the floor. But despite the movement every eye remained locked on Deidre. More than looking for guidance. Desperate to obey.

Deidre waited, gauging the crowd. She raised one hand and silence immediately reigned—except for the young boy's sobbing.

"Micah Chase!" she called the name like a queen calling for an executioner. "You have been given a reprieve. To complete your penance you will instruct and supervise the new Step Zero as she purges herself of her sins."

The crowd turned as one to stare into the corner behind Morgan. Her guard steered her that way as well. There, face to the corner, knelt a tall boy, hands behind his head, elbows out, spine held rigid by a broomstick shoved down the back of his shirt.

One of the Red Shirts leapt forward, pulling the stick out. The boy slumped but quickly righted himself before falling. Morgan sensed it was a matter of pride, but from the sweat stains on his shirt, she also had a feeling that he'd been kneeling in that corner, frozen in place, for quite a long time.

Slowly, with the agony of an old man, he pushed a palm against the wall and climbed to his feet. He kept his back to Morgan and the others, shoulders heaving as he gathered his strength.

"Almost a record," he mumbled, but no one else seemed to hear. Then he turned to face Morgan, studiously ignoring Deidre and her minions.

He was as light as Morgan was dark. Hair the red gold of a winter sunrise. A faint spray of freckles below his left eye the only hint of childishness softening his face. Eyes the color of a cloudless sky, fathomless and much too ancient for a kid his age.

No mask. Micah Chase faced the world naked, exposed. Morgan's own mask slipped for the barest of instants when she noticed that, as if in sympathy. How did he survive, vulnerable like that, when anyone could read him?

His gaze sharpened, locking on to hers. Just a flash, but she knew he'd spotted her mask. Maybe not so vulnerable after all. Or innocent. Not with the calluses thickening his knuckles or the scars across one side of his neck. Scars like that—someone had once held him in a choke hold and tried to slit his throat.

He tilted his head the slightest bit as if presenting his scars to her: trophies of a battle hard won. Gave her a nod faster than a blink—she almost thought she'd imagined it until she saw the challenge in his eyes. *Ask me*, his gaze said. *I dare you.*

She didn't try to hide her smile. Finally someone who might make being stuck here, playing this role, tolerable—maybe even entertaining.

CHAPTER 31

The new girl was a puzzle. One that Micah didn't have long to sort out if he was going to save her from Deidre's wrath. He had no idea what she'd done to piss Deidre off when she'd only just arrived.

Maybe it was instructions from Reverend Benjamin. Or maybe it was Deidre losing control. Again.

Ever since Bree left, Deidre had been bordering on psychotic, flying into rages followed by crying jags—and making the No Names suffer along with her.

Usually new Zeroes were given a day or two before being forced into the Purge. Not this girl. They were going to strip her body and soul right here and now, with no preparation. And he had no way to protect her.

Then he caught her eye. There was something about her, something almost-not-quite invisible. Like maybe she didn't need protecting after all.

Relief flooded him. He wasn't sure how much longer he could last, and he was all that stood between the others and Deidre's iron fist. It was the only good thing about his delay in getting out of here . . . maybe this girl, maybe she was the one who could take his place after he left? Just like he'd taken Bree's place, shepherding the No Names, when her mother came and took her home early.

As long as someone stood, unbroken, unbowing to Deidre and her cohorts, the rest could be protected.

Deidre's minions moved him into place behind the new girl. Handed him a fiberglass broomstick—lighter than a wooden one, it couldn't be broken as easily and didn't leave more than a welt if you hit someone with it. But it was still strong and rigid enough for Deidre's purposes.

He met Deidre's gaze. Hated the look in her eyes. Fury personified, pupils so dilated only the faintest glow of blue around the edges remained. There was no reasoning with her when she was like this—which, since Bree left, had been more and more often. Deidre was a true believer. Her faith drove her righteous condemnation, which meant it was almost impossible to escape her wrath. After Bree left, Deidre felt betrayed and became more volatile than ever.

No one could be as perfect as Deidre's God demanded. Not Bree, not even Deidre herself. Micah had once spied bloody welts on her back—the kind you'd get if someone whipped you. Or perhaps she'd done it to herself. He'd read about religious zealots who did crazy shit like that.

Either way, once Deidre targeted you as an unrepentant sinner, there would be hell to pay. For Deidre, salvation came through suffering.

He heaved in a breath, his balance still off after the prolonged kneeling, legs and knees shooting sparks of pain with every movement. He needed to stay alert if he was going to save the new girl.

The girl watched him with a wary expression. He wasn't sure if she was pretty, hard to tell with her face blotchy with crying, but she was . . . interesting. He reached her just as two Red Shirts spun her around to face the crowd and forced her to her knees.

"Everybody up," Deidre called out. She glanced at Tommy, alone in the front row.

Now Micah understood—Tommy hadn't experienced a Purge yet. Deidre had orchestrated this not only to break the new girl quickly but also to break Tommy. And with Micah forced into the role of instructor, a reluctant instrument of Deidre's torture, no way in hell would Tommy ever trust him again.

Sometimes he wondered what lay in Deidre's future. A career in politics? Bloodthirsty corporate raider? Or maybe worst of all, Mommy Dearest to innocent children.

He shuddered. Deidre glared at him, jerked her chin at the new girl. Micah approached the girl and laid one hand on her shoulder. The two Red Shirts stepped aside. Micah leaned forward, murmuring to the girl as he adjusted her position.

"Just do as she says," he whispered. "My name's Micah. I'll try my best to protect you, but this isn't going to be fun." He forced her arms out straight in front of her, palms up as if begging for supplication. "Try to hold out as long as you can—if you break too fast, she doesn't stop, she just keeps going until she's had her fun . . . or gets bored."

The crowd was on its feet, Deidre walking back and forth, whipping them into a frenzy as they marched in place, belting out "Onward, Christian Soldiers."

"I'm Morgan," the girl whispered back, barely moving her lips. "Thanks."

"Don't thank me yet," he warned. The Red Shirts watched him, obviously impatient. He stood upright, yanked the collar of Morgan's shirt back and slid the broomstick inside her shirt so that it stood vertically pressed against her spine. Deidre liked to position the stick under girls' bras—it increased their pain and humiliation. Micah hoped she wouldn't notice that he was taking it easy on Morgan.

Morgan didn't resist but looked terrified as the other kids crowded over her, shouting and clapping and waving their hands.

Micah stood at attention, gripping the stick, playing his role, half-hearted as it may be. Deidre glanced over her shoulder at him, flashed him a grin, then raised her hands. The crowd instantly went silent.

"Let us begin." She whirled on Morgan. "This is the Purge. Where you will confess all your sins and examine your life. It is only through repentance that you can be redeemed and ReNewed."

"ReNew, ReNew, ReNew," the crowd chanted, moving even closer to Morgan, blocking her view of anything except their bodies.

"You are here as a sinner," Deidre continued, using her best preacher voice. "God loves sinners but only if they repent."

"Repent, repent, repent!"

"We love you, but only if you redeem yourself by confessing your sins."

"We love you!" The crowd's scream sounded like a wild beast out of control.

That was the most dangerous thing about the Purge—when the crowd took on a life of its own. Kids humiliated and intimidated by the Red Shirts saw a chance to regain control, steal some power, even if it was at the expense of one of their own.

Micah didn't like crowds. Wild, unpredictable, and, if no one took control of them, deadly.

Deidre knelt directly in front of Morgan. She grasped Morgan's hands, bent over to kiss both palms, then looked up at Morgan as if it was Deidre seeking absolution.

"We love you. We love, love, love you," she whispered seductively. "This is for your own good. It's the only way. We must purge you of evil."

CHAPTER 32

Morgan stared into Deidre's empty eyes. The girl reflected there looked scared—she *was* scared.

At least as scared as Morgan ever got. When the Red Shirts had whipped out those broomsticks, she'd been expecting a beating, some kind of "spare the rod" type of punishment. Pain she understood; pain she could handle. All a matter of mind over body. Staying in control and divorcing herself from her feelings.

Thanks to her father, Morgan was a master of pain.

But this, this was something much worse than physical pain. Fifty bodies crowding in on her and she was trapped, unable to escape. Screams demanding answers coming from fifty different directions, making her head swarm as if a hive of wasps had been set loose.

At the center of it all, the eye of the storm, knelt Deidre. With her piercing gaze and serene expression she whispered to Morgan, trying to seduce a confession from her.

Deidre controlled the mob; Deidre controlled the noise and the fury and Morgan's fate. And Morgan despised her for it. A physical beating would be so much better than facing this, Morgan's greatest fear: trapped, at the mercy of strangers.

"What was your first sin?" Deidre asked, swaying closer to Morgan so she could be heard over the din of the crowd stomping around them. "Your original sin. I know what it was, don't I? Do you?"

The other kids were clapping and whirling and shouting in a bizarre conga line spiraling around Morgan, Micah, and Deidre. They would abruptly leap forward and push at Morgan or shout in her face or kiss her, then vanish once more as the whirling mad crowd of khaki and red pulled them back into the vortex.

Deidre kept hold of Morgan's hands while Micah anchored her with the broomstick, keeping her upright. Buffeted from all sides, overwhelmed with heat and noise and the press of unwashed bodies, Morgan felt as if she were drowning, unable to breathe. Her heart rate, always slower than a normal person's, began to throb in her temples as she gasped for air.

"I know your secret," Deidre persisted. "I know it and I forgive you. I love you, we love you, but you must confess. Purge yourself of your sins. You are a liar. Do you know your very first lie? The first one ever told, when you were such a little girl? Even then, even when you were so small that your dad could still carry you on his shoulders and your mother could rock you in her lap, even then you were a sinner."

Footsteps thundered around her, more and more hands knocking Morgan one way, then the other. The chanting coalesced into a single animal cry. "Sinner, sinner, sinner!"

Deidre nodded, a simple, single jerk of her chin, and it stopped. Silence reigned. Deidre dropped Morgan's hands and stood. Morgan slumped forward, but the broomstick kept her from falling. Her hair matted to her face and head, sweat trickled across her brow, fogging her glasses, turning the crowd into an ugly beige monster with more heads than a hydra.

"Why do we begin at Zero?" Deidre asked the crowd who had reassembled itself into rows before her.

"We are less than nothing!"

"Why are we less than nothing?"

"We are dirty, filthy sinners!"

Deidre motioned to the crowd, and as one they fell to their knees, all eyes on Morgan. She didn't try to wipe her glasses clean; it was far easier to deal with the crowd as an anonymous mass than to focus on each individual.

Morgan knew what Deidre was doing: classic brainwashing techniques designed to strip a psyche bare, break a person's will. She'd seen her father do it dozens of times. But knowing how it was done provided little protection. Morgan also knew how to manipulate people, a few at a time. That was easy. But she'd never spent much time in crowds. No formal schooling, no attending church services, no clubs or organizations designed to socialize a child.

She'd never much missed it before now. Crowds to her were simple faceless diversions, a place to hide out in. Deidre was showing her a whole new side—a mob.

Deidre paced back and forth, her gaze sweeping the crowd as her dress swirled around her like a priest's robes. "I know what your sin was, your original sin. Do you?"

"Sinner, sinner, sinner," the crowd chanted, drowning out anything Morgan could say.

Deidre whirled on Morgan. The crowd hushed. "Your very first sin, the sin that you can never be cleansed of, not until you fully repent . . . that first sin was when you told your parents that you loved them."

"Liar, liar, liar!" the mob accused Morgan, their bodies swaying in time with their words.

"I know that you lied," Deidre said, pacing once more, fists punching the air, emphasizing her words. "Because if you truly loved your parents, if you honored and obeyed them, if you truly loved God and honored and obeyed His commandments, then you wouldn't be here now!"

The crowd went wild at her pronouncement. They raised their hands over their heads, waving them in wide circles, roaring their condemnation of Morgan and her wicked ways.

One girl leapt to her feet and ran to Morgan, putting her face mere inches away. "You're a sinner!" Her words were accompanied by a spray of spittle. "Repent!"

As soon as she backed away, another took her place, this time a boy, younger than Morgan. "You're a liar and a thief," he screamed, his breath hot against her face. "A dirty, filthy whore!"

And so it went, one after another, the students berated Morgan, shouting and screaming and spitting, their words buffeting her from all directions. Until finally the youngest was shoved forward, the Red Shirt with him forcing him to lean down until his nose was almost touching Morgan's. He was crying, mucus streaming down his chin, his lips quivering. The look in his eyes was anguish personified, and she couldn't help but wonder what terrible crime such a young boy had done that his parents had exiled him here.

Morgan surprised herself. Tried to explain it away as acting, playing the role of a sheep, but that wasn't it. She could read this boy's need, and she wanted to help him.

Pulling against the broomstick that Micah held behind her, she reached her arms around the young boy and hugged him tight. "It's okay," she whispered. "You'll be okay."

Deidre spun, her back to the crowd, so that only Morgan and Micah could see her face. Flushed with fury, she scowled at Morgan and yanked the boy away, thrusting him into the arms of one of the Red Shirts.

Then she gave Micah a nod, and he twisted the broomstick.

Stress position, that's what Morgan's father called it. But even he would have been impressed by these kids and their diabolical use of a simple, lightweight broomstick.

Morgan was caught off guard as the broomstick twisted her top into a tourniquet, constricting her belly in one direction and her throat in the other. She realized Micah hadn't torqued it as hard or fast as he could have, but she still had to turn her head to catch a breath and release the pressure of the cotton material now tight against her throat.

Deidre knelt before her and clasped Morgan's hands, not allowing her to grab at the bunched-up shirt. "More," she told Micah as Morgan gasped for air.

Morgan's head was arched back far enough that she met Micah's eyes. He made a show of moving his hands up and down the broomstick as if he was working to twist it but didn't actually tighten the noose. She helped by coughing dramatically, hoping Deidre would buy her performance.

"Please—" Morgan gasped, cutting the word short with a choked wheeze.

Deidre didn't move, simply tightened her grip on Morgan's hands, her face serene. "We love you," she cried out. The crowd echoed it back, the noise thundering at Morgan from her position on the floor.

Morgan fluttered her eyelids and stopped fighting, sagging forward, as if fainting. Deidre let go of her hands. "Release her."

Micah quickly removed the broomstick, freeing Morgan. She heaved in a breath, coughed some more, enough that tears came, and opened her eyes.

"Sit up straight, arms out," Deidre ordered. Morgan struggled to obey, one hand going to rub her neck until Deidre slapped it away. Micah repositioned the broomstick so that it now slid through the arms of Morgan's top and behind her, forcing her arms out at her sides like a scarecrow. Uncomfortable as hell, but at least she could breathe.

Deidre stood, patting Morgan's cheek like she was her new pet. "Let us begin again. Tell me about how you pimped out your little friend to, what was it, three older men? And how you whored yourself to them as well. What did you get in exchange? Booze? Drugs?"

Morgan pretended to be confused. "No. That's not how it happened. We didn't know Jeremy's older brother would be home. We just went to crash, play video games, hang out. That's all. Nothing happened."

Another of those spooky smiles. A glint in Deidre's eyes prepared Morgan, but even rolling with the slap, it still stung. Micah kept a firm hold of the broomstick, not allowing her to fall.

"Don't lie to us. Your only salvation lies in telling us the truth." Deidre leaned forward. "All of it. Every. Single. Detail."

"Purge, purge, purge," the crowd shouted, sounding more and more like a hungry mob. Morgan glanced past Deidre and saw the little boy in the front row being jerked around like a puppet by the guy in the red shirt behind him. He was being forced to cheer and clap and yell . . . and watch. And she thought her dad was twisted. Hell, he would love this Deidre chick.

Deidre followed her glance and turned her smile on the boy. "Tell us everything or he'll be next," she said in a voice too low to carry past Morgan and Micah. "Start with all the filthy things you did with those three men. Every detail. And then you can tell us what you did to your little friend."

CHAPTER 33

A fter her proclamation, Caren's eyes went dead and she crumpled into the corner of the love seat. Andre had to restrain himself from rolling his eyes at her performance—she had it down pat; that was for sure.

"So you told your husband about the affair?" Nick asked gently.

Caren nodded. "I ended it and told Robert. That's why I went to bring BreeAnna home. With Tyler gone from my life and Robert on the road, this house was just so empty. I needed my little girl back home."

Translation: Caren's life was empty without her lover or her husband to make her the center of their universe. Only then did she think about her only child.

"It was your idea to bring BreeAnna home, not your husband's?" Jenna's voice was calm and level despite or, more likely, because of Caren's emotional roller coaster.

Caren scoffed. "Robert thinks every decision made under his roof is his and his alone, but no, I wanted BreeAnna home. I made the call and went to pick her up on my way to get Robert at the airport."

"Could you walk us through that day? You were telling us that you were the one who decided to pick up BreeAnna," Nick prompted her. "What was the procedure for that?"

The mother responded better to factual questions rather than more open-ended ones, Andre had noted. Funny, because her husband seemed the opposite. Whenever they'd asked him any direct questions, he'd gotten evasive.

"I don't know if there is a procedure," Caren answered, relaxing. "I simply called Reverend Benjamin—"

"The Reverend, not the administrator you met when you dropped BreeAnna off?" Jenna asked.

"I didn't want to bother with any red tape or paperwork. Not with Robert's flight coming in that afternoon—I wanted to surprise him with BreeAnna there at the airport to welcome him home."

Andre turned away again. Suddenly she was back to this all being one big happy family reunion. Maybe that was the only way she could live with herself.

He stared out the window. The sun was setting, the lawn was brown, and the trees bordering it all barren except for a few artfully placed evergreens. It was only March, so he wasn't expecting more, but somehow he had the feeling that BreeAnna's view never grew any more cheerful than what he was seeing.

If it wasn't for BreeAnna's mysterious visitor the night she died, he could totally understand why she'd kill herself. Living in this house with these people would be worse than solitary confinement.

He exhaled, his breath fogging the window and the view beyond. Wished he would have known BreeAnna before her death, wished someone would have told her that in just a few more years, once she left to live her own life, everything would be so much better. Wished someone, somewhere, had cared enough to give her hope.

"But even though the Reverend had approved everything," Caren was saying, "that other man, Mr. Chapman, he gave me such a difficult time. To the point where I threatened to call our attorney." Her voice grew strident, amazed that any mere administrator had the audacity to stand between her and her daughter. "But once I took out my cell phone and started to dial, he went and got BreeAnna and everything was fine after that."

Except, obviously it wasn't—ten hours later BreeAnna was dead.

"So you and BreeAnna went to the airport to pick up your husband," Nick said. "Was he pleased to see BreeAnna?"

Caren shrugged, her robe falling open with the movement. "He's so preoccupied with those lawsuits that honestly I don't think he even remembered she was in ReNew. Not until I explained how much effort I'd gone to, giving him a welcome-home surprise. Then we came home. And then"—a tiny frown marred her unlined forehead—"BreeAnna worked on her music, and we went to bed."

She pinched her lips tight and crossed her arms, not saying anything more.

Jenna moved from her chair to sit beside Caren, who didn't seem to notice, staring past Nick at a family portrait hanging on the wall behind him. In it, Robert Greene stood in the center of his family. Caren clung to his arm with both hands, while Robert had his other arm wrapped possessively around BreeAnna's shoulders. *Pretty much summed up the Greenes*, Andre thought.

"I just came from your husband's office, Mrs. Greene," Jenna said. "He told me the truth. About where you were that night."

Caren stiffened. "We were here, asleep. Just like we told the police."

"No. You weren't. Did you know someone came to the house while BreeAnna was here alone? Around—" She glanced at Andre.

"Ten twenty-one," he supplied.

"Around ten twenty-one. Any ideas who that was? Was it someone coming to see you or your husband?"

Caren honestly appeared shocked. She sprang up from the love seat and turned to face them. "What are you saying? Someone was here? At the house? Who?"

"That's what we were hoping you could tell us," Jenna said. "Did you see any cars when you and your husband left? That would have been just a few minutes before ten, right? Maybe someone on foot?"

Caren shook her head, at first little shakes of disbelief, then hard, violent, wide-eyed shakes. "No. There was no one."

"Tell us about the man you had the affair with. Could he have come here that night? Maybe to see you or confront Robert?"

"That's impossible. No."

The door opened and Robert Greene entered. Andre turned away from the window but kept his back to the wall and his hands free. He didn't like the look on Greene's face. Not at all.

Superior. Smug. Satisfied. In charge.

"Evening, sweetheart," he said, bending over the back of the love seat to kiss Caren's head. "Fancy meeting you all here." Jenna moved off the love seat and took the chair beside Nick while Greene took his place. "Did I interrupt something?"

Greene ignored everyone except Jenna. As if his question was aimed directly at her.

"Caren was just telling us about the night BreeAnna came home from ReNew," Jenna said. She leaned back in her chair, looked relaxed despite Greene's challenge, but Andre knew she was faking it. Obviously something had happened between the two of them—something while they'd visited ReNew? He wished he'd a chance to confer with Jenna in private.

"Oh, I thought you were talking about that boy of Caren's. What was his name again?" He ruffled his fingers through Caren's hair, but the gesture seemed more controlling than intimate.

"Tyler," she mumbled.

"Right. Tyler." He focused on Jenna once more. "But I'm not sure what he has to do with anything."

Nick stood, stepping between the staring match Greene was holding with Jenna. "Mr. Greene. We learned that your daughter was not alone the night she died. Someone came here, to the house, at ten twenty-one, and she spoke to them. Do you have any idea who that could be?"

For the first time Andre saw Greene grow flustered. His eyes widened, and a crease of surprise formed between his eyebrows. "Someone was here? At the house?"

"Yes. That's why we're asking about Tyler. We need to know where he was that night."

Greene shook his head and stood, pacing behind the love seat. Caren sat up and watched him with a wary gaze. "No. You don't understand," she said. "Tyler couldn't have come here."

"Why not?"

She sagged against the back of the love seat, hands twisting the belt of her robe into a knot, her eyes never leaving her husband. Greene stopped, stared at the floor for a long moment, then raised his head and nodded to her. "Go ahead, Caren. Tell them."

"Tyler couldn't have come here." She stumbled over the words, obviously uncertain. Stopped and glanced once more at Greene, seeking his approval. He jerked his chin in a nod. "He couldn't because—" She shook her head, tears choking her, and buried her face in her hands.

"Because that's where we went that night," Greene finished for her. "I made Caren take me to his place. Then I beat the crap out of him." An eerie smile lit his face. "And then I showed him how real men make love to their women. After that Caren and I drove into the woods and celebrated my homecoming just like I told you."

The only sound was Caren's sobbing. Greene marched around from behind the couch and, ignoring Nick, took a position over

Jenna, too close to allow her to stand up from the chair. Andre moved forward, ready to intervene.

"So if he didn't kill my daughter and she didn't kill herself, then who the hell did?" Greene thundered down at Jenna. "Answer me that!"

CHAPTER 34

Morgan totally understood why Deidre called it a Purge. A fitting name for Deidre's incessant inquisition, prying into every minute detail of Morgan's fake persona, grilling her so intensely that she made up events more and more lurid simply to satisfy Deidre's never-ending appetite.

Deidre was unrelenting. Whenever Morgan slowed down or backed away from confessing illicit activities, Deidre would hit her with one of the lightweight broomsticks. Morgan, caught in her kneeling scarecrow position, couldn't duck or fight back. The blows stung but only left faint reddish welts, marks that faded long before the pain.

When Deidre tired, the others took turns barraging Morgan with questions, popping up from their position on the floor, shouting at her, then dropping back down like a bunch of meerkats.

"How many men have you had sex with?"

"When's the last time you shot heroin?"

"How many drinks do you have a day?"

"What's the last thing you stole?"

"How many three-ways have you had?"

"Are you a lesbian?"

Ridiculous. Morgan didn't even bother to keep track of her answers, simply threw the first thing that came to mind out to the inquisition. Now that Deidre had the crowd back under control, Morgan quickly grew bored. She stole stories from her father's exploits, made up the most outrageous shit imaginable. It was either play along or break free of Micah's grip and ram that blasted broomstick down Deidre's throat until it came out her ass.

It was Micah who decided for her. His knees buckled against her back until she was holding him up more than he supported her. Whatever they'd been doing to him before she arrived had taken its toll. So she played the good sheep. Besides, she kept telling herself, it was the best way to get what she came for, info about Bree. After this silly initiation rite, the others should accept her as one of their own and be willing to talk. She hoped.

She had no idea how much time had passed—there were no clocks or windows in here, but finally Deidre called for a break. The kids rushed to grab chairs, while others went through a swinging door in the rear of the room and returned with trays piled high with sandwiches and milk cartons. No plates or utensils. The way the kids grabbed the food, eating so fast Morgan was surprised they didn't choke, Deidre obviously had been starving them.

No food for her or Micah. The Red Shirts had sandwiches twice as thick as the others, swollen with cold cuts, but also no plates or utensils, while Queen Bee Deidre sat in a chair directly in front of Morgan and Micah, knees together, ankles crossed beneath her, and was served on a plastic plate with a plastic glass and plastic silverware. Which told Morgan a lot about how much power Deidre really had at ReNew—not enough to be trusted with real silverware.

"Let's share our rules with our newcomer," Deidre commanded.

A Red Shirt nudged the little guy whose name Morgan had heard whispered as Tommy. He stood, cheeks full, clutching at his food as if afraid someone would steal it, swallowed, and said, "No Names do not speak without permission."

A girl from the row behind him jumped up. "No Names do not eat without permission."

And down the row it went. "No Names do not sleep without permission." Or bathe or pee or cross a doorway . . . yeah, yeah, she got it; Deidre ran a tight ship. Down to deciding how many pieces of toilet paper each child was allotted. The litany went on, but Morgan quickly tuned it out.

Deidre ate slowly, savoring every bite. Never once losing her infuriating smirk. Morgan tried to lick her lips, but she'd been talking for so long that her tongue felt like a piece of corrugated cardboard.

"Water," she croaked. "I need water."

The crowd of kids glanced up from their food, aghast. Several shook their heads, and a few put their hands over their mouths in warning.

Too late. Deidre's smirk turned into a Cheshire grin. She finished the last of her food, patted her mouth daintily, and handed her plate to a Red Shirt. "Of course, you can have water."

One of the female Red Shirts brought a large plastic cup, the kind designed to hold a day's worth of soda or convenience store slushie. Sixty-four ounces, thirty-two ounces, it didn't matter—it only took an ounce or two to fool a body into thinking it was drowning.

Micah's hand slipped to the back of Morgan's neck, hidden by her hair, and patted her reassuringly. As if she didn't know what was coming next. If she was a Norm, she might be surprised by Deidre's sadistic techniques, but Morgan was her father's daughter. She knew what Deidre wanted to see, what would end this ridiculous inquisition. If she wanted to keep her cover intact, she'd just have to give it to her.

Deidre carefully filled the cup with water from the pitcher another Red Shirt handed her. The rest of the kids cringed, staring down at their laps, edging their chairs back away from Deidre and Morgan.

Deidre stood and was joined by two male Red Shirts. "Micah, you're relieved. Sit."

Micah didn't leave Morgan until the two Red Shirts pulled him away. He slumped into a chair beside the youngest boy—the one Deidre had threatened earlier—and stared at Morgan, one hand worrying at the scar on his neck.

The two Red Shirts weren't as gentle as Micah. They each grabbed the broomstick restraining her arms and jerked her upright. One twisted his fist in her hair, pulling so hard that pain shot across her scalp, yanking her face up. The other slammed her jaw shut with his hand, holding her chin tight.

Deidre approached, carrying the cheap plastic tumbler as if it was a chalice. She handed the cup to the female Red Shirt and positioned herself in front of Morgan. "You wanted water. So much that you spoke without permission. Here you go."

The female Red Shirt had a grin that matched Deidre's as she tilted the cup, fitting its rim around Morgan's nose and mouth, then pushed Morgan's head as far back as possible. The cup's contents gushed directly into Morgan's nose.

The pain of the water hitting the nerve endings in Morgan's sinus passages was blinding. Primal reflexes engaged, closing off her airways and alerting her body to the threat of drowning. Stress hormones flooded her system, designed to produce panic and jump-start a person's fight-or-flight reflex.

A normal person. Not Morgan. She blocked out the pain. Used the stress hormones to energize and focus. Thanks to her father, she'd had plenty of practice. Nick had described the sensation correctly when they'd spoken yesterday: dissociation. As if her body and mind were separate.

Her chest heaved and her limbs jerked, desperate for oxygen, but her mind wandered free. Bach's Little Fugue crescendoed through her brain. Her father may have been an uneducated long-haul truck driver—when he wasn't torturing and killing women—but he believed in the right music for the occasion, and Bach seemed appropriate now, the organ's deep rumbling matching the thunder pounding in her head.

She focused on the ceiling above her. Acoustic tiles. Suspended. Also a sprinkler system. Which meant a crawl space above the ceiling. A crawl space that would avoid locked doors and allow her access to the rest of the complex.

Nice. She'd been worried she'd have to use her hidden lock picks to escape, travel around the outside of the building, and let herself back in. Not too difficult, but it was damn cold outside at night, and without shoes or a coat, she'd be risking hypothermia. Plus, she hated being cold.

Plan of attack formed, she brought her consciousness back to her current situation and scanned the faces before her. Her eye-glasses were skewed and fogged with water droplets, but below them she could see Deidre smiling at her, Micah leaning forward in his chair, three more Red Shirts holding him down, his face twisted with fury—ready to sacrifice himself to rescue her? Why? He barely knew her—and finally Tommy, also held down by a Red Shirt, terrified and crying again.

Her lungs strained. She could hold her breath a long time, but no sense risking blacking out—that's where the real danger of waterboarding came, risking death by aspiration. She didn't trust Deidre and her clowns to be smart enough to know that. Morgan choked and gagged, heaving her body in every direction, making a good show for Deidre.

"Enough," Deidre commanded. The Red Shirt removed the cup, water cascading over Morgan, soaking her hair and shirt. She went limp, gasping for air, making it look as if she'd been close to drowning. The two Red Shirts behind her dropped her, and she fell to the floor. They slid the damn broomstick free, and she gave Deidre what she knew Deidre wanted: surrender.

Morgan curled up into a fetal ball, coughing, hands clutching her throat, not making eye contact with anyone. To her surprise, Deidre joined her, gathering Morgan onto her lap and rocking her as if Morgan was a child.

"Breathe, little sister!" Deidre chanted. "Feel the warmth and light of our love. You've taken your first step to redemption and ReNewal."

"ReNew, ReNew, ReNew," the crowd chorused all around Morgan. They stood over her, blocking out the overhead light. "We love you, we love you, we love you!"

Their roar still felt more frightening than uplifting, especially as they edged closer until their legs pressed against Morgan's body. Deidre on one side, clutching her tight, the faceless throng on the other. If Morgan were claustrophobic, she'd be panicked. Above her, the other students wrapped their arms around each other's shoulders and began swaying and singing again, this time a softer tune, ragged at first, but then it coalesced into "Silent Night."

It was three months past Christmas, but obviously the kids' repertoire was limited and the sentiment fit as well as anything. Rebirth, renewal . . . Deidre was orchestrating Morgan's recruitment into her brainwashed zombie legion by tugging at multiple emotional and physical chords. Very effective.

If she were a Norm, Morgan wouldn't have to think and decide how to react to Deidre's manipulation—it would have simply happened. But she was no Norm, so she had to bide her time, calculate how long was long enough without pushing Deidre's patience past her limit. When the time was right, she threw her arms around Deidre, forced more fake sobbing, and cried out, "Thank you!"

Deidre smiled down upon her, and all was right with the world.

One step closer to gaining their trust. Now all she needed was a few minutes alone with students who knew Bree. That Micah guy, he seemed a good place to start.

Then Deidre pulled her even closer, her hands squeezing Morgan's shoulders so tight they dug into her flesh. She lowered her mouth until it was next to Morgan's ear and whispered, "You don't fool me. I know what you are."

CHAPTER 35

Morgan stared at Deidre, stunned. No way had her cover been blown. She'd played the role of sheep perfectly.

Maybe Deidre had meant something else? If so, what?

One way to find out—and to get Morgan herself closer to an exit strategy in case she needed it sooner than anticipated. She glanced around. Who to target? Micah. He'd moved to stand beside her, as if to protect her from the crowd. He might have the answers she needed. She began coughing and choking again, twisting her body away from Deidre. Then she vomited all over Micah's legs.

Deidre and the Red Shirts jumped back in disgust. Micah bent to support Morgan's heaving body. "Are you okay?"

He didn't even seem to notice that they were both covered in the foul-smelling remnants of her lunch. She nodded weakly, tried to stand, but fell back against him. He helped her to her feet.

"Clean up. Both of you," Deidre said. "Everyone else, to the music room." Escorted by her Red Shirts, she paraded out the doors on the opposite side of the room, followed by the other students, while Micah guided Morgan back the way she'd entered.

To her surprise the doors to the intake room were unlocked. Good thing because they were fire doors. Not that Morgan cared much about fire safety, but if she did have to make her way through the crawl space above the ceiling, it meant any wall containing fire doors would block her path. If these were routinely left unlocked, it was one less barrier to work around. She could simply climb down from the crawl space and walk right through them.

Micah held the door for her, and Morgan shuffled through, still playing sheep-ish. Somewhere along the way she'd lost her flip-flops, and her feet squeaked against the gym mats that covered the floor of the intake room.

"You sure you're okay?" Micah asked.

She wiped her mouth with the back of her hand and nodded. "Yeah. Sorry about that. Hope it didn't get you in trouble."

He shrugged. Just one shoulder, more of a backward heaving off a potential burden than an upward motion. "The women's showers are over there, behind those cubbyholes."

It was her first chance to get an uninterrupted view of the intake room in full light. His and hers locker rooms, she realized. With the wall separating them and all the lockers and benches removed, leaving a wide open space between the two shower and toilet areas. Guess whatever ReNew taught, modesty wasn't an important tenet.

The half walls that partially blocked the view into the shower areas were simple plywood, nailed together to form the cubbyholes that held the ReNew khaki uniforms along with an assortment of underwear and flip-flops. Micah moved behind the wall on the male side of the room; it barely came halfway up his chest.

"You're lucky," he said as he stripped off his scrub top. "Usually we only get to shower with the rest of our level group while Red Shirts watch."

Morgan selected clean underwear and scrubs, this time in her proper size, and moved behind the cubbyholes on her side of the room to the women's showers. Typical school locker room: an open area surrounded on three sides with shower nozzles and a central drain. There was no shampoo, only liquid soap in wall-mounted receptacles. She made fast work of cleaning up, wanting more time to check out the space.

There were no towel racks—too easy to use as a weapon—no paper-towel dispensers, either. She used her dirty clothes to dry herself off before changing. Beyond the shower were four toilet stalls, all with their doors removed. Ugh. There was more privacy in prison.

She glanced behind her at the clock over the door leading out to the administration area. Only 6:51? She'd been here less than four hours and was already going nuts with the effort it took to stay in character.

Then she spotted one more thing—a camera in the center of the clock. It was behind the glass enclosure, so no microphone; that was good. She made an act of appearing exhausted as she shuffled across the room to slump down on the wall beside the door. Below the clock and out of view of its camera.

She knelt and examined the lock on the door. Nothing she couldn't handle when the time came. Micah emerged from his shower. He'd already put on pants and was in the act of pulling his top over his head. He had the kind of physique older men worked so hard to maintain: six-pack abs and well-defined back and shoulder muscles. No scars to match the ones on his neck, but bruises in various states of healing glowed yellow-green-purple against his pale skin.

He looked up, spotted her, and smiled. "Feel better?"

She didn't answer. He joined her, sitting beside her. "The first day is always the worst," he assured her. "Plus, you came at a bad time. It's not always like this."

Morgan pulled her knees to her chest, hugging them like she'd seen so many of her father's victims do. Trying to become smaller targets. Never worked. But it was a sheeplike posture, and Micah responded to it, placing his arm around her shoulders and letting her lean against him.

"What is this place?" She added a tremor to her voice. "Some kind of cult?"

"No. Not a cult. Just a bunch of kids with nothing to do, bored out of their minds, and a girl in charge who is a little—"

"Crazy?"

"Unstable. She didn't used to be this bad. Deidre's been here longer than anyone. Her brother enrolled her when she was twelve."

"Twelve? But she's at least, what, twenty?"

"Nineteen."

"Seven years and no one has let her out?" She turned to him. "Does that mean we'll never get out of here? My parents, my friends, I'll never see them again?" She forced a pretend sob. "I have to talk to the Reverend, he seemed so nice, I know he'll understand, this is all a mistake—"

Micah gave a short laugh. "Good luck with that. You won't be seeing the Rev again—unless he selects you for one-on-one counseling. And that's only until he gets what he wants from you. Then you'll be stuck here with the rest of us."

Hmm . . . she wondered if Bree had been one of the chosen selected to receive Reverend Benjamin's personal attention. Sounded like he might be interested in something more than saving souls. She made a note to find a way to ask about that later, once she'd gained Micah's confidence. Right now she needed him feeling strong and protective.

She hugged her knees tighter. "But there must be adults. Guards, teachers, counselors?"

"Nope. Just us chickens caught in the chicken coop. Deidre does her best—she's a true believer, actually thinks she can save us all. Sooner or later kids leave. Usually when their parents run out of money. Never before the Rev is sure they won't talk about what really goes on in here. Except once . . ." His voice trailed off. "Bree. Deidre hoped she'd change everything. Somehow got it in her crazy mixed-up mind that Bree would stay here. She was so angry when she found out Bree was leaving. Felt abandoned. You see, Deidre is just as trapped as the rest of us, even though she's in charge."

The way his words gushed out, Morgan wondered when the last time was he'd had any chance to talk to anyone in more than the monosyllabic responses Deidre commanded. It felt as if Micah needed to unburden himself. And Morgan was very happy to hear it all. "If Deidre couldn't change things after seven years of being here, what made her think this girl Bree could?"

"Bree was supposed to save us all. When her mother came to get her early, she promised she'd let the people in the outside world know what was happening here. She said she'd tell our families, tell the cops, whoever it took. She and Deidre were especially close—they'd sit up all night singing together and Bree told Deidre about all the things she'd missed. I mean, can you imagine spending seven years with no TV or phone, no Internet, nothing but a bunch of mixed-up kids that you had to keep from killing each other? Bree painted a whole new world for Deidre."

"She gave her hope." A dangerous thing in Morgan's experience.

"Exactly. But." His shoulders heaved again. Micah's shrugs were more expressive than most people's smiles, she'd noticed. "But, she left and it's been a month and nothing's happened. Except for Deidre starting to lose it. For real. I'm worried. She's going to go too far—or lose control of the Red Shirts, which would be even worse. Deidre wants to save our souls, but Red Shirts just want to have fun. Bullying the rest of us is the only entertainment they have."

Boredom. As dangerous as hope. Especially in people like Morgan. She craved stimulation like a drug, needing more potent doses with each hit. Being locked up with a bunch of sheep, if you were a person with Morgan's proclivities, or worse, her father's . . . not a pretty picture. And if Deidre was losing control—

She realized that Micah was watching her again. It was unnerving, the way he allowed every emotion to rest on his face, exposing himself to the world. Inside the commons room he'd been protective of her, worried, and a bit frightened.

Not now. Now he regarded her with curiosity.

"Just who are you, Morgan? The truth."

"You first," Morgan countered. "How'd you end up here?"

Another shrug, this one nostalgic. "A bunch of us got into a bar over on the North Side. We thought we were so cool, sneaking in with the crowd after a Steelers' game. Stupid dive bar, they didn't care how old we were as long as we could pay for our beer. Anyway, there was this guy. He hit a girl. Slapped her so hard it knocked her down." His breathing edged between clenched teeth at the memory. "No one was doing anything; they all just watched."

"Except you."

"Guess I was the only one sober enough—or stupid enough. I told the guy to back away—he was getting ready to kick her while she was down—and next thing I knew he had a broken bottle in his hand and there was blood all over me."

"He could have killed you."

"Not like he didn't try. He got me in a choke hold, cut me, then dropped me to the floor and went on about his business. I don't know what came over me, some kind of berserker rage or something. I saw the blood, saw the girl crying, saw his smile—he was laughing—and everything else was a blur. I grabbed a cue stick, lunged at him, and he rushed me and—"

"You hit him—did you kill him?"

He touched the scar on his neck. "No. Stupid drunk. He tripped over the girl, fell on the bottle. Didn't kill him but it cut him up pretty bad, needed more stitches than I did. But I was underage, had a beer, in a bar, holding a deadly weapon in my hands. Worse, the girl testified against me, said I started it, said I was the one who hit her and her boyfriend. Good thing they had video that showed otherwise. So all I got was ninety days for the underage drinking. Just dumb luck this place was next up on the residential treatment program rotation."

Dumb luck? He was the one who'd rushed in, decided it was his responsibility to defend a woman he didn't even know. She had met other Norms like this—in fact, her life suddenly seemed full of them, saints and martyrs intent on showing her the light as they tried to take responsibility for every wrong in the world and set it right. Nick, Andre, Lucy . . . not Jenna. Jenna barely took responsibility for her own actions and always had her own agenda, a lot like Morgan that way. And now, Micah.

He was only a kid. She had to stop him before his hero complex earned him an early grave.

"Where do you draw the line, Micah? Or are you God, all-knowing, the Holy Father taking the world's sins onto His shoulders?"

He rolled his eyes, but his shoulders still slumped in anguish. "You're thinking of the Son, not the Father."

"Right, the guy who ended up nailed to a cross. That what you're aiming for?"

He was silent. Morgan waited.

"I just want to live my life without regrets," he finally said.

Exactly what she wanted. No regrets, like the blood on her hands ending with her locked up in a cage . . . or a prison. She glanced around and laughed. Off to a helluva good start.

He jerked his head up. "Are you laughing at me? Ending up in this hellhole protecting a woman who didn't want or need it?"

"No. I'm laughing at myself." She wrapped her arm around his, drawing his body back to her until their sides touched. Usually she didn't like people in her space, but somehow she didn't mind with Micah. And it wasn't because she'd already cataloged his vulnerabilities and was confident that she could kill him before he could hurt her.

For once—for the only time she could remember—it was because she simply wanted another warm body next to hers.

But then he slid his arm free of hers. She sucked in her breath, disappointment chilling her, waiting for him to reject her, abandon her.

Instead he pressed his body closer and wrapped his arm around her shoulders, holding her to him. "We're a pair, aren't we?"

Morgan said nothing. If he only knew.

"Now you know my sob story," he said. "Your turn. Why are you here, Morgan?"

She lowered her face, avoiding his scrutiny. Debated on maintaining her cover. But if he could help her get out of here faster...She followed her impulse to trust him, looked up, and met his gaze.

"I'm here because BreeAnna Greene is dead."

CHAPTER 36

"Bree is—" Micah couldn't finish his thought. His chest felt hollowed out, as if an Arctic wind had swept through him, snatching up his heart and leaving nothing but ice in its place. "No. She can't be."

The ice dropped deep into his gut while his throat closed with anger. He wanted to hit something; he wanted to hit someone. He wanted Morgan to take back her words, to say it wasn't so, to tell him she was a liar. He wanted to leap up and rip the clock from the wall above him, tear it apart, and turn back time.

He wanted so many things as tears filmed his vision, sparking rainbows in the glare of the overhead lights. Most of all, he wanted none of this to be real, because even if that meant that Bree wasn't real, that she was just some crazy messed-up hallucination, then she wouldn't be dead. Gone forever.

"What—how—why—" Single syllables were all he could manage.

Morgan didn't move to comfort him but neither did she move away. Instead she simply watched, staring at him with that unnerving expression that was no expression at all. As if she wore a mask labeled "Teenage Girl."

Not at all like Bree. Bree's face was a constant symphony, changing faster than clouds rolling in before a storm or butterflies swirling in a summer breeze. He'd drawn her in his mind so many times, and yet, he'd never really been able to capture her. Had hoped maybe someday he could try again in person . . . "What happened?"

"She hung herself. The same night she left here." Morgan's tone was as chilled as her words.

"No. Bree would never—" Again he stopped himself. His shoulders heaved so hard and fast he felt as if he was going to be sick. Suddenly his heart returned, pounding fast like thunder in his head, and he felt flushed.

"No. She was going to save us. She wouldn't kill herself." He pivoted on his knees, facing Morgan, gripping her shoulders tight. Wanted to shake the truth from her but stopped himself. "Bree did not kill herself."

Morgan kept staring at him. No fear despite his hands on her body, able to bash her head against the wall or throttle her or do anything. Or do nothing. He dropped his hands, looked at them as if they belonged to a stranger.

"Okay," Morgan said, more like talking to herself than to him. "Maybe she didn't. But she died. Less than twelve hours after leaving here. And it looked like suicide. Who would want her dead? Did something happen while she was here? Something more than—" She waved her hand at the doors on the opposite side of the room, the ones leading to the commons room. "Did Deidre break her?"

Micah shook his head back and forth, whipping his vision until the world blurred. "Bree never broke. Not for Deidre, not for the Rev. Never."

"But they tried?"

"Deidre did at first. But something happened—" He stopped, staring into the ceiling, hands dangling uselessly between his knees. How to explain, how to possibly explain what life was like here? How could this strange girl from the outside ever understand?

"What happened, Micah? Did someone hurt Bree?"

"No. Just the opposite. Bree saved us. From ourselves."

✦

Jenna stared up at Robert Greene's fury-filled face. He wanted her to feel intimidated, dwarfed by his larger body, trapped in her chair. To hell with that.

Andre stepped toward her, ready to tackle Greene, but she waved him off. She met Greene's gaze calmly and said, "Maybe if you and your wife are done keeping secrets, we can do our job and find out who killed your daughter."

Silence as he glared down at her. Finally he turned away. "It was Benjamin. You know it was."

"No sir." She leaned back, kept her voice calm. He stood, looking away from her, shoulders hunched. "We can suspect anyone— well, anyone except you, your wife, and her former lover since apparently you alibi each other—but we need proof."

"I don't care about proof." He grabbed Caren's arm and yanked her to her feet. "You. This is all your fault. You took her there, to that place."

He shook her like a rag doll. She made a sound between a sob and a screech. Andre moved to intervene, placing his hand on Greene's shoulder and wrenching him away from his wife. Caren fell back onto the love seat as Greene raised his fists, ready to attack Andre.

Andre backed off—not in surrender but to give himself space to maneuver. Jenna knew from the way he held his body that he was restraining himself from giving Greene the fight Greene so obviously wanted.

She pushed to her feet, ready to step between the two men, but it was Nick who defused the situation. He touched Greene's elbow—a simple, nonthreatening touch—and brought the man's attention to bear on him.

"Your little girl didn't kill herself, Mr. Greene," Nick said in a low tone, each word rocking Greene like a blow. "Maybe you could sit down and help us find out who did?"

Greene wavered, hands bunched into fists, but then his face lost focus and he sank onto the love seat beside his wife. Caren immediately draped her arms around his shoulders as Greene ignored her, burying his face in his hands, shoulders heaving. "My baby, my poor baby," he moaned. "I wasn't here for her. She was all alone."

Jenna gave him a few minutes of self-pity. Hoped it might soften his need to control the investigation and let her finally do her job without interference. She waved Andre and Nick back and crouched beside him.

"Mr. Greene, is there any way someone associated with your lawsuits could have come here that night?" She couched her words carefully in order to not expose the fact that Greene was using his daughter's assault to blackmail a federal judge.

He shook his head, still staring at the floor. "No. Like you said earlier, why would they? I still have all the leverage I need . . ." His voice choked, and he paused to swallow. "With BreeAnna gone."

"BreeAnna opened the door that night. Would she have done that for a stranger?"

Caren answered. "No. Never. Even if it was a police officer, she wouldn't have opened the door without seeing some kind of identification."

"So it was someone she knew."

Greene finally raised his head to meet her gaze. "It was Benjamin. Had to be."

"Why?" The simple question was impossible to answer.

"I don't know. I don't care. It was him. I know it." He shook free of Caren's clingy arms. "Good thing I already have someone on the inside."

Jenna stood. "Who?"

He stood as well, facing her. This time he was calm, but despite that, Andre still stepped closer, ready to defend Jenna. "After our discussion this afternoon, I knew I couldn't trust you to get the job done. So I hired your associate."

"Morgan? You paid Morgan to go undercover at ReNew."

"Why not? We were all set up to do it until you got cold feet." His smirk returned. "I even paid extra for an expedited pickup, same as how they took BreeAnna."

Jenna rocked back on her heels, speechless.

"You sent men to grab Morgan?" Andre demanded. "Do you have any idea—"

No. Of course, Greene didn't. Damn it. Totally her fault, she knew who, what Morgan was.

"Relax. I followed them to the school, she was fine."

"She was fine," Nick echoed. "Despite being jumped and dragged into a van." He was trying to reassure her and Andre, Jenna knew.

"Of course, she was fine," Greene said. "We walked in together. My point is, we now have eyes and ears in place at ReNew. Thanks to me."

"When?" Jenna asked.

"A few hours ago. How are we going to listen in?" Greene was eager now.

Jenna took a breath, tried in vain to decide exactly when she'd totally lost control of the situation. "You and your wife obviously have a lot to discuss," she said, using her voice of command.

Greene bristled at that, but Nick took the hint. "I'll stay."

"Good. Andre, you and I are heading back to the office to monitor those transmitters." Technically they could listen to the bugs from any smartphone or computer, but she needed to get out of this house, away from Greene and his manipulations.

"I want to hear—" Greene protested.

"You've done enough for today, Mr. Greene," Jenna said.

Before he could argue, Andre brushed past him, inserting his body between Greene and Jenna as they walked out.

CHAPTER 37

Morgan waited for Micah to explain more about Bree, but he sat in silence, his face shuttered by grief. Maybe it was a mistake telling him the truth. Too late now. She tried a different tack. "Were you here when Bree arrived?"

He nodded. "I'd been here a week, was still overwhelmed, trying to find my footing. Didn't help that other than Deidre and Nelson, the leader of the Red Shirts, I'm the oldest here—guess that made me threatening. I spent most of that first week in isolation. But then Bree came and they turned their attention to her."

"Like they did with me?"

"No. No. You're the only person—" He stopped then began again. "Bree began at Step Zero like everyone, but she seemed to understand Deidre, saw right through the games and stupid challenges. Bree didn't let Deidre or anyone manipulate how she felt, but it was clear she already felt bad about something. She never confessed, at least not to the group, but—"

"She never went through the Purge?"

"I guess she made her own variation. That very first day she was here, she begged the rest of us to help her. Said she needed to earn our love."

He turned his face away, staring up at the far corner of the ceiling. "Bree was just so . . . lost. First time I saw Deidre cry—really cry, like weeping, tears that wouldn't stop. I'll never forget the two of them sitting on the floor surrounded by all of us, holding each other, crying. After that Deidre and Bree were inseparable. Until the day she left, that was."

She bet the Red Shirts didn't like that bond between Deidre and Bree. Upsetting the balance, gaining access to the person with the most power, circumventing the normal chain of command. "How did Nelson feel about that?"

"He was jealous of Bree—before her, he was the one Deidre confided in, kept close."

"But nothing bad happened to Bree while she was here?"

"Nothing anyone else did to her. We all loved her. She brought us music—no one here played, but Bree convinced Deidre to open the music room, and she would play for hours and hours. Anything. Silly songs we all could sing along to. Music I'd never heard, not classical but rich like that, complicated. Bree would be like in a trance when she played that stuff, but she never finished the song, she'd always wake with a jerk, notes crashing around her."

He stopped, rubbed his palms against his knees, as he remembered. "It was like waking a sleepwalker from a dream. The look on her face, startled by the real world—and desperate to return to the dream."

Morgan restrained her impatience. She already knew Bree played the piano. She needed to understand more. "What about the Reverend? Did he single Bree out for special attention?"

He nodded slowly. "Yes. He saw her every day. Would keep her for hours. I thought maybe—I was afraid, I mean, an old guy like that—but she said nothing ever happened. Said he never touched her, he only wanted to make her talk. Said she never did and that's why he kept making her come back."

"And you believed her?"

"Yes. She never acted afraid to go when he called for her. Treated it as if it was some kind of game and she was winning." A tiny smile flitted across his face. "I had the feeling Bree never had a chance to feel like a winner before."

"Did she ever talk about why her parents sent her here?"

He shook his head. "No. You could ask, but she'd never answer. Just said she needed to become a better person before she could go home."

Didn't sound like a rebellious teen to Morgan. Sounded like someone who'd been pounded down so hard that she blamed herself for everything.

"I'll tell you one thing, though," Micah continued. "Bree wasn't excited about going home. If it wasn't for helping Deidre and the rest of us, she would have never agreed to leave when her mother came. Especially after she saw how upset it made Deidre. Deidre accused Bree of abandoning her. I've never seen her so angry. Bree was torn—she wanted to stay with Deidre, but had no way to stop her mother from taking her."

Okay. She hadn't been expecting that—she was more than ready to blow this joint and she'd only been here a few hours, not two months. Maybe Bree's time here at ReNew had nothing to do with her death? If so, then Morgan was wasting her time.

"She never said why she didn't want to go home? Maybe she and Deidre were more than friends?" Their relationship sounded intense, maybe a love affair? It would explain why Deidre had grown so angry and volatile after Bree left her.

Micah shook his head and gave another one of those shrugs, this one enigmatic.

Okay. She needed more answers. And she wasn't going to find them here. She pushed up to her feet. "Let's go."

Micah seemed reluctant to leave the quiet of the intake room. "Are you some kind of cop or undercover investigative reporter? What do you think really happened to Bree?"

"Not a cop or a reporter. And I have no idea." When he remained sitting, she lowered her hand to help him up. "But I'm going to find out."

They pushed through the doors to the commons room together. The room was empty except for two Red Shirts and Tommy. One of the Red Shirts, Nelson, watched and snickered as the second held Tommy's face down to the puddle of vomit Morgan had left.

"Stop it," Micah called out.

The two Red Shirts spun around. Tommy tried to escape, but Nelson grabbed him by his shirt collar, twisting it viciously to hold the boy in place.

"You're a Zero again, Micah. You can't talk to me that way," Nelson said.

"And you can't touch him," Micah protested. "Deidre said—"

"Deidre isn't here. She's off getting saved by the Rev. How come he never sends for you, Micah?"

"Deidre must give better head," the other Red Shirt snickered.

"Let's see how good this one is." Nelson wrapped his arm around Tommy in a choke hold. The little boy whimpered. His face twisted as he tried to prevent the noise from escaping. He seemed to realize that showing weakness would only encourage these two hyenas.

Micah stepped toward Nelson. "Let him go."

The second Red Shirt, a beefy red-faced wrestler-type, grabbed Micah's arm and pivoted him into a wristlock, forcing Micah to either bend forward or risk dislocating his shoulder.

"Maybe the new girl here wants to volunteer." Nelson leered at Morgan and nodded to the other Red Shirt who twisted Micah's arm harder to pivot him toward her. Micah had no choice but to comply, the Red Shirt shoving him until Micah's face was in Morgan's cleavage.

"How about it, Micah?" Nelson sang his name in a high-pitched approximation of Deidre's voice. "All that time you two spent in the showers. She must have been mm-mm good. Why don't you two give us a demonstration?"

Morgan assessed her options. No weapons within reach—if you could call those damn broomsticks or the plastic chairs weapons. The Red Shirts took her silence as fear. Fools. She rubbed her right side, her fingers dancing over the fake scar above her right hip, and decided the one holding Micah would be the first to die. Then, with Micah free, it would be two against one.

"Leave them alone," Micah said, his words gritted with pain. "Take me. Do anything you want."

The Red Shirts laughed. "What makes you think we won't, anyway?" said Nelson.

"Stop it!" Deidre's voice sliced through the air like a machete. "Let them go." She stood in the doorway, the light from the hall silhouetting her, making her seem taller, majestic.

Nelson released Tommy who scurried to Morgan, hiding behind her, clutching her waist. She shook him free, needing to be able to move without him holding her back.

"How was your personal salvation lesson, Deidre?" Nelson asked with a sneer. "Did you see the face of God?"

Deidre strode forward and slapped him so hard he rocked back. His partner in crime took advantage of the moment, released Micah, and sidled out the door. Hopefully not to get reinforcements. Morgan doubted it; the guy had seemed like strictly a follower, not an alpha. Micah moved to stand with Morgan, Tommy behind them.

The silence that followed the slap seemed endless. Deidre and Nelson were trapped by some unseen force. Nelson raised his hand. Micah stepped forward, ready to defend Deidre, but instead of striking her, Nelson touched his cheek in surprise. He blinked, opened his mouth to say something, then fell into Deidre's arms.

Deidre wrapped herself around Nelson, and together they sank to the floor.

"Nelson," Deidre crooned, soothing her hand across the Red Shirt's face, pulling his head onto her lap. "Why? You were my strongest warrior. How did you lose your faith?"

Nelson shoved her hands away and pushed onto his knees, facing Deidre. "I'm aging out of this joint next week. My parents left me here for almost two years. Left me here to rot. In all that time, the Rev never called me in for any personal salvation. What's that mean? My soul isn't worth saving and yours is? Or is it because you're fucking the old man?"

His voice broke with unshed tears. It was obvious where the real source of his anger and pain lay. He was in love with Deidre. Faced with being forced to leave her, knowing she would never follow or reciprocate his love, it had driven him to rage. He wanted to hurt her, destroy everything she'd built.

Morgan knew the feeling. It was exactly how she felt about her father. A twisted love-hate that couldn't be put into words.

Deidre wrapped her arms around the Red Shirt and pulled him to her. Morgan couldn't hear what she whispered into his ear, but his shoulders twitched with silent sobs.

Micah took a step to the door. Deidre glanced up, not at Micah, at her. The newcomer. The one who'd upset the delicate balance of the sizzling stir-fry of adolescent emotions that was ReNew.

"You three. Wait for me in the room across the hall. I'll deal with you in a minute."

Morgan followed Micah and Tommy into the classroom across the hall. There were no desks or chairs. The only decor consisted of more ReNew banners with their promise of a rainbow sunrise. In the corner a group of khaki-clad students sat in a circle on the floor, passing a Bible and reading from it under the watchful eye of a Red Shirt.

"Why did you do that?" Morgan asked in a low voice. "Offer yourself to him? You can't show them any weakness or they'll slaughter you."

Micah gestured for Tommy to join the others as if hoping that by blending in, Deidre might forget him. When he started to follow Tommy without answering her, Morgan grabbed his arm, tired of all this nonsense and more than ready to get out of there.

"I don't need any of your paternalistic crap," Morgan snapped.

Micah was silent. He didn't look at her. He watched the other kids around them, especially the Red Shirts.

"Need me to explain what paternalistic means?" she asked, annoyed when he didn't answer.

"It means treating someone like they're a child." His gaze met hers, then slid off again. "I wasn't treating you like a child, Morgan. I was treating you like you were one of us."

"I told you, I'm not." Last thing she wanted was him playing hero, getting in her way.

"Doesn't matter why you're here. While you are here, you're one of us." He turned and faced her, accepting the weight of her stare without flinching. "And in here, we watch out for each other. Nothing paternalistic about it—it's the only way to survive."

CHAPTER 38

Nelson entered the classroom and beckoned to Morgan. To her irritation, Micah stepped forward between her and the Red Shirt. Had he heard nothing she said?

"Deidre wants to talk with you," Nelson told her. He placed a palm against Micah's chest. "Just her."

The two boys faced off, but Morgan ignored them and walked to the door. She remembered Deidre's rules: not looking a Red Shirt in the eyes, not speaking, not crossing a threshold without permission. It worked, because Nelson left Micah alone and joined her.

"Follow me," he ordered.

They left, but not without Morgan looking back and giving Micah a nod, letting him know she was in control. It did nothing to ease the worry from his face. If he only knew what she was capable of . . . of course, if he knew, he would have never let her get close to any of these kids, kids he obviously cared about and felt responsible for. He would have made sure she was locked away, to protect them from her.

It was the first time she could ever remember feeling regret about the truth of who she was. Just an instant, but it was an instant of weakness that she despised. Can't change the past, she reminded herself as she shuffled down the hall behind Nelson.

He led her to what could only be the music room. An empty classroom, identical to all the others she'd seen, barren of all furniture, not even any gym mats or plastic chairs, the only thing in it was a small upright piano without a bench. It was positioned facing away from the windows so that whoever played could sit on the radiator grill.

No one played it now. Deidre leaned over the back of the piano, staring across the keys out the window to the March landscape appearing stark and cold in the glare of the spotlights ringing the school's exterior. A no-man's-land between winter and spring filled with brown grass leading to a brown forest, barren twigs scratching a moonlit sky. Deidre stroked the keys as if stroking a lover's cheek, gentle enough that she caused no sound.

Morgan watched Deidre out of the corner of her eye, waiting. Nelson shifted his weight in the doorway behind her, made a small sound. "Do you want me to stay?"

Deidre shook her head without turning around. Nelson waited a moment longer, then finally left, closing the door behind him. The sound of the latch catching seemed abnormally loud, but Deidre didn't flinch. Her fingers caressed the keys, forward and back, forward and back.

Finally she pressed one white key. A single tone filled the space before dying.

"I imagine you're confused," Deidre said, her voice soft but loud enough to carry to Morgan.

"Yes," Morgan answered, still not looking up.

"You don't know what to expect."

"No." Morgan let the silence grow, sensing Deidre wanted to talk—just as Micah had earlier. It was a useful tool, silence. Norms hated it, always wanted to fill it up, would tell you their deepest, darkest secrets just to end the silence.

Deidre sighed, turned to face her. "I'm sorry you heard that. What Nelson said. He's upset about leaving his family."

"I thought he was going home next week," Morgan ventured.

"You don't understand. *We're* his family—not the parents who abandoned him. Just like we'll be your family. If you follow the path and truly repent. You want to repent, don't you, Morgan? You want to shed your sinful ways and be ReNewed?"

Morgan nodded, an eager sheep. "Yes, yes, of course."

"Good. That's all I want for you—for everyone here. That's all the good Reverend Doctor wants as well."

"But Nelson, what he said—"

"He was wrong. The good Reverend Doctor isn't interested in carnal knowledge. All he's interested in is saving souls. Cleansing us all from evil." Deidre's shoulders sagged as if she carried a heavy burden. Her palms went to her belly. "It's my job to carry your sins, to cleanse them."

Morgan nodded even though she had no idea what the hell Deidre was talking about. The silence lengthened, Deidre's attention wandering back to the piano.

"Do you play?" Morgan asked.

Deidre shook her head. "Not me. There was a girl, Bree. She made such sweet music—it was the sound of angels come to dance among us. She understood."

More silence. Deidre didn't seem to mind it, so Morgan pressed her. "Understood what?"

"Bree understood me. My job. How important it is that someone lead. The price to be paid. She was willing to take up my burden, to help me escape. All we needed was a little more time—"

Again her hands moved to her belly. Morgan doubted she was even aware that she did it. Deidre reminded her of Bree's mother, Caren. Emotions zigzagging in every direction from the raging lunatic fanatic attacking Morgan earlier to healing lover comforting Nelson and now to quiet, reflective true believer. Which was the real Deidre?

The girl had been here seven years, she reminded herself. Maybe they were all part of her—maybe she had no idea who she was or what was real anymore, a shattered mirror, each piece reflecting a sliver of the truth but never the whole.

"She left without you?" Morgan risked asking. "This Bree? She left you behind?"

Deidre jerked her head up. "No. You don't understand." Her tone sharpened, slicing through the air between them. "I was the one who was meant to go. Bree was meant to stay, take my place. It was my time to be free."

Morgan stood silent, letting the emotions settle around them both. Did Deidre really think that? That Bree would stay and take her place here rather than return home, to the freedom of the outside world? It sounded like the delusions of a desperate woman. And if there was one thing Morgan's father had taught her to know and use, it was desperation.

"What did you mean? When you said you knew who I was, that I didn't fool you?" It was a risk, challenging Deidre's delusions, but Morgan's curiosity got the better of her.

Deidre whirled on her, her glare piercing. "I know you. I see the truth. You are a sinner, just like me. You know sin, you know blood, you revel in it. You understand salvation only comes through pain."

She stepped toward Morgan, her face flushing with excitement. "I was wrong about Bree. She wasn't who I've been waiting for. It's you. You're the one. The sacrificial lamb. You'll carry the sins, the blood for all of them. Just like I've done."

Sacrificial lamb? Morgan? Deidre was mad, utterly mad. Morgan stared, half-tempted to slap the other girl back to reality. Her hand rose, but then she dropped it. Challenging Deidre wasn't going to get her any answers about Bree.

None of these kids could help her. Best thing she could do was find those records and get the hell out of here.

Deidre paced a circle around Morgan, scrutinizing her. "You'll do. You're strong enough. You'll carry the blood."

Suddenly she stopped and clapped her hands like a child getting ready to blow out her birthday candles. "Nelson! Take her away."

Nelson popped inside the door so fast Morgan knew he must have been listening.

"Take her to Iso. Her and Micah Chase. No one is to speak to her. No one except me." She grabbed both of Morgan's hands, just as she had earlier. Morgan resisted the urge to jerk away. Deidre's eyes shone, as she squeezed tight. "Don't worry. I'll prepare you. The good Reverend Doctor will be so very pleased with your offering. I just know it."

Then she let go, spun on her heel, and danced away, leaning over the piano and randomly hitting notes with gleeful abandon. Nelson took Morgan by the arm and ushered her out of the room.

"You tell anyone what you saw, what she said, any of that crazy shit, and I'll kill you," he told her. "No. Better. I saw you with Micah. You step out of line, do anything to hurt Deidre, and I'll kill him." He shook her so hard she almost lost her balance. "Do you understand?"

Morgan looked down before he could see the fury in her eyes and nodded sheepishly. She followed meekly, memorizing their path. What did she care about his threats or Deidre's madness? She was getting out of here. Tonight.

CHAPTER 39

A ndre listened to the two transmitters Morgan had placed, while Jenna drove them back to the city and not so silently fumed at the sudden upheaval of their plans.

"This is exactly what I predicted," Jenna finally said. "Morgan rushing off, doing things on her own, screwing us."

"Doesn't sound like Greene gave her much choice." He surprised himself, defending Morgan.

"No way in hell Greene forced Morgan to do anything she didn't want to do. A phone call? Would that be too much to ask? Save us from being embarrassed by our own client."

"She got the job done, planted the bugs." Andre played Morgan's initial conversations from her intake at ReNew for her.

Jenna ID'd the voices. "That first one is Chapman, the director. The other is Benjamin."

"The guy Greene thinks killed BreeAnna." What a mess. Yet, Jenna didn't seem at all worried.

"Yeah, but I met Benjamin. I don't think he'd kill anyone. More likely he'd convince someone else to do his dirty work for him."

She inhaled, her grip tightening on the steering wheel. "Let's go through this once more. Maybe we missed something."

"It all started with that party."

"Right. BreeAnna started acting out after that. We already knew that."

"Not so much acting out. Most of that Caren made up. More likely a reactive depressive episode, according to Nick. He said it would be common after a trauma like what happened to her at the party, especially if she didn't get any counseling afterward."

"Plus going to school and seeing the people who'd abused her every day, knowing they'd never be brought to justice."

From her tone, it sounded like she might have some personal experience there. Andre filed that away for future exploration—times like this, he realized just how little he knew about Jenna or her life before they met. She never spoke of her family or growing up or really much of anything that happened in her past, other than cases she'd worked.

"Yeah, I'm sure that didn't help. Then she found the pregnancy test and realized her mom was having an affair—"

"It was Caren who had the pregnancy scare, not BreeAnna?"

"Right. Caren lied about that as well. Anyway, that's why she shipped BreeAnna off to ReNew. To give her time to calm down before she did something they'd both regret and ruined Caren's marriage."

"Prenup."

"Yep. Caren said it was her idea to bring Bree home early—that she missed her, especially since she'd ended the affair."

"Funny. I got the feeling it was Greene's idea."

"Think that's important?"

"Not sure. I guess not—not if someone outside the family is responsible for BreeAnna's death."

"Our mysterious midnight visitor."

"Which brings us right back where we started." She thought for a moment and jerked her chin up as a thought occurred to her. "How sure is Nick that BreeAnna didn't actually kill herself? I mean, she'd been locked up for two months with unstable kids, that alone might have been enough to push her over the edge after being raped and having to keep silent about it."

"Plus keeping her mother's secret—she didn't know that Greene knew about her mother's affair," he reminded her.

"So she's fresh out of ReNew, all screwed up by these secrets she's got locked away, her folks leave her alone, and someone comes and they make things worse—" She broke off, leaned forward over the steering wheel. "What if whoever rang the doorbell was one of the people from the party? Maybe one of the guys heard she was home, figured she was easy prey—you know how word gets around at a school like hers. They would know all about ReNew. Kids like that, entitled, privileged, they'd see her as the perfect victim. Defenseless."

Actually, Andre had no clue how rich kids going to an exclusive prep school acted, but it was clear Jenna did.

"I'd buy that, except how did they know she was home alone?" he argued. "No one except Caren knew she was picking Bree up that day, and they came straight home after getting Robert at the airport. There's no record of Bree calling anyone. And it's not like Caren and Robert advertised that Robert dragged her out for the night so he could beat the shit out of her lover."

"Yeah, okay. But damn, that would be a good reason to keep suicide in the mix." She thought for a moment. "How did whoever came know she was home alone? Or home at all? And why would BreeAnna open the door to them?"

"They must have been watching the house. Which meant they knew Bree was home from ReNew."

"Who would BreeAnna let inside at ten o'clock at night?"

"Had to be someone she knew. Someone she trusted." He rolled his window down, sucked in the cold night air hoping to clear the clutter from his brain.

"Or someone she was used to obeying."

"Which brings us back to ReNew."

They hit the Fort Pitt Tunnel, the yellow glow of lights hitting the tile walls reflecting against the windshield like incandescent ghosts. As they sped out the other side of the mountain and over the bridge, Andre didn't even notice his favorite nighttime view of the city's skyline. "Jenna, we need to get Morgan out of there. Now."

"Why would I want to do that?" she asked, sounding truly puzzled. "You can't still be worried about those kids? If Morgan didn't fight the goons who grabbed her"—and from the recording it was clear she hadn't—"then she'll be fine."

Andre turned to glare at her. Why was he the only person who saw the danger? "We've just discovered that BreeAnna was killed. Most likely by someone at ReNew."

"Exactly. And Morgan is right there where we need her."

"Locked up. With a killer."

She glanced at him. "Can't have it both ways, Andre. Either you trust her or you don't. Personally, if our guy is the kind of coward who waits for a girl to be alone and wheedles his way inside her house, kills her, makes it look like suicide, then my money's on Morgan."

"What about the other kids?" He wished he had the words that would make her see reason. He couldn't even explain it himself, this itch jangling his nerves. Exactly what it felt like to have a sniper's sights land on his back.

"Who better to protect them than Morgan?"

"I don't like it. What if the killer figures out she isn't who she says she is?"

She blew her breath out. More exasperated and tired of arguing than agreeing with him. "We'd only blow her cover if we went tonight anyway. But," she continued when he started to interrupt, "we'll go first thing in the morning and get her out. Happy?"

No. But it was the best he could do for now.

✦

"What's Iso?" Morgan whispered to Micah as Nelson and a second Red Shirt led them down a corridor of empty classrooms. Several of the rooms were strewn with gym mats and blankets—the so-called dorms?

"Isolation," Micah whispered back. "Observation is more like it. Lights on twenty-four-seven, someone sitting in the door watching you every second, but no talking. You're not allowed to do anything except meditate on your sins."

Last thing Morgan needed was someone watching her that closely. She needed privacy to break out of the locked wing and reach the computer files. She'd considered skipping getting the files, except she was curious about what Bree said that had Greene so worried. And it would be nice to get enough hard evidence to bring Reverend Benjamin, that cheesy administrator Sean Chapman, Deidre, and her Red Shirts down.

"So Iso, it's the worst punishment?" she asked a little louder, hoping Nelson would hear and follow Deidre's instructions. But he was too far ahead of them.

Micah shook his head. "Worst is the Hole. Locked up, no contact, total darkness." His face grew pale. "Don't worry, Iso isn't so bad. Just find someplace in your mind and go there. I paint. Bree composed music—began humming it so loud that Deidre heard and let her out that first night." A wistful smile crossed his face. "Things weren't so bad when Bree was here with her music."

They came to a row of rooms, smaller than classrooms or offices, smaller even than a jail cell—maybe storage closets? They had no doors, no furniture except for a single gym mat on the floor, no pillow, no blanket, bare walls—not even a ReNew logo. Across from each doorway there were comfortable-looking office chairs. Where the guards sat to watch their prisoners.

Nelson shoved Micah inside the first tiny room. "Stand in the corner until you're given permission to move."

Micah gave Morgan an encouraging smile, then did as he was told, settling into a position with his hands above his head, elbows out wide, touching the wall, as if this was a familiar routine. The second Red Shirt positioned one of the office chairs opposite Micah's doorway and slung his weight into it, acting as if he was already bored with his guard duty.

Nelson shoved Morgan forward to the next room. She resisted at first, digging her heels in. He chuckled as if amused that a girl half his size would even try to disobey. He pushed harder. Morgan used her momentum against him, letting him push her far enough away that she had room to spin around and punch him in the groin so hard that he doubled over. She darted past him and ran back down the hall.

"No!" she screamed. "I'm not going in there. Don't make me go in there!"

"Get her!" Nelson yelled to the guard at Micah's doorway. The Red Shirt leapt to his feet and lunged for Morgan as she tried to zigzag past him.

She could have escaped, but that wasn't her plan. Micah almost ruined things by emerging from his cell just as the Red Shirt caught her in a crushing bear hug.

"Don't hurt her," Micah cried out, raising a fist.

Nelson tackled Micah from behind and sent him sprawling against the wall. "You get back inside there, or we'll do more than hurt her."

Micah whirled, ready to fight. Morgan caught his eye and shook her head. Nelson was facing away from her, so she risked a wink. Micah looked confused but lowered his fists. That didn't stop Nelson from punching him in the gut.

Morgan kept up her act, kicking and screaming and clawing the air as the second Red Shirt lifted her off her feet.

"Take her to the Hole," Nelson ordered. "Let her see what happens to troublemakers."

CHAPTER 40

The Hole was a janitor's closet around the corner from the Iso rooms. The door was solid wood, no window, making it ideal for Morgan's needs—just the fact that it was one of the few rooms left with a door in this damn place made it worth any potential discomfort she suffered for the short time she'd be imprisoned there.

The door was secured by a simple hasp with a long padlock dangling from it, hanging open. Morgan wondered who had the key—was glad she didn't need to worry as she had an alternate exit strategy.

Nelson opened the door. The room was small, about six by six, naked walls and floors, no comfy gym mat here, and the only things inside were a large janitor's sink and a fluorescent light fixture suspended from the ceiling. Morgan focused on the sink; it was too low to the ground for her to be able to stand on it and reach the ceiling, but there was a thick pipe secured to the wall leading from the sink to the ceiling. Perfect.

She made a show of resisting Nelson. "Please, I'm afraid of the dark. Please, no, don't turn the lights off," she cried after he pried her fingers from the door and threw her inside. He closed the door, and she pounded on it as he flicked the lights on and off from outside, laughing.

The lights went off, and she shrieked, an unnerving sound despite the solid door between them. "Shut up!" he yelled, but the lights came back on and stayed on.

Morgan leaned against the door and smiled. Time to get out of this place.

She climbed onto the janitor's sink. A quick shimmy up the pipe and she was at the ceiling. She pushed one of the tiles aside and raised her head up to assess the crawl space.

Typical suspended ceiling on a flimsy metal grid held by wire ties. Useless except for access. What she was looking for were the stronger elements that could bear her weight: the interior metal two-by-fours that framed each room she could balance on, the heavy-duty sprinkler pipe she could hang from, the overhead trusses she could use as guides.

Finding her way to the intake room's fire doors would mean a zigzag route following the exterior room elements with at least one monkey crawl along the pipes to cross a corridor, but as long as she didn't get lost, she could make it. Only problem was the lack of light.

She pulled herself the rest of the way out through the ceiling and perched on one of the two-by-fours that framed the wall that held the pipe. Hanging on to the pipe with one hand, she reached out, pushing as many ceiling tiles as she could reach out of their supports, dropping them to the floor below. They made some noise, but no one came to investigate. Most importantly, they released a swath of light into the crawl space, enough to get her across the corridor where she could hopefully find another empty room and repeat the process.

The roof trusses in this part of the building ran parallel to her path, so it was fairly easy to use them to brace herself with as she toed across the two-by-fours like a gymnast crossing a balance beam. Stray nail heads and bits of metal scratched at her bare feet, but she ignored the pain.

She made it to the corridor wall. Leaving the security of the truss behind, she slowly edged along the top of the wall until she could reach the sprinkler pipe that crossed the corridor. The light was almost nonexistent, but she knew it had to be the corridor and not another room by the row of light fixtures dropping down through the suspended ceiling.

Too risky to knock out tiles above a well-traveled corridor. She'd have to wait until she reached the other side and hope she found an unoccupied room that she could pull ceiling tiles from and steal more light. Then she could proceed to a room far enough away from where the guards sat keeping watch over Micah that she could drop down through and make her final escape. Which meant, she closed her eyes, building a map inside her mind, going to the left along the two-by-four studs, then turning right, heading to the empty rooms across from the commons room.

Hanging on to the pipe like a monkey, her ankles crossed above it, she pulled herself across the corridor. She could barely make out the gleam of the steel studs that marked the top of the opposite wall. She lowered her feet to balance on the framing element, hung on to the pipe with one hand, and leaned forward as far as she could to raise the corner of a ceiling tile. The room below had its lights on, but she heard no noise.

She pulled the ceiling tile up higher and lowered her head to scout below it. The movement released a stray piece of metal bracing that had rested on the tile. Before she could catch it, it fell through the opening, landing with a clatter on the linoleum floor.

Shit. Morgan eased the ceiling tile back into place and froze, listening. Her toes cramped with the effort of curling around the narrow metal stud, but she held her position.

Footsteps came down the hall. The door below her opened. More footsteps inside the room.

"What was it?" someone called from the hallway.

"Nothing. Probably a bird flew into the window."

The lights clicked off, and the door slammed shut. The foot-steps headed back down the hall and faded away.

Morgan remained still, making sure no one was returning. She'd planned to use the concealment of the crawl space to get her all the way past the Red Shirts over to the commons room, but without any light it was too risky. And since they'd just cleared the room below her, odds were, they wouldn't be back.

She hoped.

She pried the ceiling tile loose once more, slid it up to lie across the suspension grid, gingerly lowered her weight onto the door frame, then dropped down onto the floor below. The only sound was a soft thud.

Her shoulders and feet ached with pain, but she immediately rolled onto her feet and waited behind the door, listening once more. No one came.

She cracked the door open. The corridor was empty. All the rooms were dark. Moving as silently as possible, knowing that Micah's guards were just behind her and around the corner, she crept toward the commons room. She looked back once, cha-grined to see smears of blood from a cut on the bottom of her foot. They were small and in the shadows where the wall met the floor, but . . . she pulled her top over her head and used it to mop up the blood and apply pressure to her foot until the bleeding was stopped, then pulled her shirt back on and retraced her path.

One more turn and a short length of corridor. Unfortunately it was the corridor with the rooms where the kids slept—rooms with no doorways.

She came to the turn and snuck a peek around the corner. Two Red Shirts coming down the hall. Hide? Or take them out?

No weapons but also nowhere to hide—she'd never make it back to the last room she'd passed in time. Okay, if they didn't pass, she'd try to bluff her way through.

Flattening herself against the wall, she waited. But then the lights overhead began to flicker. "Lights out!" the Red Shirts cried. "Lights out!"

Kids streamed from the rooms where they'd been congregated, all segregated by their levels, toward the sleeping rooms—exactly the direction Morgan needed to go. She smoothed her top down and joined a group, passing the boys' room, then the girls', following two Red Shirts as if she had ordered to go with them—only they never spotted her dogging their footsteps.

The Red Shirts turned down a hall, away from the commons room, and she moved into the doorway, glancing through the window to make sure the room was empty. No strange prayer circles or mop handle tortures tonight, she was pleased to see. She ran through the first door, sprinted across the room to the doors leading into the intake room, and was home free.

Except for the locked door across from her. Hoping that no one was monitoring the camera in the clock, she crossed the room and crouched down below the clock, where she and Micah had talked earlier. It was only nine o'clock—but if Deidre had kept them up all last night, she guessed the ReNewers deserved an early bedtime. Better for her that they were out of the way as well.

She peeled back one edge of the theatrical putty that created her fake appendectomy scar and slid out the thin wire and flat sliver of metal that were her lock picks.

Easy-peasy, she thought as she worked the lock. She'd get what she wanted from the files and be home sleeping in her comfy bed before Deidre and her Red Shirts even knew she was gone.

She thought of Micah suffering a sleepless night in Iso because of her, but promised herself he wouldn't mind. Not when she was able to close this place down for good.

CHAPTER 41

The administrative wing was quiet, but it didn't feel empty, so Morgan took her time as she edged her way down the hall. Since she hadn't seen any signs of computers or a file room near the entrance this morning, she turned to explore the rest of the area behind the main offices.

These rooms were smaller than the classrooms. *Probably meant to be administrative staff offices*, she thought, given that they were on an interior corridor and had no windows. The first was furnished with a desk and chairs, giving off a distinct vibe of guidance counselor.

The second surprised her. Behind its door was a man's bedroom. The bed, with its rumpled sheets that from the smell hadn't been washed in quite a while, took up most of the space, leaving room for only a small dresser and a clothing rack with several suits dangling from it. A door opened onto a single-stall bathroom strewn with dirty towels and shaving gear.

Sean Chapman, the administrator she'd met earlier, had mentioned something to Greene about living on-site. Providing the children with therapeutic guidance day or night, he'd put it. As director, he'd have access to the files. Definitely no room for them here, though.

She tried the next door. This room was a living area, probably also for Sean, given the large-screen TV, gaming console, leather recliner with a well-worn butt dent, and empty beer bottles on the floor. It appeared as if it was originally meant to be the staff lounge with its small kitchenette at the back of the room. She crept inside, scanning the area for any signs of a laptop or other computer equipment.

A man's voice sounded from the hallway. "Where do you think you're going?"

Morgan spun. The door was closed; he hadn't seen her. Yet.

"No. He can wait. We need to talk."

There was nowhere to hide—no closets, no large piece of furniture to duck behind, no room between the refrigerator and the wall. Last resort. She opened the bottom cabinets below the countertop between the sink and the refrigerator. Most people filled the top ones first—easier to reach than squatting down low—and she didn't expect Sean to have a lot of dishes to store.

Bingo. The cabinet was empty except for a few empty plastic food containers, tossed randomly onto the shelf. Morgan slid inside, folding and flattening her body along the bottom shelf, closing the cabinet doors just as the room's door opened.

"Get in there." She peered through the crack between the hinges. Sean Chapman, still in his suit, shoved Deidre inside. She stood, facing away from him, shoulders slumped, as if waiting orders. He entered behind her and closed the door. "Look at me."

Deidre slowly raised her head and turned to face him.

"What the hell were you thinking?" he shouted, mere inches from her ear. Deidre took a step back, but he grabbed her shoulder and held her in place. "That stunt with the new girl? I told you a thousand times you need to back off."

"You needed her to confess." Deidre's tone was meek. "She confessed."

Sean made a noise of frustration and raised one hand. Morgan thought he was going to hit her, but instead he pushed her away and ran his fingers through his hair. "When are you going to get it through your thick skull? Bad intel is worse than no intel."

He spoke as if ReNew was in the business of interrogating prisoners of war. Morgan blinked, realizing that was exactly what their business was. They weren't satisfied with just raking in the dough they made off their exorbitant tuitions, even though they spent no money on actually teaching the kids exiled here. They also used the secrets divulged by the kids during their Purge and so-called counseling sessions to blackmail their parents.

After that, no matter what the kids reported about how awful their stay had been, no way would the parents take action.

That's why Micah said no one was released until they broke—except Bree. She hadn't broken. At least not here, not until she'd gone back home.

So what was the data in the files Robert Greene wanted her to destroy?

"My job is saving souls." Deidre's voice was soft, but from her expression, it was clear she understood that her words were an act of defiance. "The good Reverend Doctor says—"

"Your good Reverend Doctor is about to turn us out on the street if you don't get your shit together," he snapped. "Any more complications and he'll shut this place down and move on. Without either of us."

Deidre stepped back as if he had slapped her. "No. He'd never—I'm meant to be with him. He promised me."

"You're no good to him, bringing lawyers and cops in to nose around. We barely survived that fiasco with the Greene girl. One more screwup and . . ."

She spun away, arms flying around her chest as if hugging herself. "He can't leave me. We belong together. If I can find the one, maybe this new girl—"

Sean stared at her in disgust. "Don't you see? Benjamin doesn't love you. He'll always be the one to leave you."

Then he surprised Morgan. He stepped forward and wrapped his arms around Deidre, pulling her into a tender embrace. "Not me. I'll never leave you, Deidre," he crooned in a low voice. "Never."

She burrowed her face into his chest.

"We've got it good here, little sis," he said, fingers combing through her hair. "Don't screw it up."

Little sis? Morgan pressed her eye against the crack. There was a definite resemblance, although Sean was several years older than Deidre. But the way he touched her, talked to her, it wasn't what she expected from a big brother protecting his little sister. More like a pimp convincing a reluctant whore to seduce a john.

Sean disengaged from her and stepped away. Deidre stood, still with her arms wrapped around her chest, staring at the floor. "I won't mess up again. I'm sorry."

"Good." He opened the door. "Go. Get ready for him." She shuffled to the door, still looking down at her feet. "Remember. Whatever he wants, whatever it takes. Make him happy. Our future depends on it."

She nodded and left. Sean stood in the open door, watching, a scowl on his face. He glanced inside the room as if debating returning inside, but then turned toward the administrative offices and let the door bang shut behind him.

Morgan waited a few minutes before crawling out of her hiding place in the cabinet. She opened the door and scanned the hallway. All clear.

She resumed her progress down the hall, heading away from the main offices. There was nothing on the ReNew blueprints specifically labeled as a file or records room, but it was obvious that

Benjamin and his people cared little about what a room's original intended purpose was.

The corridor ended in front of the main doors to the school's chapel. To the right was a narrow passage that led behind the administrative offices. The only major landmark in that direction that she could remember from the floor plan was a door at the very end, which was a side door that led into the back of the chapel. Inside the chapel there was another door on the opposite side leading into the classroom area, no doubt locked.

She doubted the Rev would use a chapel to house his computer storage, but that still left the rooms lining the corridor as possibilities. The first was a storage closet for office supplies. It was pretty much just empty shelves and a few reams of paper—of course, since there was no actual classroom instruction going on here, not much need for many office supplies.

The next was stacked with more of the lightweight plastic chairs and tables that she'd seen beyond the locked doors in the student area. Across the hall, though, she hit pay dirt: a windowless room containing several desks with computers and hard drives. No paper files, but given the audio and video recordings the Rev and Chapman collected, why would they need them?

She settled into one of the workstations and accessed the computer. No security to speak of, her main obstacle was finding Bree's files scattered among seven years' worth of folders. They were coded by date and time stamps, so Morgan chose the date BreeAnna arrived at ReNew.

Even for that date there were thirty-four separate recordings. She remembered seeing cameras in the Rev's counseling room, the intake room, and the commons room. Who knew where else he was eavesdropping on the students' secrets? She clicked on one, hoping it wouldn't be bathroom porn.

A woman's cries pierced the air. Morgan stabbed the "Mute" button and held her breath, pivoting to watch the door. She left the chair and checked the hall. Empty. When she returned to the computer, she saw who the woman was—Deidre.

She was naked, kneeling on some kind of single-person pew, flogging herself so hard that Morgan winced with each stroke even though she couldn't hear it. Pacing around her, gesturing to a large cross hanging above them, his mouth open as he screamed at Deidre, urging her to hit harder, to purge her sins, was Reverend Benjamin.

Morgan didn't need the sound on to know what he was yelling at her—Deidre's tortured expression of self-loathing was enough. Finally she slumped over the railing, exhausted, the flail dangling from her hand. The Reverend snatched it from her and took over, striking her so hard that he drew blood. His hand slid to his crotch as he smiled at the camera. The camera panned to a table beneath the cross. It held a variety of whips, scourges, and other instruments of torture, as well as large containers of salt and vinegar.

No wonder Deidre was so screwed up. She'd been here seven years, since she was twelve—had the Rev been using her as his whipping girl all that time? Brainwashing her into truly believing she was evil, probably the same bullshit that had made Deidre feel responsible for the sins of the other students as well. Anything to twist her mind and keep her compliant.

Morgan knew the routine all too well—it was what her father did with his fish. He'd play games, turning them on each other, would even make them hold each other down while he or another fish tortured them. *Survival of the fittest*, he'd tell them. Only, of course, none of them survived. He didn't care; he had his fun. Just like the Rev.

Carrier of the blood, salvation through pain, sacrificial lamb. Now Morgan understood why Deidre had been so desperate to convince Bree to take her place. And when that failed, she'd now fixated on Morgan as a possible replacement.

Morgan clicked on another file from the same date. The intake room. Bree was shoved inside, the door closed behind her, leaving her in the dark. She'd pounded against the door, calling for her mother, until the doors behind her opened and Deidre and the Red Shirts appeared.

Morgan knew what happened next, so she opened the folder for the next day and found a file from the Rev's first session with Bree. The girl sat in her flimsy plastic chair, eyes sunken and glazed over, as he interrogated her, tearing her life apart, trying to get her to admit to the transgressions her mother had accused her of.

But Bree appeared more stunned than guilty. She said nothing, merely shaking her head in denial with each accusation. The Rev stormed and yelled, showering down eternal damnation on her and her family, until tears streamed down Bree's face, but still she said nothing.

Morgan noted the code for the Reverend's sessions and flicked through the next several days. Same shouting and screaming, but Bree simply sat, never saying a word. Toward the end she no longer appeared stunned. Rather a shy smile crossed her face. Triumphant in her silence.

Whatever Greene was afraid his daughter had disclosed, he need not have worried. From what Morgan could tell, Bree never confessed to anything.

She pulled the stem from her glasses, revealing the USB plug. Greene had loaded his scrubber program, but it wouldn't run until she activated it. Morgan plugged her glasses into the computer, which read it as an external drive. First, she deleted Greene's program—no way in hell was she erasing the pain and suffering these kids went through. With this evidence, she could close ReNew for good and finally get some measure of justice for Bree.

Her glasses didn't hold enough memory for all the files, so she copied most of Bree's and a few of Deidre's onto the drive and uploaded the rest into a cloud account. It would take several hours for all of the material to be saved—after all, the Rev and Chapman had been doing this for over seven years—but there was no reason for her to stick around that long; the program could run automatically.

Using a voice over Internet protocol, she called Greene. "It's done. Come get me."

"Really? Already?" Greene seemed surprised.

"You aren't paying me by the hour. How long before you get here?"

"You made sure the program uploaded properly? Everything is erased?"

"All the digital files. I haven't found any hard copies yet."

There was a long pause. "Have you spoken to Jenna Galloway since you arrived?"

Jenna? How the heck would she talk with Jenna? "No. Why?"

"Never mind, if you've done your job, then I can handle any loose ends."

What the hell did that mean? "Are you coming to get me?"

"Don't worry." His voice turned warm, soothing. "I'm on my way."

He hung up. Morgan frowned at the screen. Then she called Andre. "It's me."

"Morgan. Is everything okay?"

He sounded worried. "Why wouldn't it be?"

"Nick discovered that BreeAnna was home alone the night she died. And she had a visitor. Someone rang the doorbell, and she let them inside the house, right around the time the medical examiner said she died."

"Bree was murdered?" That explained so much. But who killed her? And why? "You're sure it wasn't her parents?"

"No. They have an alibi."

"Greene's on his way to get me out of here. But I'd appreciate it if one of you came as well. I don't trust him."

"I'll grab Jenna and head right out. Are you safe?"

Footsteps sounded from the hall outside. Morgan hung up without answering his question and turned the lights off, hiding beside the door.

"Did you see what your sister did to that new girl?" Reverend Benjamin's voice came. Sounded like they were right outside the door. "You need to man up as head of the family and control her."

"Like you do?" Sean Chapman answered. "You've got her so twisted, she believes your crap. Thinks she's saving souls."

"What goes on between us is none of your business. Your job is to make sure things run smoothly around here. Which means no more lawyers, no more parents raising hell, no more curious eyes prying into our business."

"Then we might have a problem. The release papers came through on Micah Chase. We can't stall any longer. He's out of here tomorrow."

There was a pause. Micah was being released? Morgan was torn. It was a strange feeling. She wanted him out of this cesspool. But she wanted him here. With her. Good thing she was leaving as well.

"Exactly my point. If you kept your sister in line like I told you, stopped all this Purge crap, he wouldn't have seen anything and we could have pocketed the county's money, sent him on his way."

"So you want me to let him go?"

"I want you to do your job and take care of the problem. I don't care what it takes. Make sure he doesn't talk." The two men continued down the hall, out of range of her hearing.

Make sure he doesn't talk. What did that mean? Didn't matter. She was on the wrong side of the locked doors to help Micah.

She could finish her job, wait for Jenna and Andre or Greene to arrive, and hope they were in time to save Micah.

Or she could forget about her own escape and go back and save him.

Save herself or save a sheep? No-brainer. At least it should be. Yet, she hesitated.

With the evidence she had to shut down ReNew, she'd save not only Micah but all the kids held here if she stuck with her plan.

Weird. She couldn't remember ever needing to talk herself into doing anything before. Usually she did what she wanted, dealt with any consequences later. Second-guessing wasn't in her nature.

She shook her head. Micah would be fine.

Another set of footsteps passed the door, this time headed down to the end of the hall where the door to the chapel was.

When the hall went quiet again, she eased the door open. The corridor was empty. She stepped out and sidled down the hall, away from the chapel. The office supply closet would be a good place to hide and wait—it was obvious no one had been there in a long time. No. Better to sneak out of the building and catch her ride beyond the security perimeter.

She glanced down at her bare feet. Maybe a quick stop at Chapman's room to steal a pair of socks and a coat first. She'd almost made it to the end of the corridor when Reverend Benjamin came barreling around the corner, colliding with her.

CHAPTER 42

The good Reverend Doctor may have been a self-proclaimed man of God, but somewhere along the line, Morgan would bet good money that he'd worked as a bouncer in a not-so-nice bar.

Her first instinct was to dodge past him, make a run for it. For most men caught off guard, that would have worked and she would have had a nice head start.

Not the Rev. As Morgan moved one way—playing the odds and going for his presumed weak side, his left side—he pivoted with her, lunging and grabbing her shoulder and elbow, twisting her arm behind her so that her own momentum worked against her.

She didn't try to resist—there was a damn good reason moves like that were called compliance holds. Fighting it would only lead to a lot of pain and a dislocated shoulder. Instead she played the sheep and went limp, faking a whimper.

"What the hell are you doing here?" he demanded.

Morgan thought fast, putting together the pieces Deidre and her brother had dropped like bread crumbs, and bluffed, "Deidre told me to come to the chapel. Said you wanted to see me for a special counseling session?"

The Rev straightened, pulling Morgan along with him. "She did, did she? We'll just see about that. Come along." He dragged her down the hall to the side door leading into the chapel.

It didn't look much like a place of worship on the inside. Other than a small single-person kneeler in front of the altar, there were no pews. Instead there were fancy lights, like what professional photographers used, and two cameras on tripods. Which spoke volumes. Morgan remembered the clip of Deidre she'd seen earlier. The Rev had had his hands full, whipping her, yet the camera had panned in.

Deidre's brother, Sean? And she thought her family was sick.

Keeping her head low and her posture submissive, hiding behind her hair as it fell over her face, she scanned the room. Above the kneeler, chains hung from the ceiling, ending in thick manacles. In the far corner, near the door leading into the locked student area, was a dog bed. Hanging from hooks on the walls near it were several dresses. So this was Deidre's home when she left the students.

But what most attracted Morgan's attention was the table between the kneeler and the altar. It was covered with a white cloth, and arranged on top were a variety of torture instruments, including one of Morgan's own favorites: a curved-blade fillet knife.

If she could get close to that . . . But the Rev didn't give her a chance. Keeping a tight grip on her, he hauled her to the center of the room near the kneeler.

"Deidre!" he bellowed. "Get out here!"

A door beside the main doors opened. There was a tile-walled bathroom behind it. Deidre appeared, wiping her face with a paper towel. Her color was pale, and one hand rubbed her belly. Morgan had a feeling she had a pretty good idea why Deidre was so desperate to escape ReNew.

She almost felt sorry for the girl. Almost. Except Morgan made it a rule to never feel anything for fish, and that's what Deidre really was.

Deidre didn't want to save herself. Deidre wanted to save them all. She was a true believer. And someone along the line—probably her brother or the Rev, or both—had convinced her that the only path to salvation lay through pain and suffering. Through being broken.

All those "confessions" she'd purged from the kids at ReNew, Deidre truly believed them. Because her own world was so twisted and corrupt, she imagined all of the other kids at ReNew were also sinners, deserving of punishment.

"I came like you asked," Morgan told Deidre, hoping the other girl would play along. "I came to carry the burden."

"Is it true?" the Rev asked. "You asked her to come here?"

Deidre looked from Morgan to the Rev and back, still wiping her face with the paper towel. Then, she slowly nodded, her gaze locked with Morgan's, not the Rev's.

Morgan knew she'd won. Her first impression had been so wrong. Deidre wasn't like Morgan's father, not at all. She was more like one of his victims—no, he'd never been able to warp any of his victims' minds so completely, except one: the woman he'd married, his ultimate accomplice.

Deidre's mind had been warped by two men: the Reverend and her brother. Morgan suspected Bree had begun to sow seeds of doubt—could Morgan capitalize on those now?

The girl dropped the paper towel and stumbled across the space separating them. She reached a hand to stroke Morgan's arm as if overcome and beyond words. Then she took Morgan's hand in hers, and the Rev released Morgan.

"Well, now," he said, moving to set up the cameras. "This is an unexpected present." His tone was one of a man totally focused on his task—a task that unfortunately put him between Morgan and the knife.

"I only ask one thing, Deidre," Morgan said. She'd have a better chance taking down the Rev if she didn't have to worry about

Deidre—the girl was too unstable to rely upon. "He sent your brother to kill Micah. You can't let that happen."

The Rev scoffed. "I sent Sean to counsel him. Deidre knows there's a price to be paid by the wicked. Micah Chase refuses to repent. He can't leave here until he does."

"He's done nothing wrong except refuse to let you break him."

"Of course, that's what a sinner like yourself would say. Deidre knows better."

Doubt crossed Deidre's face. "Please," Morgan whispered. "Save him."

"I can't do that," she whispered back, her voice filled with fear rather than condemnation. Then she straightened and said in a loud voice, "Micah must finish his penance before he can leave. We can't let sinners like you loose on the outside world." Deidre's words emerged like the recitation of an automaton. The Rev grinned in victory and turned to face them both, hands on his hips and a wide grin on his face.

Morgan could almost see him relishing the possibilities. Two girls, his to break. She needed him focused on her and her alone.

"Micah's not who you should worry about," Morgan said. Time to act the wolf rather than the sheep. As a wolf, she had something of value to offer the Rev. If she could convince Deidre to give her something in return.

"There's only one sinner here worthy of your attention." Morgan focused on breathing in time with the Rev, blinking at the same slow speed, mirroring his posture, until he finally began to nod in time with her. She knew what he wanted, and it had nothing to do with salvation or forgiveness, but she needed to keep up the act for Deidre's sake. And to buy time. How long would it take Jenna and Andre to get here? Or Greene? "The greatest sinner of all. Me."

"You?" Deidre gasped in confusion.

"Me. Do you know who my real father is? I'm sure you've heard of him. Clinton Caine."

Deidre looked puzzled. Seven years with no contact with the outside world, Morgan reminded herself. That was okay; Deidre wasn't her target. Benjamin was—and he took the bait, eyes wide, mouth gulping open and shut again like a goldfish.

He threw his hands into the air. "Thank you, Lord, for this opportunity to redeem this sinner." He smiled as if accepting a gift from heaven above, then turned to Morgan. "Daughter of Eve, you carry the greatest sin of all. I can't risk you carrying the serpent's venom to the innocents of the world beyond."

"It's okay, Deidre," Morgan said in the same low, hypnotic tone she'd been using on the Rev. "Everything's okay. I understand now. I need my sins purged. I'm ready." She dropped her voice and turned her head so the Rev wouldn't hear. "Now's your chance. Go. Save Micah and the others. And your baby." She nodded to Deidre's belly.

Without waiting for Deidre's response, Morgan faced the Reverend and did the one thing she never dreamed she'd ever do. She knelt and raised her hands in supplication. "Please, Reverend Benjamin. There's no time. Please save me. Cleanse my soul. Erase my sins."

A shiver raced down her spine. His smile was exactly the same as her father's when he caught a particularly juicy fish, one who would pleasure him for a long, long time.

✦

"With his house being closer, Greene has a twenty-minute head start on us," Andre said as Jenna drove them out of the city. Andre tried calling Robert Greene again. So far, no luck. Greene, like Morgan, had gone radio silent.

Leaving Andre with a bad feeling. A nervous itch, like he used to get before going into battle.

"What makes you think that Greene getting there first is a bad thing?" Jenna countered. "Doesn't that mean the cavalry is arriving faster to save poor defenseless Morgan?"

Andre didn't take the bait. They both knew Morgan could be in trouble. He gave up on Greene and switched to monitoring the transmitters Morgan had planted. Nothing but silence from the one and normal background noise from the other.

His phone rang again, the sound shrill against the hum of the highway beneath their tires. He answered and put it on speaker. "Morgan?"

"No. It's Nick." The psychologist's voice was strained. "Caren tried to kill herself. An overdose."

"Shit. Is she okay?"

"The paramedics think so. But that's not why I called."

"What?"

"While I was dealing with her, Robert took off."

"Morgan called him; he went to get her out of ReNew."

"I don't think so. Andre, he had a gun."

Andre's itch disappeared. No time for worry when there was an objective to achieve. "We're on it."

Jenna gunned the engine, although Andre knew there was no way they'd make it in time. He called 911, but the ReNew compound was on the far edge of the county sheriff's territory; the dispatcher estimated that it would be at least twenty minutes to get a car there—about the same time it would take Jenna and Andre.

Until then Morgan was on her own.

CHAPTER 43

The Rev smiled down at Morgan, his eyes aglow with desire. Morgan played into his need. "I'm the biggest sinner you'll ever meet," she said, talking to him as if they were the only two people in the universe. A universe defined by his need.

"All that crap I told you earlier? Nothing compared to the real truth." She leaned forward, the Rev mirroring her movements. "Make me bleed, suffer for my sins. Purge me of this evil. Ask me how many people I've killed. I'll confess everything, but only to you."

The Rev's eyes narrowed, and his head bobbed like a cobra getting ready to strike. "You." He didn't use Deidre's name; she was nothing to him, not compared to the promise of extracting Morgan's confession. "Put her in the cuffs. Make sure they're tight."

Morgan allowed Deidre to maneuver her onto the kneeler and stretch her arms overhead, locking one manacle around her left wrist. Deidre was taller than her, leaving the second cuff beyond Morgan's reach. At least it would appear that way to the Rev.

Impatiently, he pushed Deidre out of the way. "One's good enough."

He ran his hand through Morgan's hair, down her neck, his fingers wrapping around her flesh. Not tight enough to choke her, simply a reminder of who was in control here. "I'm going to make you repent."

Then, finally, the tell she'd been watching for. A furtive brush of his hand against his crotch. She had him where she wanted him.

Morgan knew her role as a fish required her to act afraid, jiggle her chains, maybe sob or scream in fear. This man was driven by a need for power, to decimate his prey mentally and, in Deidre's case, physically, until they obeyed his every command.

A need Morgan was uniquely prepared to exploit.

Measuring the Rev's attention—she needed all of it, if this was going to work—she settled for an enticing whisper. "I'll tell you everything," she promised him. "But are you certain you want a witness?"

He jerked as if remembering Deidre's presence for the first time. "You're excused," he told her. "Go, now."

Deidre moved in a half bow, half curtsy, and left. But not before meeting Morgan's gaze and giving her a quick nod. Micah would be safe, she knew.

Too bad she wasn't as sure about herself. Not with the gleam that lit the Rev's face as he trailed his fingers across the torture instruments aligned on the table. He smiled and paused, finally reaching for the knife.

He twisted the blade so it glinted in the bright lights, preening for the cameras. Then he held it before her face, smiling when she responded with an expression mimicking fear. He sidled behind her, tracing the edge of the knife down her cheek, along her neck, back to her spine.

She held still, waiting. He'd want to take his time, but once stupid emotions and hormones took control, things became unpredictable. It was one of her father's greatest failings, his inability to maintain control. Sometimes the kill was over so fast, as if he was caught in a frenzied blood fever, that he'd rage all the more because he had no chance to savor it.

The Rev's breath came hot and fast on the back of her neck as he sliced Morgan's top down the back so it fell away, leaving her skin bare except for her bra. Then he returned to the table and exchanged the knife for a leather flail.

The first lash hit Morgan like a dozen hot needles burrowing beneath her skin. *Not too bad*, she thought, biting her lip against her gasp. She wasn't going to give him the satisfaction of showing any pain—if she did, this would all be over too soon, and the whole idea was to buy enough time for the cavalry to arrive. She couldn't wait until they got the video from her glasses and the cameras into the hands of the authorities. The Rev better enjoy this, his last dance, because if she had her way, he'd spend the rest of his life locked up with men like her father.

Another strike, this one rocking her body against the chain that held her in place. Morgan grabbed the manacle with her free right hand, masking the move to look like a desperate attempt to stabilize herself. The Rev paused, his fingers caressing the welts he'd just raised.

"We can do better than that." He switched from the first flail to one constructed with strands of barbwire woven into the leather. He struck her again, this time pausing before yanking the flail back, all the barbs embedded in Morgan's skin first digging in deeper, then ripping through her flesh as he pulled them free.

Harder to keep from screaming, but Morgan somehow managed. Pride more than anything—or maybe, in her own way, she was just as crazy as he was. She twisted her pain into a cackle of derision. "That all you got?"

In response, he struck again, viciously wrenching the barbed hooks as he pulled them free. Morgan felt warm liquid streaming down her back, knew it was her own blood. Good. Blood would keep him happy and distracted. Making this a simple waiting game.

As the Rev focused on the best way to make her suffer, she inched the thin blade of her pick from between the fingers of her right hand and into the manacle's lock. The filleting knife would be within easy reach as soon as she was free.

The image of that knife protruding from the Rev's throat kept the pain at bay as he struck again.

"BreeAnna, she didn't break either, did she?" Morgan asked. "Is that why you killed her?"

Another blow rocked Morgan's body. If she wanted, she could kick out at the Rev, knock him to the ground. But then he'd just get up, madder than ever, and she'd risk dropping her lock pick, so why bother?

"Not me. Wish I had. That bitch—a little more time and I would have had her. Just like all the others." He punctuated his words with more blows. Morgan lost count, focused instead on her lock pick. It was tricky work with each strike spinning her body one way or the other, but she'd practiced a lot—she could even pick law enforcement handcuffs with her hands behind her back. Which made it all the more frustrating that these stupid kink-shop-bought manacles were being so stubborn.

"Why don't you have sex with them? All those children in your control," she taunted, hoping to distract him long enough that she could brace her body and finish with the lock. "You can't, can you? Only with Deidre? Or is this as close to sex as you get?"

The next blow landed so hard the Rev had to leverage his weight against the embedded barbs to tear them free—and along with them, a good portion of Morgan's skin. *Pound of flesh*, she thought with giddy abandon. Was that blood loss or endorphins kicking in?

Focus. Buy time—which meant keeping his attention on her without getting him so angry that he killed her. Fine balancing act. But she had learned from a master. Her father.

Another blow, this one spinning her around to face the Rev, her arms caught in the twisted chains overhead. The lock pick slipped, and she had to squeeze her hand into a fist to keep it from dropping.

The flail whipped across her exposed belly, once, twice, leaving ribbons of blood in its wake.

"You know Deidre is pregnant, right? She's trying to escape. Is that because she loves you and wants to be with you? Or because she knows you'll kill the baby before you give up your little fun and games?"

"Satan's whore!" he screamed, his face turning dark red. She hoped he wasn't having a stroke—it would deprive her of fun once she got free. Carefully, she twisted the lock pick back between her fingers and into the manacle. "You lie! Confess and repent!"

Morgan's laughter crackled between them. He really was funny—no comparison at all to her father. Once started, she couldn't stop; flashes of all the blood and screams and death gurgles her father had created sped through her mind like a warped highlights reel. The Rev was a pathetic, broken toy of a man beside Clinton Caine.

The more she laughed, the angrier the Rev got. He spun to the table, searching for a new and better weapon, so furious that he crashed into it, toppling it over. Morgan was suffused with hilarity as he scrambled, hands and feet on the floor, butt in the air, until finally he stood, holding the knife before him.

He stumbled toward her, his gaze fixed on hers, arm raised.

A piercing alarm shrieked through the air, stopping him midstrike. A killing strike if the gleam in his eyes said anything. He whirled to the door to the student area. Smoke poured through the cracks around the door frame.

The Rev squinted at her for a moment, then stepped away. He crossed over to the door and opened it. More smoke roiled through, making Morgan gag.

He glanced at the knife in his hand, then out to the blaze that filled the hallway beyond. And then he smiled. "God always has an answer." He turned to Morgan. "Burn in hell, bitch."

He raced out the main doors on the opposite side of the chapel, away from the fire.

Morgan braced her feet against the kneeler, straining to see through the smoke that surrounded her. Her eyes watered; her fingers were numb as she fumbled with the lock. *C'mon, c'mon.* Flames now twisted along the polished wood of the doorway, climbing up the walls to the ceiling, marching toward her.

CHAPTER 44

There was no "lights out" in the Iso hallway. Here, the lights stayed on day and night. Micah often wondered if Deidre had chosen to do that to protect the No Names or the Red Shirts guarding them. Either group could have used darkness to their advantage.

Or maybe she just loved messing with people's heads. Keeping them awake until they didn't know if it was day or night.

Whatever her reasons, Micah didn't mind. He actually liked Iso—the chance to sleep alone without worrying about rolling over onto someone else. And the quiet. You couldn't beat the quiet. No snoring, no coughing, no crying.

Just him and his guard. And the light beaming ruby red through his eyelids. He painted with the light, turned it into a canvas of alizarin crimson and naphthol scarlet.

He'd just finished a gleaming portrait of the new girl, Morgan, when a shrill alarm pierced the silence. Micah jerked upright, then sprang to his feet. Somehow in the almost-sleep driftwood of his mind, Morgan and the alarm went together. Shit. He never should have let them take her away—even if it had been her idea. She had no clue what the Hole was like or how unstable Nelson was. The guy had tried to burn down his own house with his little brother inside—rich parents helped him avoid any criminal charges, but he'd ended up in here until his eighteenth birthday.

The alarm kept wailing, its noise worse than a dentist's drill. Micah broke all the rules, crossing the threshold of the Iso room and approaching the Red Shirt guarding him. A kid named Joey who took orders just fine but had no clue otherwise. Joey hadn't even gotten up from his chair, although he was busy swinging his head up and down the hallway, as if expecting divine guidance to come running up to him.

"It's a fire, you idiot," Micah yelled over the din.

"Can't be," Joey yelled back, still not abandoning his comfy chair. "If it was, the sprinklers would have come on."

"How do you even know they work?" Micah said. Tendrils of smoke drifted down between the ceiling tiles and light fixtures above them. No flames, but who knew how long they had. "Come on, we need to help get the others out."

"My orders are to stay here."

"Screw your orders. Nelson locked Morgan in the Hole. We have to let her out."

More smoke snaked along the ceiling overhead. Joey stared at it in confusion. Micah grabbed his shirt collar and jerked him to his feet.

That's when it hit him. He'd been so proud, not breaking, not bowing to Deidre's will. But she had won. Because he didn't need permission to do the right thing, he just needed to do it.

He let go of Joey, who immediately scrambled toward the commons room and the exit. Micah turned the other way, toward Morgan. The smoke was thicker the closer he got to the janitor's closet where she was locked up, but he didn't let that slow him.

From the smoke at the end of the hall a figure emerged. Not Morgan. Nelson. Barreling toward Micah with raw hatred fueling his charge.

"You bastard," Nelson shouted. "This is for what you did to Deidre!"

Before Micah could respond, Nelson slammed into him so hard, Micah's head cracked against the wall and his vision sparked with pain.

"You raped her." Nelson aimed a wild punch at Micah. It connected with the side of his face, but Micah was able to duck so that it was only a glancing blow. Still hurt like hell, but that made for good motivation.

"You're crazy. I never touched her," Micah said as he shoved Nelson off him and moved to put room between them.

"Did you even know she's pregnant? Do you even care?" Nelson charged again. Micah realized the larger boy was trying to herd him past the janitor's closet and down the hall. He risked a glance over his shoulder and saw why.

The room at the end of the hall, beside the door leading to the chapel, was the source of the smoke. Not just smoke. Bright, iridescent flames reaching out toward him.

✦

The fire was distracted by an overhead air vent, but that didn't stop the smoke, which was far more deadly. Where the hell were the sprinklers? Morgan wondered as she kept trying to pick the lock.

Obviously not working, came a calm reply. Despite the smoke choking her every breath, her entire body went still. She craned her neck back and squinted at the manacle restraining her. Idiot. Sex-shop toy—the lock wasn't real, had no tumblers. She gave up on the lock picks and instead felt around the housing until she found the release catch. Of course. The Rev would have no patience for real locks and keys.

The manacle snapped open, and she fell to the ground. Her left hand was numb from being restrained overhead, her shirt fell open in the back, her stomach and back were smeared with her own blood, and she could barely see through the thick smoke that had turned from grey to black.

Still, she didn't panic. Instead she oriented herself to the main doors, crouched low to the floor where the air was still clear, and crossed the space between her and freedom. A few seconds later, she pushed through the doors, shoved them shut again before the smoke or fire could escape, and sat down hard, focusing on the simple act of inhaling.

Her reprieve was short-lived as smoke began filling the corridor leading from the computer room. She pushed to her feet and began down the hall, past Chapman's living quarters, smoke billowing behind her, pushing her faster.

She reached the intersection with the administration corridor and sped around the corner, smoke choking her from every direction. She quickly oriented herself. There was Benjamin's so-called therapy room. A few steps farther and she'd reach the corridor leading to the main exit.

She stumbled forward but stopped again. The sounds of children screaming and fists pounding undercut the piercing wail of the fire alarm. She turned toward it. Through the windows of the doors to the intake room she saw faces pressed against the glass.

"We're trapped," Deidre shouted. "Find the keys. Let us out!"

To hell with keys. Morgan knelt to begin work with her lock picks. The sounds of the kids coughing and crying urged her to hurry, but she ignored them. She knew what she was doing; rushing it would only lead to mistakes and wasted time. Calmly, she felt the last tumbler fall into place, and the doors unlocked.

She held one door open, releasing a mass of humanity as the kids raced out. "Go down the hall, to the left," she told them. A few of the Red Shirts pushed their way to the front and took off running, abandoning the others. But most of them helped each other, fighting their way through the blinding smoke, coughing, and choking.

"Where's Deidre?" she asked as the last made their way out. Somehow she'd lost track of the other girl. The kids shook their heads, turning toward freedom.

Morgan should have followed, but she also hadn't seen Micah. She entered the intake room in time to see Deidre go through the doors on the opposite side, the ones leading to the commons room. Morgan ran after her.

The smoke was thicker in the commons room, pouring through all the air vents as well as between the light fixtures. Morgan pulled what was left of her top off and wrapped it around her face. She caught up to Deidre on the other side of the room. The older girl had slumped against the door, gasping for air.

Morgan helped her through the door into the classroom corridor. Not as much smoke here, but now the lights were flickering ominously. "Where's Micah?"

Deidre coughed, pointed toward the Isolation rooms.

"Why didn't he leave?" Morgan asked as she hauled Deidre with her. As they reached an area with less smoke, Deidre's breathing steadied and she was able to walk on her own.

"Nelson."

Shit. The state Nelson was in, he'd rather stay behind to beat the crap out of Micah than run for his life. She remembered Benjamin's orders to Chapman about getting rid of Micah—had Chapman sent Nelson to deal with Micah while he started the blaze? The chaos of the fire would make a damned good diversion, and the panicked mob of kids would easily cover up a murder.

They rounded the corner to the hall where the Iso rooms were. At the far end, past the janitor's closet where Morgan had been imprisoned, Micah and Nelson were grappling, shoving each other against the walls, throwing wild punches, perilously close to the flames. Morgan glanced around, searching for a weapon. The only thing handy was the long padlock dangling from the janitor's closet. Brass knuckles?

"Stop it," Deidre shouted, trying to get between the two combatants. "We need to get out of here."

"Is it true?" Nelson said, whirling on her. Blood streamed from his nose and a split lip. "Your brother said Micah raped you."

Micah took the opportunity to rush Nelson, plowing into him, both of them slamming against the wall. "I never touched her!"

Nelson responded with a knee to Micah's groin and an elbow to the side of his head. Micah stumbled back, groaning, doubled over in pain. Nelson swept his feet out from under him, and Micah went down.

Morgan tied her shirt around the lock. Just as Nelson leaned back, ready to deliver the final blow with a kick to Micah's head, she struck him with her improvised mace. She swung it hard enough that when it landed against Nelson's chest wall there was an audible crack.

He fell, off balance, landing on his butt. Before he could recover, she pounced on him from behind, placing him into a choke hold, just like her father had taught her. A few seconds later and he slumped, unconscious.

"What did you do to him?" Deidre cried, racing to his side.

"He'll wake up in a second or two." Morgan turned to Micah. "Are you okay?"

He nodded, climbed to his feet with her help. One of his eyes was already swelling shut and the other cheek was cut and bruised, but he seemed to be moving okay. She retrieved her top, untied the padlock, sliding it over her knuckles, ready to use it again if

Nelson didn't behave himself. She slung the top, now more a rag than clothing, around her neck.

"You're hurt," Micah said. "What happened? Who did this?"

Morgan glanced over her shoulder and down at her belly. The barbs hadn't done serious damage; she doubted she'd need any stitches, and the bleeding had already stopped. But she had to admit, the welts and abrasions along with the blood made for a nasty sight. "Looks worse than it is."

Deidre knelt beside Nelson and soothed his forehead. Nelson jerked awake, startled. No choking or gagging, Morgan noted, pleased with herself. There was always a risk of crushing the larynx with that hold if you did it incorrectly. He gasped and held his side—a cracked rib or two from where the heavy padlock hit him, but he was breathing okay.

"Get him up. We need to move," Morgan ordered.

The smoke had found them, billowing in through the overhead ventilation grills. And it'd turned black, which couldn't be a good sign. It also smelled worse, if that was possible. More acrid, it burned Morgan's throat.

Deidre and Micah hauled Nelson to his feet. He pushed Micah away. "It's okay," Deidre told him. "Micah never hurt me. My brother lied."

"But—why?" Nelson turned to the room where the fire was coming from. "I thought he'd hurt you. I wanted to kill him."

"So you started a fire?" Micah's adrenaline could be heard in his roar of anger. "With all these kids trapped inside?"

"I knew they'd get out. Everyone would get out. Except you."

"I didn't do anything!" The two boys glared at each other, both with their elbows back and fists ready to strike.

"Stop it!" Morgan said. She didn't shout. Instead she used a tone borrowed from her father. One low and venomous, promising lethal consequences if you didn't obey. "Now. Where's the nearest room with a window?"

"The music room." Deidre pointed to a room a few feet down the corridor.

Morgan led the way, tying her shirt back around her face and crouching low to avoid the smoke overhead. Just as she reached the door to the music room the lights went out.

CHAPTER 45

Jenna hated driving these Pennsylvania farm roads at night. At least in LA they understood the concept of streetlights. Or there'd be plenty of other traffic to help guide you through sudden curves that always seemed to appear while negotiating steep mountainsides.

"The sheriff's deputy is still twelve minutes out," Andre said as he hung up the phone. "We're her only backup."

"I'm going thirty miles an hour over the speed limit." While praying she didn't hit a deer—at seventy miles an hour that would not be a pretty sight for either of them. "Besides, Morgan can take care of herself."

Andre leaned forward, his back rigid. More than adrenaline, anger. Shit. She didn't need this, not now while their client might be on a homicidal rampage and she had to decide how to best protect both him and their firm.

"My point is." His words flew out clipped, as if he was taking aim. "She shouldn't have to. You need to decide, Jenna. Right now. Is Morgan part of the team, or not?"

Right. Damn marine code. Leave no man behind and all that jazz. Why couldn't he understand that there were some people in this world who simply weren't cut out to be on any team? A mercenary. That was what Morgan was. Someone you used for their particular talents when you needed to and then you cut them loose.

Except cutting Morgan loose might be more dangerous than keeping her close. "She is," Jenna finally allowed. "Which is why I'm risking our lives to—" They crested a hill and saw the lights ringing the ReNew compound. The building itself was dark. "We're here."

"You drilled for active shooter response while with the Postal Service?" Andre asked. Jenna could almost hear his mind calculating lines of sight and approaches.

She didn't have to ask about Andre's preparation—his unit had seen some of the worst door-to-door urban combat fighting of the war in Afghanistan. She steered the Tahoe into the ReNew drive, surprised to see the entrance gate open.

"Jenna, watch out!"

A group of kids ran in front of the car, skirting the edge of the headlights. Jenna slammed the brakes, and they scattered. She swore under her breath, fear sending her pulse into a gallop. The SUV screeched to a stop.

Andre rolled down his window. "What happened?" he called out to the kids who'd dived to his side of the narrow drive. "Why are you running?"

"Fire," a boy gasped. "The building is on fire!"

Andre glanced at Jenna. "Guess that's Morgan's call for help. Just like you told her to do."

"I didn't mean for her to panic a bunch of kids."

"Why aren't the fire guys here?" He pulled out his phone.

"Don't bother them for a false alarm. We know it's Morgan." She eased the Tahoe down the road to the parking lot. More kids were running from the building, but what caught her attention was the white Lexus SUV pinning a middle-aged man against a Jaguar sedan.

The headlights were so bright they made the man's skin appear a ghastly blue white. He held his hands up against the Lexus's grill as if he thought he could stop the SUV, the movement revealing a white clerical collar visible against his dark shirt.

The good Reverend Doctor Amos Benjamin. Although the blubbering fear that twisted his face made him look nothing like the charismatic man she'd met earlier today.

Robert Greene leaned out the driver's side window to shout at the trapped man. "Tell me why, Benjamin. Why did you kill my daughter?"

◆

Morgan led her ragtag group into the music room. Nelson had his arm wrapped around Deidre's shoulders. It was a protective gesture, but it was also clear that he was limping and breathing heavily. Maybe she'd done more damage with her improvised mace than intended.

Once inside the room, she closed the door, but that didn't help—the smoke was weaseling its way down through the ceiling tiles and light fixtures.

"You started the fire in the crawl space?" Micah asked as they stumbled over to the piano.

"Figured it would be the best place. That way I didn't have to worry about the sprinklers putting it out right away."

"If they worked in the first place."

Morgan ignored their chitchat, climbing onto the radiator in front of the windows. "There are no latches. We'll have to break one out."

She reattached her padlock to her shirt once again. Turning her head away and shielding her eyes, she swung it as hard as she could against the lower corner of the window. It bounced back, almost hit her. She leaned forward and felt the window. Barely a faint crack.

The smoke was drifting down, a thick blanket choking and smothering them. Deidre and Nelson leaned against the piano, coughing.

"Let me try," Micah said. He took the makeshift weapon from her and twisted his body to put his full weight against it and swung. This time there was a definite thud and a crack. He swung again, and the padlock went through the glass, producing a hole.

The night air rushed in. Morgan filled her lungs, relishing it. A crackling sounded overhead. Ceiling tiles began dropping around them, coated with flames. More flames roared in through the gaps they left, searching for the oxygen.

"Hurry," she urged.

Micah swung again, grunting with the effort. He broke through the glass a few inches away from the first hole. Quickly he wound up and hit it again and again until a thunderous crack pierced through the wail of the fire alarm. The glass crashed down, shattering against the windowsill, flying in all directions.

Morgan grabbed Micah, pulling him back and spinning them both away from the glass. A gust of wind swept in, feeding the fire. The room now was choked with smoke and flame.

She took her shirt and the padlock back from Micah and wrapped the cloth around her nose and mouth. "You go first," she told Micah, her voice hoarse from the smoke and the need to shout. "That way you can help Nelson down."

Micah nodded and climbed onto the radiator. He swept as much glass off with his legs as he could, but there were still plenty of shards poised to cut them. As he twisted around to lower himself through the window, Morgan took his arms to help brace him. She had no idea how far down it was.

"My feet aren't touching," he confirmed her suspicions. "Let go, I'll have to drop."

She did and he vanished into the night. Too late she remembered that none of them wore shoes. She leaned out the window, trying to stay away from the sharp edges at the rim. "Are you okay?"

There was enough light between the fire and the moonlight that she could see him push up from the ground to his feet. His head was about two feet below the window. "I'm fine. A bit sliced up, nothing serious. Go ahead and pass Nelson through."

The fire seemed frustrated by the lack of fuel in the empty classroom, crawling along the remaining ceiling tiles and the walls. But the air was heating up to the point where it was hard to take in a breath, and the smoke was blinding.

Morgan didn't waste energy on talking. Instead she tapped Deidre's arm and grabbed Nelson by the shoulders. Together they helped Nelson, who was breathing shallow and fast, up onto the windowsill, then held his arms to lower him as Micah guided him from below. He cried out in pain, but there was nothing else they could do.

Deidre was overcome with a coughing spell and let go abruptly, leaving Morgan holding all of Nelson's weight. He slipped through her grasp and fell with a loud scream.

"Shit," Micah said. "He landed on a piece of glass, sliced up his leg."

Morgan didn't have time to do anything—Deidre had collapsed, and the smoke was so thick, Morgan had lost sight of her. She dropped to her knees and felt around with her arms spread wide, listening for Deidre's coughing. Finally she found her.

Grabbing Deidre by the arm, Morgan hauled her up and onto the radiator. The flames were so close their roar was louder than the fire alarm. She pushed Deidre out the window, hoping she wouldn't land on top of Micah and Nelson, then she jumped as well, trying to spin her weight to one side to avoid hitting the others.

She landed hard, but remembered to bend her knees to absorb the shock and rolled with her momentum. Pieces of glass bit into her knees and palms, but nothing too large or deep. Gasping for air and relishing how cold and fresh it was, she climbed to her feet and turned to the others.

Flames shot out of the window above them. Deidre was still coughing, but not as badly. She sat beside Nelson, picking glass from his hair. Micah had taken off his shirt and tied it around Nelson's right thigh. "I can't get the bleeding to stop. We need to get him help."

"Can you carry him?" Morgan asked. They were at the back of the building, near the forest. Out of sight of the road.

"Yeah, help me get a good hold on him." Micah squatted and she maneuvered Nelson into position for a piggyback. Then she let Micah lean against her as he straightened. His weight landed on the welts on her shoulders and hurt like hell, but it was only for a moment.

"We'll be right behind you," she said.

Micah took off into the night, and Morgan turned to help Deidre who sat stunned on the ground. Her flowing dress had been singed and torn so it fluttered around her like ribbons. She looked up at Morgan, nose dripping with mucus; the fire reflected from her eyes making her appear like a madwoman.

The fire burst through one of the other windows, showering them with glass. Deidre didn't move. Morgan grabbed her hand and hauled her to her feet. Both of them were slicked with sweat yet also shivering in the cold night air. They stumbled away from the building, feet crunching through the glass. Deidre slipped and fell to the ground. Morgan let her catch her breath—they were far enough from the building that they were safe for now.

She was too sore and exhausted to risk sitting down herself, afraid she might not find the strength to get back up again. She unwound her ruined top and rewrapped it around her arm where glass shards had left some bloody cuts, squeezing the padlock in her hand. Damn thing had saved her more than once tonight; she wasn't about to let it go now.

"You okay?" she asked Deidre after a few minutes. "We need to get moving before we get hypothermia."

The girl stared at her without comprehension. She ignored the hand Morgan reached down to her.

"Deidre, c'mon. We have to go now."

Deidre shook her head. Small, quick shakes as if trying to deny reality. Morgan wondered if the girl had finally had a mental breakdown. Not like she was all that stable to start with. But then she realized Deidre wasn't staring at her—she was looking at something behind Morgan.

She whirled, the padlock gripped in her fist her only weapon. No match for the large semiautomatic pistol Sean Chapman had aimed at her heart.

CHAPTER 46

Jenna positioned the Tahoe to maximize the amount of cover it provided. She got out on the driver's side and drew her Sig Sauer. Andre slid across the front seat and climbed out beside her, his own weapon, a Beretta 9-millimeter, in his hand.

"How do you want to handle this?" she asked him. When it came to tactics, there was no one she trusted more than Andre.

"Can't risk a shot. If we kill him and his foot slips off the brake—"

"Then the Reverend is toast." She glanced over the Tahoe's hood. Greene was screaming obscenities at the Reverend, and he was also now aiming a pistol at the man.

"He's not our only problem." Andre tapped her shoulder. Behind them more kids emerged from the building. Accompanied by thick billowing smoke.

"Damn it. She started a real fire. What the hell was she thinking?" Jenna muttered. Andre called the fire department. Greene finally sputtered to a stop, and she saw her chance. "Mr. Greene," she called. He swung his head to face her but didn't point the gun at her. A good start. "I need you to put the gun down and back the car up."

"Jenna!" Greene seemed relieved to see her. "He did it. This sonofabitch came to my home and killed my little girl."

Benjamin saw his chance, twisting his torso as much as possible to face Jenna. He raised his hands as if surrendering. "No. I'm innocent. I never hurt his daughter. I never hurt anyone. I love them all. Can't you see? I'm trying to save them."

"Liar," Greene spat the word. "You used my own daughter against me. Tried to blackmail me. And when I wouldn't pay, you killed her!"

Andre edged away from Jenna, skirting the rear of the Tahoe, aiming for a position closer to the Lexus where he could take a head shot without risking the children.

Benjamin clasped his hands in prayer. "I swear to God, I did no such thing. I've never met you or your daughter before today. I only did what she asked me to. I was only trying to save her soul."

Greene was livid. "That wasn't my daughter. My daughter is BreeAnna Greene. And you killed her."

He revved the engine, but thankfully the SUV didn't move. He must have it in "Park." Which might buy them time and the ability to use lethal force if need be. She glanced at Andre, still not in position.

"Mr. Greene," she called out again. "Obviously there's been some confusion. Why don't you let me take it from here? The police are on their way. We'll make sure BreeAnna's killer pays for what he did."

Hostage negotiation wasn't exactly Jenna's forte, but Greene seemed to consider her words.

"No." Or not. "I want to hear him say it. I want to hear his confession. About how he used my daughter's own words, e-mailed me blackmail threats with messages from BreeAnna, and then he . . . he—" Greene's voice sputtered away, choked with tears.

Benjamin appeared confused. "BreeAnna Greene? I never even—you don't understand—it wasn't me. It couldn't be. I never use a computer, my assistant does. I never e-mailed you, and I certainly didn't kill anyone."

The Reverend managed to pull himself together, standing tall despite the automotive steel pinning his body. "I'm a man of God, sir. If someone used my good name to do you harm, then we need to work together to find him."

Greene considered the Reverend's words. Then he shook his head and aimed the gun at him once more. "No. I don't believe you. You're lying."

Shit. They were losing him. Jenna glanced at Andre. He was in position for a kill shot. No sign of the cops. Damn, damn, damn. She did not want to make this call. Getting her very first client killed had not been the plan. Damn Morgan, this was all her fault. Stirring things up, creating this chaos.

She held a hand up to Andre, telling him to stand by. No one could fault them for that, for trying to defuse the situation, waiting for the authorities to arrive.

Engage the subject. Connect with them. The heart of any negotiation.

"Mr. Greene," she tried again. "Robert. Would BreeAnna want you to do this?" Stupid question. Never give them a chance to say no, she reminded herself. She quickly regrouped. "What would BreeAnna want? For you? For your family?"

He hesitated, the pistol drifting down. She thought she had him when a man stumbled out from around the building, into the glare of the Lexus's headlights. And the line of fire.

Not a man, she saw. A teenage boy. Carrying another. He carefully laid the second boy onto the asphalt. "Help me," he called. "I can't stop the bleeding."

◆

"Get up, Deidre," Sean ordered, his gaze locked on Morgan's. At this close range, any shot would be lethal. "You two are coming with me."

Behind Morgan, Deidre obeyed and climbed to her feet.

"Sean." Deidre's voice filled with surprise and dismay. "Put that gun down. What are you thinking?"

"I'm thinking you really screwed up, that's what I'm thinking. I'm thinking I need to cut my losses." He gestured for them to move toward the tree line and the side of the building farthest away from the road and any help. "I'm thinking a hostage wouldn't hurt."

They walked around the far corner of the school. There was a service drive here and a Cadillac ATS parked, its engine running. Sean realigned himself so that the girls were trapped between him, the building, and the car.

Morgan braced herself to rush him, but he was still too close. If the gun went off at this distance, he'd surely hit her. Because it was her he was aiming at, not his sister.

He gestured for them to move to the car. Clicked a remote and the trunk popped open. "Inside, Ms. Renshaw—or whatever your name is."

"No." Sean appeared as surprised by Deidre's defiance as she herself did. "Let Morgan go. She doesn't belong here, mixed up with you . . . you," her face twisted as she searched for the right words, "you heathen. I see now. The truth. Using these children, twisting God's word, making a mockery of everything you profess to believe in. For what? Money?"

She was practically spitting the words at her brother by the end. Sean's attention shifted to his sister, but unfortunately his aim remained on Morgan. He understood who the real threat was here.

"What would you know of it?" he snapped back. "All your life you've been coddled, taken care of. After Mom left, who went out and stole food for you while going hungry himself? Who sat in the rain in the gutter and begged so you could have a coat to keep you warm? And these past years, safe inside here—"

"Inside here where you imprisoned me. Was that the deal from the beginning? Was I the price you paid the Reverend so you could have a roof over your head?" Deidre paced in a small, tight circle, her fists circling through the air, not unlike the movements she'd inspired in her flock during Morgan's Purge. "You used me, Sean. Just like he did."

Sean studied his sister as if seeing her for the first time. "You didn't figure that out by yourself. The Reverend had you totally under control—he had everything under control until that fat cow, BreeAnna Greene, came along."

"Don't you blame her! Don't you even say her name!"

If only Sean would take a step back or to the side. If only his aim would waver for an instant—it was all Morgan needed to escape. Because there was nothing here she could use to fight—nothing except Deidre's wrath. And her baby.

"Did you know she's pregnant?" Morgan threw the words into the silence between brother and sister, gasoline on a fire. "Did you know your sister is having a baby?"

She braced herself, ready to make a run for it. But Sean didn't take the bait. Instead he let loose with a small, exhausted exhalation. "Of course, I knew. That's why I had to kill BreeAnna."

CHAPTER 47

Y ou killed Bree?" Deidre's voice was strangled. She rushed Sean. He whirled, the gun now pointing at her belly.

Morgan could have run. She should have run. All she'd been thinking about was when to run.

Her body faced the tree line where she might escape into the forest. It was far, maybe too far to outrun a bullet. But it was her only hope. Somehow her feet took her in the other direction. She charged between brother and sister, pushing Deidre aside before Sean could use the gun and inserting her own body between them.

They were now so close, Deidre pressed against her back, her sobs shaking both her and Morgan. In front of Morgan, Sean's chest heaved as he fought to regain control. Which left Morgan trapped in the kill zone, a pistol mere inches from her heart.

"Why?" Deidre cried out. "Why did you kill her?"

"It's your own damn fault. You told her. Everything. What were you thinking?" Sean's voice rose in pitch, sounding more like a scorned lover than a con man cutting his losses.

"Bree was going to help me. She'd stay here so I could marry Reverend Benjamin. She was going to save us both."

"You're an idiot. Benjamin doesn't love you—he loves to hate you, to hurt you. And BreeAnna, she was going to tell. About the baby, about everything. She was going to ruin everything. I'd be in prison for the rest of my life. Is that what you wanted?"

"No. Of course not. But it has to end, Sean. Can't you see that? We can start over. You and me, just like it's always been. You and me and the baby."

Sean shook his head in regret. His mind had been made up as soon as he aimed the gun at his sister, Morgan knew.

"I'm sorry, Deidre. I thought by silencing BreeAnna, I could save you, but she's ruined that." He glared at Morgan as if this was all her fault.

Stall, she had to stall. Someone would be here soon—if not Jenna and Andre, then Greene. Or a helpful fireman. Surely someone cared about fifty kids alone in the middle of nowhere.

No. Of course not. That was the point, wasn't it?

Finally she understood what Bree had found so compelling about ReNew. More than a chance to fit in with other outcasts, misfits. Bree believed she could help those kids. That they needed her.

Unlike her own family.

Robert and Caren Greene had used their daughter like a dog's chew toy, a plaything for their egos and marital power struggle. They'd taught Bree that she was worthless, that she didn't matter.

But here, at ReNew, where her gift of music had made such a difference, where her gift of friendship helped Deidre find a path to salvation for her and her unborn child, where her willingness to pay the price to protect the others from the Rev's twisted needs . . . here, Bree had mattered. She'd had the chance to change everything.

Here at ReNew she'd never be alone again.

Morgan's mind whirled, sifting through a myriad of possibilities. Bree might have found hope and fellowship here at ReNew, but Morgan was on her own. She couldn't count on anyone arriving in time to save her.

Just like all those hours waiting in the dark for her father to finish his business, trying to block out any tiny remnant of fear or emotion that would betray her to him, she was all alone.

"You don't need to do this, Sean," Morgan tried again. "I'm here to expose the Reverend. He made you use those kids to blackmail their families. You had no choice."

His face twisted into a sneer. "You have no idea what the hell you're talking about. The Reverend didn't use us—we used him. At least we did until she"—he waved the pistol at Deidre—"went and got religion, fell in love with what Benjamin was feeding her. All that bullshit about purging sins and being purified. You two deserve each other; you're both twisted freaks."

Deidre lunged forward. Morgan grabbed her arm, holding her back. "Don't you say that, don't you dare say that about him! He's a good man, a great man. He can lead us all to salvation."

Clearly still conflicted about the good Reverend Doctor. Which wasn't helping, not at all.

"A good man? How can you still believe that? The old man gets his kicks out of torturing kids and breaking them down until they're mindless pools of self-pitying jelly. Oh and his idea of sex is seeing how much pain you take before you pass out."

"He's trying to save my everlasting soul," Deidre protested.

"You've been locked up here since you were twelve. What the hell could you have done that takes seven years of his sadistic torture to cleanse your soul?"

Deidre drew in her breath so sharp and fast that Morgan felt the hairs on her neck bristle. "You know what I've done, you know my sins can never be forgiven," she said in a tight whisper. "I'm wicked, as wicked as Eve when she seduced that serpent into giving her the apple and then turned her evil wiles on Adam. I deserve to be punished."

"Fine by me. You want to be saved, to meet your Almighty Maker? Glad to oblige. Get in the trunk, and it will all be over with real soon. They'll blame the fire, say it spread to the car. Then I can get the hell out of here while Benjamin takes the fall."

Morgan had no idea what they were talking about, but there was no mistaking the threat in Sean's voice as he detoured from hostage taking to outright murder. She'd lost her chance to reason with him, thanks to Deidre making it personal. Why did people have to let their emotions run wild like that?

He jabbed her with the pistol. "Move. Both of you."

What emotion drove Sean? Self-preservation, obviously. And greed.

"We can create a diversion, Sean. So you can get away with all that money. You were the one behind the blackmail scheme, right? Smart guy like you, I bet you have all that money socked away in some offshore account. You need us to buy you time to get to the airport. Let us go and we can do that."

"No," Deidre screamed, darting around Morgan to get at Sean. "He killed Bree; we can't let him get away with that."

Sean aimed at his sister, but instead of shooting her, he hit her with the gun butt so hard that she staggered back, knocking Morgan over before Morgan could take advantage of the opportunity.

"Get up and get in the car," Sean repeated, his voice now devoid of emotion. "I won't ask again."

There was no ignoring the gun he pressed against Morgan's temple. Maybe there was a weapon in the car trunk that she could reach, one better than the padlock she still held—and it would get Deidre out of the line of fire.

Morgan led Deidre, who was now weeping silently, to the trunk. Sean remained behind her, the muzzle of the pistol digging into Morgan's bare neck right at the top of her spinal cord. She was freezing, out here in the night air dressed in nothing but a sports bra and torn scrub pants, no shoes, but she embraced the cold. It numbed the pain from the lacerations crisscrossing her back and kept her focused.

She helped Deidre climb into the trunk. Deidre knelt in the opening, unwilling to let go of Morgan's hands. "I'm so sorry, Morgan. It's all my fault."

All Deidre's fault? For what? Letting herself be used by the Rev? Or . . . something else?

"Deidre, who's the father of your baby?"

The other girl said nothing. But her gaze left Morgan's to search out Sean.

"I'm so sorry. I'm evil, I know I am," Deidre wailed. She released Morgan's hands and covered her face.

Morgan wanted to lash out at the girl for her self-pity and weakness. But she held back. For one thing, it wouldn't do any good. And for another, she hated to admit how alike she and Deidre were. Both molded to be the perfect fish for their respective father figures. Both trained to obey without question.

And in the end, both victims.

CHAPTER 48

Micah knew he was taking a terrible risk. But Nelson had passed out, and he could barely carry the larger boy's weight another step, and if that really was Bree's father holding the Rev prisoner, then maybe Micah could reason with him, unlike the lady—she must be some kind of a cop—behind the Tahoe across the parking lot.

Nelson didn't have time to wait, he realized as he laid him down in the headlights and saw how much blood covered Nelson's pants and Micah's own body. "Mr. Greene," he called to the man in the Lexus, ignoring the others. "I was a friend of BreeAnna's. She was so proud of you. Said you were the kind of guy others could count on in an emergency—said you even once got caught in a cave-in while working a mine."

Greene blinked, startled by his words. Good. Anything to end this fast so Nelson could get the help he needed.

"I was your age," Greene said. His voice sounded as distant as the memory. "Just turned eighteen. Roughnecking it, trying to find veins of coal in an old mine, long stripped bare. It put food on our table, barely. Me, my dad, uncles, and cousins, we were all there when the roof crashed down on us."

"Bree said you saved them all. Said you were the one who got them out. Can I count on you to help me save my friend?" Micah swallowed, his spit tasting of soot and blood. "Please, sir. Help us."

He locked his gaze with Greene's, ignoring the tall black guy who crept up on Greene's blind side, a gun aimed at the older man. Greene nodded, slowly, then blinked fast as if holding back tears. "They killed my baby."

"I know, sir," Micah said. "I miss her, too. Help me and I'll tell you all about her time here. Your daughter—she's just like you. She saved us all."

Tears streaming down his face, Greene's gun slipped from his hand and clattered against the blacktop. Sirens sounded in the distance, but the black guy didn't wait. He lunged forward, popped the SUV's door open, and grabbed Greene, spinning him to the ground.

The lady with the gun came running around. She pulled a pair of plastic handcuffs onto Greene's wrists and tugged them tight. "Help the boy," she told the black guy. "First-aid kit's in the back."

Micah pressed down with his entire weight, trying to slow the blood seeping from Nelson's leg. The black guy ran to the Tahoe, then back to Micah just as the bright lights of a fire truck and cop car appeared at the far corner of the fence line. The guy crouched beside Micah, ripping open a bandage from its plastic packaging.

"My name's Andre," he told him. "Don't worry, your friend will be fine. I've seen this QuikClot work wonders with worse wounds."

Micah released his makeshift bandage and sat back to give Andre room to work. For the first time since escaping the fire, he shivered, feeling the cruel March wind against his bare chest. The ReNew building was now totally engulfed, flames crowding through windows and the roof, reaching to the sky.

His ears rang with the noise—not helped by the shouts of the firemen and the police officers. He shook his head to clear it and looked around.

Where the hell were Morgan and Deidre?

✦

Every instinct in Morgan's being screamed at her to run, run, run. Yet, she stood her ground, despite Sean's gun jabbing into the flesh at the base of her skull.

Not because she was any kind of hero. Not because she was willing to risk her life to protect Deidre and her unborn child. Not because she was frozen with fear.

No, it wasn't fear Morgan felt searing her veins. It was anger.

Hiding her motions from Sean, she slowly unfurled the tattered length of material that secured the padlock to her wrist. She was no sheep. No fish. She was Clinton Caine's daughter. A natural born killer. A wolf.

No way in hell was she about to allow a weak, cowardly bully like Sean Chapman to defeat her.

"Get in." Sean jabbed the pistol into her skull. Behind them came a thundering crash as part of the roof caved in, showering them with sparks and a blaze of embers.

Morgan took full advantage of the distraction, pushing off the car fender, forcing Sean to step back. His gun arm went up to protect his head. She swung the padlock, all her energy and power behind the movement.

Her aim was off—the padlock's unbalanced weight made it impossible to accurately predict its trajectory—and instead of cracking his skull as she'd intended, the padlock struck his shoulder and glanced off, the damaged fabric finally tearing and the padlock spinning away into the darkness.

The blow was enough to send Sean another half step back, which gave Morgan the room she needed. Allowing her momentum to carry her in an arc, she followed her first blow with an elbow to his ribs and then spun a back kick to his knee. He dropped to one knee and was bringing the pistol to bear on her when she tucked her head down and charged him, head butting his chest, forcing him off balance, and following up with a blow to his throat that he dodged, turning it into an uppercut to his jaw.

He grabbed her with both arms as he fell to the ground, pulling her down with him. Sean rolled his weight onto her, knee pressed against her chest with his full weight bearing down so she couldn't breathe.

"I'm so fucking tired of you, bitch," he muttered, his words spitting blood at her and sounding garbled. *Must have bit his tongue.* The thought flashed through her brain even as she fought to get a fist or knee or elbow free.

He raised his gun.

A blur of motion like a dark shadow speeding through the firelight appeared in her peripheral vision. At first she thought it was an oxygen-deprived hallucination, but then Micah tackled Sean, throwing him off of Morgan. They hit the ground, tumbling.

Once again Sean got the upper hand, landing on top of Micah. Micah had both his hands fastened around Sean's wrist, trying to force the gun free. Sean grabbed Micah's hair and slammed his skull against the asphalt.

Morgan leapt to her feet and threw herself against Sean's back. He had his chin tucked tight to his chest, giving her no room for a choke hold, but that still left her with plenty of other vulnerable targets.

She clapped both palms hard against his ears to disorient him, then pressed her fingers into his eyes, pushing hard enough that he howled in pain.

"Let him go or I'll rip them both out," she told him in a voice steeled with lethal fury.

He froze for a moment. Long enough for Micah to haul in a breath and wrench the gun free. As it clattered to the ground, Sean slumped into her arms, hands up in surrender.

"Let go, let go," he screamed, sounding like one of her father's fish.

Micah scrambled to his feet, but Morgan didn't release her grasp. Not until Micah touched her wrist and gently removed one hand. "It's okay, Morgan. He's not getting away. Not this time."

She glanced up, met his gaze. He looked—proud? Of her? For what? Not finishing what she'd begun and killing the man?

Slowly, she released Sean. He slumped forward, hands covering his eyes, body rocking in pain. Micah extended his hand, and she took it, letting him help her up.

CHAPTER 49

P retending to be a Norm is harder than it looks," Morgan began her session with Nick two days later. He'd requested the session—to evaluate her after the "stress" of everything that had happened at ReNew. She'd agreed—to evaluate his response to her answers. If she could fool Nick, she could fool anyone.

"What was the hardest part for you?" he asked. "Being inside ReNew, under their control? Playing the role of what you'd call a sheep?"

See. Here. She'd have to start with the lying right away. She'd promised Nick she'd always be truthful during their sessions, but promises were made to be broken. No way in hell was she going to admit that there at the end she hadn't been acting the role of sheep—she'd become worse, a true victim. It had only been for a few moments when Sean Chapman held her life in his hands. But, for the first time ever in her life, she'd realized that she was just as vulnerable as any Norm.

Morgan was not about to admit that to anyone. Especially not to Nick. "Pretending to let them control me was tough. I had to keep reminding myself that I was there because I wanted to be, that I had a goal. But the hardest thing was the boredom. I wanted to scrap the plan, to lash out, have some fun—anything to relieve the damn boredom."

"You know you need more stimulation than other people. Is that why you let the Reverend do that to you?" He nodded over her shoulder.

The Rev and his twisted perversions—that's all anyone wanted to hear about: the cops before she slipped away from them, Micah, Jenna. Andre was the only one who hadn't asked.

Funny thing was, Morgan didn't give a shit—barely thought about it at all until she leaned back against something and felt the pain. She hadn't even needed any stitches; the Rev obviously knew what he was doing. But Nick hadn't asked about what the Rev had done to her, had he? No. He'd asked *why* she'd let it happen.

Man was smart—which made him dangerous. Because Morgan wasn't ready to go there. That way led to a minefield.

So she told the story of the *what*, emphasizing the Rev's delight at her pain. "But Deidre told me later that it wasn't always about the pain for him. She said half the time he'd call her and all he wanted was to cry, beg for her forgiveness, or he'd read Bible stories to her, tell her she was special, some kind of holy offering, and if he could take her pain on himself, he would, that he truly regretted her needing to suffer."

"I suspect the Reverend suffers from a rather complicated pathology. But we're not here to talk about him—except—" He interrupted himself, took a beat to look her straight in the eye, taking the bait she'd dangled. "You're not intending to go after him, are you, Morgan? Seek revenge?"

"How about protecting his next innocent victims from him?" she countered, irritated that he assumed she'd break her vow of nonviolence so easily. "No. I don't have anything planned for the Rev—don't need to. Deidre's going to testify against him, and we have tons of video of what he did to her when she was younger."

Nick sank back, obviously relieved.

"What I don't understand," Morgan said, both to fill the silence and to gauge his response. "Is why or maybe it's how, they all could believe that crap? Deidre I get, she was pretty much brainwashed between the Rev and her brother. But how many hundreds of kids went through there in the past seven years—and they all came out believing, having faith in ReNew. Jenna said no one she talked to would speak against the program, even kids and families who weren't being blackmailed by Sean. And on the news there are tons of former students defending the program, saying it saved their lives, gave them faith, something to believe in."

"Everyone needs something to hang on to," Nick said. "It's not about the words. It's about accepting that there are things beyond your control, believing in the future."

"You mean all that higher power bullshit."

"So you don't believe in anything?" Nick pressed.

Morgan snapped back in annoyance. "With a father like mine, I've no need of God or Satan. I have faith in myself, that's more than enough."

He raised one eyebrow—she hated when he did that, so she mimicked his expression perfectly, something he in turn despised. "If the only person you trust is yourself, then why did you let them lock you away in that detention center? Why put up with the inconvenience, the suffering, if you're only looking out for your-self, Morgan?"

"Because I let you talk me into it. Trying to be a team player, fitting in, remember?" Not quite the truth, but close enough.

"You can't have a team without trust."

"I trusted myself. I could have gotten out of that damn hellhole anytime I damn well pleased, and you know it."

"My point is, you didn't." He sat back and let the silence swirl between them. Doing that shrink thing again.

"You think I went there because I had faith that you, Jenna, and Andre wouldn't let me down?"

"All I know is that you are driven by a need to not end up like your father. You've said that being locked up is the one thing you fear. And yet—"

She almost laughed, but it would have been cruel. If he was a stranger, maybe, but she liked Nick—and she needed him. So she swallowed her snort of derision. "And yet, I got myself out of there. Truth is, Nick, I went because I was bored. You can't imagine how damn boring it is wandering around all you sheep, playing by your rules, and never having any fun."

Again, not quite the truth, but all the truth she felt safe in his knowing. Or her knowing. Whatever. The session was a success—they'd spent the entire hour without a single mention of Micah.

She stood up. "I think that's enough insight for one day."

"Where are you going?" She liked that there was the slightest edge to his voice, as if he was afraid she was going to race out to start a killing spree.

"To see my father. Like I said, I don't need faith or God or Satan, so I think it's finally time to say good-bye once and for all."

His startled look tasted like sweet victory.

✦

Morgan didn't leave for the prison, not right away. She wasn't even sure why, but figured Nick had done enough probing of her psyche for one day, why not give herself the night off?

Micah was easy to find. Even easier to sneak in after visiting hours. He'd suffered a skull fracture and concussion, but the surgeons hadn't needed to operate, she learned from a peek at his chart. Amazing what access a white coat and stethoscope gave you.

She waited until the nurses ushered his mothers out. One was Asian, petite, despite the fact that Morgan knew from her background check that she worked as a welder, specializing in underwater work on the bridges that surrounded the city. The other must have been Micah's biological mother—she shared his ash-blonde paleness. She taught English to sixth graders.

They made for an interesting couple. She liked the way they moved together, in sync, their conversation continuing even through silent pauses. They held hands as they waited for the elevator, leaning in so that their shoulders touched.

She could easily imagine Micah with them, the center of their world—so unlike Bree and her parents. And she'd learned, with a little breaking and entering into the juvenile justice system's electronic records, that they'd fought vehemently to visit Micah and get his early release from ReNew, despite the reports from ReNew that he'd been violent and had lost all privileges. Sean's false reports had even convinced the judge to twice add more time to Micah's sentence.

But his mothers had never given up on him. She hoped he knew that.

The elevator came and the women left. Morgan entered Micah's hospital room, wrinkling her nose against the barrage of smells. Hospitals. Almost as bad as prison. Tied to a bed by wires and tubes, forced to obey orders.

She stood at Micah's bedside. He was sleeping, his face at rest—the first time she'd ever seen him without a collage of emotions dancing across his features. It was disconcerting.

She'd intended to simply check on him, make sure the doctors were treating him right, and leave again, but something drew her closer. She lowered the bed rail separating her from him.

Morgan wasn't sure what she felt—it was so entirely foreign. Definitely not guilt. Talk about your waste of energy, pretending you could play God and change the past, present, and future—and when you found you couldn't, dissolving into a cowering puddle of would've, could've, should've.

No. Not guilt. She stroked Micah's hair, admiring his beauty—despite the scars. A lot like Andre that way. Beauty more than skin-deep, which made it all the more precious and rare.

Not remorse, either. She didn't want to take back her actions, but she realized that the only reason why Micah was hurt was because of her choices. And she wished there'd been another way she could have done things.

Not that she would have done things differently, just a feeling that in the future she would try to do things better.

Regret? Maybe. How the hell would she know? But if this niggling new thing inside her made her stay on the side of the angels and out of prison, then she'd use it.

Morgan didn't care how she got what she wanted. She'd use anyone and anything to achieve her goal: never again would she be a fish. She'd rather die first.

As she studied Micah with his one eye swollen shut, his nose crooked, a ribbon of gauze hanging from one nostril, and the variety of bruises covering his head and arms, she realized that she needed to add a new category to her classification of Norms. People like Micah weren't sheep, could never be fish.

No. People like Micah and Lucy and Nick and Andre, they weren't sheep. They were protectors. Driven to guard against predators like Morgan.

How would Micah feel if he ever recognized her for the wolf she was?

There was a sketch pad on the bedside table. Curious, she opened it. Drawings of her. Over and over again, as he strained to capture her.

The way Micah drew—it was just like the way he walked around without a mask. Open, honest. He poured his soul into every line, tossing bits and pieces of himself onto the page like feeding bread crumbs to pigeons. She flipped through the pages to find similar drawings of his mothers, BreeAnna, Deidre, and even

Nelson and Tommy. All rendered with so much energy that she felt Micah's presence leap from the page.

She closed the book but couldn't shake a strange fear that Micah had wasted all his energy on his art, that she'd look at him and be able to see right through him, nothing left.

Greed. That's what she felt. Greed. She wanted Micah to be paying attention to her and her alone. She didn't want him wasting this glorious energy on anyone else.

Was that what her father had felt? What had driven him?

She stole into the bathroom and ran the water, cupping it in her hands, gulping it down, splashing it over her face, feeling sweaty and feverish. Her father's lust had driven him beyond control. She wanted no part of that. Not ever. The red "Exit" light above the door gleamed not ten feet away from her. Should she leave? Abandon Micah?

Or gamble that she had more control than her father and risk hurting him?

She returned to his side. Turning the chair so her back was to the exit, she stayed, watched, and listened to the reassuring sound of his heartbeat on the monitor. She deserved this—besides, it was all part of playing the role of a Norm, right?

You're no Norm, her father's voice mocked her. *You and me, baby girl, we're special. Rules don't apply, not to us.*

Despite the noise of the hospital, she drifted to sleep. When she woke, Micah was awake, watching her, his eyes clear.

"I'm sorry, Morgan," were his first words—words she never wanted to hear from him.

She stood, not sure if she should move closer to him or farther away. Was he telling her to stay or to go?

"I don't have any regrets. Do you?" For once in her life, she knew exactly what she wanted, but she didn't act on that want. Instead she waited for his answer.

Carefully, he sat up in the bed, a grimace of pain crossing his face, and reached a hand across the space between them. He touched her shoulder, then her hair. Not even a touch, more like sunlight gliding over her skin.

"No. I don't believe in regrets."

She smiled and stepped closer. "Neither do I."

His hand landed on the back of her neck. She knew what was coming next and suddenly a frisson of—she wasn't sure, fear? Anticipation? Anxiety? Whatever it was, it was unfamiliar and unwelcome as it fluttered through her veins.

She looked away. He froze. "What is it?"

She hated this, this uncertainty. Not knowing what she felt, not knowing what to do about it. But she knew what she wanted. Was she going to let these silly, weak emotions stop her?

Leaping into the unknown, trusting her instincts for survival, that's where the rush was, that's what made life worth living . . . so why the sudden hesitation? She knew what she wanted. Why wasn't she grabbing hold, to hell with the consequences?

"Morgan. What's wrong?" Micah's voice echoed her own uncertainty.

The truth is never the wrong answer, Nick always said. Morgan decided to give it a try. "I'm not very good at this."

It was the truth. She'd never been kissed. All those years with her father, witness to every kind of depravity, she'd felt certain that part of her was cauterized, scorched by the blood and pain that passed for her father's idea of sex.

She had no clue what Norms did—or felt—when they fell in love. Not just the emotions but the logistics. Who turned right and who turned left? Who decided when to start and stop?

Or if it was good? Who decided that?

"I have a hard time believing there's anything you're not good at," Micah said, tracing her jaw with his thumb.

"Would it matter?" she hated herself for even asking. Sounded like a damn sheep. "If I'm not any good at it? If I don't—"

His thumb slid across her lips, silencing her. "Tell you what. I'm going to kiss you, and you tell me if you like it or not. Then we'll go from there. As fast or as slow as you want."

He moved his thumb away, and before she could answer, his lips were pressed against hers. Soft yet firm, a gentle pressure that she yielded to, wrapping her arms around his shoulders, pulling him in for more.

She wasn't sure how long it lasted—usually she was an excellent judge of time because her heart rate was so slow and steady, never rushing or jumping with excitement. Until now.

He broke away, his palms cradling her face between them. "Was that okay?"

She nodded.

"Want to try again?"

She nodded again. "Yes. I'd like that very much."

His smile filled her vision, and he lowered his face to hers once more.

A shrill ring shattered the spell. Her phone. No one had that number except Andre, Jenna, and Nick.

Micah pulled away, chuckling. "Saved by the bell."

Morgan grabbed the phone from her pocket. Unknown caller. She almost hung up, but curiosity drove her to open the connection.

"You don't write, you don't call, if I didn't know any better, I'd think you'd forgotten all about me," her father's voice came over the line.

"What is it?" She fought to keep the venom from her voice. Not for her father, but for Micah's sake. Failed.

"Don't you take that tone with me, young lady," he said. "You give any thought to how you're gonna take care of business for me?"

Calls from prison were regulated. They came collect, and you had to accept the charges and acknowledge that they were coming from an inmate. Unless, of course, someone got their hands on a smuggled cell phone.

"No," Morgan snapped, annoyed that even from behind bars, Clint still had the power to reach her. "I decided not to."

"You're not going to take care of the Feds for me?"

"No. I'm not," she said, defying her father for the first time ever. She didn't feel jittery or anxious or any of those Norm feelings, but she did feel tense. Caught herself holding her breath the tiniest bit as she waited for his reply.

Not because she was nervous. Because she wondered what her rebellion would cost her. Micah picked up on her feelings and slid his hand down her arm until his fingers were intertwined with hers, sharing his strength with her.

The silence stretched out, and she thought the call had been dropped. It hadn't. Finally Clint's voice returned. No longer bright and cheery. This time it was low and throaty, the alpha dog growling to warn others in the pack to stay away from what was his.

"We'll just see about that, baby girl," he said. "Maybe I'll have to find a way to come visit you sooner rather than later."

As long as Clint was behind bars, he couldn't hurt her. She could handle him. Then the sound of a truck's air brakes blasted through the airwaves.

"Where are you?"

"Wouldn't you like to know," he chuckled. "Turn on the news, see for yourself. Don't forget to leave a light on for me, baby girl. We're going fishing again. Just you and me, like the old times. Real soon."

NOTE TO READERS

Dear Reader,

This book would have never happened without all the fan letters after Morgan first appeared in *Blood Stained*, asking for "more Morgan, please!"

I'll let you in on a secret. I almost killed off Morgan in that first book—but her character simply wouldn't die. Just as so many of you were, I was fascinated by the potential of a teenage psychopathic killer.

Especially the question: After living through her father's depravities, could she ever be redeemed?

Morgan took a few baby steps toward redemption in *Kill Zone* when she saved Jenna's life, but she has a long, long road ahead. And, of course, it's not going to be an easy one.

Which is why in *Fight Dirty*, I forced Morgan to face her greatest fear—being imprisoned under the control of others. Of course, she's still not redeemed, but she's taken another baby step, leaving her feral life behind and heading into an uncertain future as she lives among Norms.

As a pediatrician, I worked with juvenile defendants and a juvenile detention facility, but it was nothing (I repeat, nothing!) like ReNew. To create ReNew, I combined my experiences along with those of my research advisers, Mercy Pilkington, 2010 National Juvenile Detention Association Teacher of the Year, and Cyndy Drew Etler, author of *Straightling*, a memoir about her own experiences as a student detained in a private residential facility. I also used reports from several major news organizations (including the *New York Times*) as they uncovered abuses in both private and publicly run juvenile facilities.

While the abuse in *Fight Dirty* (in particular Deidre's relationship with the Rev) is totally fictional, the other depictions of extreme behavior such as the isolation, enforced stress positions, food withholding, coed showers and strip searches, beatings, and use of restraints, are all based on real-life events.

I hope you enjoyed the start of Morgan's journey. Look for more to come in future installments of the Renegade Justice series.

As always, thanks for reading!

CJ

ABOUT THE AUTHOR

New York Times and *USA Today* best-selling author of twenty-five novels, former pediatric ER doctor CJ Lyons has lived the life she writes about in her cutting edge Thrillers with Heart.

CJ has been called a "master within the genre" (*Pittsburgh Magazine*) and her work has been praised as "breath-takingly fast-paced" and "riveting" (*Publishers Weekly*) with "characters with beating hearts and three dimensions" (*Newsday*).

Her novels have won the International Thriller Writers' prestigious Thriller Award, the RT Reviewers' Choice Award, the Readers' Choice Award, the RT Seal of Excellence, and the Daphne du Maurier Award for Excellence in Mystery and Suspense.

Learn more about CJ's Thrillers with Heart at
www.CJLyons.net.